"Send Us Back, Ross? We Can't Go Back!

There's nothing to go back to!" Susan exclaimed.

He turned to face her, a look of irritation on his face. "You don't have a man to take care of you. I can't have you holding up the wagon train."

Angry and stunned, Susan watched him begin to chain the oxen to the wagon.

"I can do without your help," she said stiffly. "I'm perfectly capable of hitching the animals."

He shrugged. "Suit yourself."

She watched him walk away before she started to struggle with the harness chains. Tears of frustration burned her eyes as the animals shifted away from her.

But at last the oxen were hitched. Her dress was ripped where it had caught on a chain, and her hands were raw. She clenched her teeth against the billowing dust and cracked the whip over the heads of the lead animals.

"Get up there, now," she shouted.

The wagon creaked forward and she got into line at the very rear. But she had done it once. Tomorrow it would be easier. She didn't need anyone's help, not even Ross Morgan's. . . .

Valley of Dreams

CAROL DANIELS

PUBLISHED BY POCKET BOOKS NEW YORK

For Eldoris Provan—who believed

Another *Original* publication of POCKET BOOKS

POCKET BOOKS, a division of Simon & Schuster, Inc.
1230 Avenue of the Americas, New York, N.Y. 10020

ISBN: 0-671-46071-4

First Pocket Books printing April, 1984

10 9 8 7 6 5 4 3 2 1

POCKET and colophon are registered trademarks
of Simon & Schuster, Inc.

Printed in the U.S.A.

Chapter 1

White tents and canvas-covered wagons were scattered across the meadow like giant mushrooms. Never had Susan Baker seen so many people and so much activity.

Children ran between the wagons, their voices raised in boisterous shouts. Their mothers gossiped over washtubs or campfires while the men stood in clusters arguing the merits of oxen versus mules.

They had been camped here on the outskirts of Independence for more than a week. At first they had been on the fringes of the encampment, but each day's new arrivals had hemmed them in and now everywhere Susan looked there were wagons and people. It seemed as though in this spring of 1849 everyone was heading west.

Idly she listened to the conversation between her mother- and father-in-law. For once their words echoed her own thoughts.

"Never seen anything like it," Ellie marveled, her soft Virginia accent more noticeable than ever. "Seems like there won't hardly be room in Oregon for all these folks, George."

"There'll be plenty of room. Problem's gonna be

1

finding enough grass for the stock along the way," Susan's father-in-law grumbled. "'Sides, most of 'em are headed for the gold fields, same as Adam."

At the mention of her husband's name, Susan stared into the distance. She had no desire to reach Oregon if it meant a reunion with Adam. His absence these last few months had been her only relief. No longer did he stumble to their bed at night reeking of cheap whiskey and cheaper perfume, demanding her attentions. No, she would be happy if she never saw him again.

Ellie sighed. "I hope he's all right."

"'Course he's all right. Stop your fussin'." George kicked an ember into the fire. "He's prob'ly in California by now, fillin' his pockets with gold nuggets."

"People do get sick on those ships," Ellie persisted. "I've heard tell of all kinds of terrible diseases."

"He can take care of himself. And come fall he'll meet us in Oregon City, just like we planned."

"If we could just get started. Did you see that Mr. Taggerty yesterday?" Ellie asked.

"Said I would, didn't I?"

"But what did he say? When do we leave?"

"Said it'd be another week yet afore we could head out. Grass ain't ready. If I'da known that, we could have waited."

"But then everything would have been picked over. Why, just this morning Mrs. Jordan in the next wagon was sayin' how much they paid for their supplies and how they couldn't get everything they need."

"Well, we have everything we need and more. I'm ready to go, not just sit here doin' nothin'."

Susan remained quiet. The longer they stayed the better she would like it. Even life in the cramped wagon was preferable to the endless hours of jolting she had endured on the trip from Illinois to Missouri.

The front half of the narrow wagon was laden with furniture and tools for their new life in Oregon. The remainder of their belongings were distributed as evenly as possible. Cooking utensils, clothing and lanterns hung from the wooden ribs of the wagon frame. At night George slept beneath the wagon while Ellie and Susan were allowed the questionable luxury of two bedrolls spread precariously on top of their cargo of boxes and trunks.

A group of children ran past, followed by a pack of yapping dogs. Their own dog, Sam, rose from the shade, a low growl in his throat.

"Shut up, dog." George aimed a kick at the animal, but Sam was too quick. He skittered under the wagon and watched Susan with mournful eyes.

"Worthless animal. Shoulda left him behind." George gave Susan a scornful look. "Would have, too, if you hadn't made such a fuss. 'Be a good watchdog.'" His voice rose as he mimicked her words. "Ha! All he'll do is bark at the moon, chase coyotes and get underfoot."

"He'll earn his way. You'll see."

"Like you will, I suppose." His tone was cutting.

Susan felt a flush creep up from her collar, but she knew better than to answer her father-in-law. Even at the best of times his temper was short and he was quick to flare out at anyone who crossed him. She turned her back and began to toss chips of wood into the smoldering cook fire.

3

It was no longer possible to hide her pregnancy. Even in the wavy reflection of her old mirror, she recognized how her looks had faded. The reddish glint was gone from her hair, leaving it a dull, lifeless brown, and dark shadows ringed her topaz eyes. Her pale skin stretched taut across prominent cheekbones and her wide mouth no longer curved up at the corners. Her once-slender body felt heavy and unfamiliar as she moved around the camp, and there were still more than two months to wait.

She faced the future with a mixture of fear and fatalism, helpless to change the course her life had taken. The child she carried had been the only bright hope in her bleak existence and now even that was shadowed by her growing dread of the journey ahead.

Susan yearned for the day when she could hold her child against her breast, marvel at its tiny features. The love that Adam had made a mockery of was focused now on the baby she carried. She tried to quell her apprehensions. They said it was bad for a baby if the mother worried—yet how could she help it?

Unconsciously she placed one hand against her stomach, as if to shield her unborn child. It'll be all right, she promised herself, but her thoughts held no conviction. How could she have a baby in the middle of the wilderness that spread from here to Oregon City?

She remembered with shame how she had begged Adam to take her with him by ship to California.

"You're being foolish," he had told her. "Ma'll look after you, better than I can. It won't be any picnic for me either, you know. The ships are so crowded I don't even know if I'll have a decent place to sleep."

He had been unmoved by her pleas, even when in desperation she confided her fears.

"Adam, I'm afraid I'll lose the baby." She had searched for the words to make him understand. "I . . . I've been bleeding and having cramps. I'm sure I'll lose it if I have to travel by wagon."

The tears that seemed to threaten her constantly spilled down her cheeks as she spoke. She had felt so alone. Adam should care—if not about her, at least about the baby.

"If you're having trouble, talk to Ma. She knows about those things. You'll be fine by spring."

"I won't. I know it. If I'm forced to jolt across the country in a wagon—"

"You don't have any choice." Adam's voice was curt.

Susan had narrowed her eyes against her tears and stared at the man she had once promised to love. She felt nothing for him but a sick hatred. She spoke slowly and carefully.

"If I lose the baby, I'll never forgive you. You'll pay for it somehow—some way. Because if I lose it, it will be your fault."

He had laughed harshly and turned his back on her.

"Stop the playacting, Susan. You're not going with me and that's final."

All her arguments had been futile, as she had known they would be. Adam thought only of himself and the gold in California. There was no room for her in his thoughts; she wondered if there ever had been.

And now Adam's father dared to imply that her condition would be a hindrance on their journey. If only she had had a choice, she would gladly be anywhere else.

"I'm going into town," George announced.

Susan watched him stride away from the wagon. His shirt gapped open over a stomach that hid his belt, his pale hair was uncombed and he hadn't shaved for several days. In a few years Adam would look just like that.

When George was out of sight, Ellie sighed.

"I sure do wish we could go into town for a while. I'm so tired of this old wagon. Once we leave Independence it'll be months before we see a proper town."

"Why can't we go?" Susan demanded.

Ellie looked startled. "Oh my, we couldn't. Not alone."

"I don't see why not."

"How'd we get there? Must be at least a mile."

"That's not far. We can walk—it'd probably do us good. Besides, if we have to, we can always get a ride back."

"Yes." Ellie's tone was hesitant. "I'd so like to get away for a little while." She smoothed her graying hair back from her face with one work-roughened hand. "Well . . . maybe it wouldn't hurt none if we just sort of strolled in that direction."

"Of course not. Let's go."

Soon they were walking beside the well-traveled road. Susan held the hem of her faded calico skirt above the dusty grass and picked her way over the uneven ground. Wagons and horses flowed by in an endless stream and so did Ellie's constant chatter.

They passed shacks set back from the road in yards bordered by split-rail fences. Children hung on the fence posts and called out to them.

"You goin' west with the wagon trains?" one little girl asked.

Susan smiled and nodded.

"Wish I was goin'." The child was no more than seven and her gaze was wistful.

If I were that age, I'd want to go too, Susan thought. If things were different, I might even want to go *now*.

She kicked a small pebble and watched it bounce into the road. If only there were something to look forward to at the end of the journey. Her shoulders sagged as she thought of the years ahead she would spend trapped as Adam's wife. There had to be another way. Maybe in Oregon she'd find it.

"Will you look at that?" Ellie's voice was taut with excitement as they reached the edge of town.

Ahead lay total confusion. Boardwalks on both sides of the street were jammed with shoving people. Carriages passed farm wagons and prairie schooners, while mangy dogs darted between wheels and hooves. Teamsters shouted and whips cracked. A blacksmith's hammer rang in the distance. A gunshot echoed from the far side of town but no one took any notice.

"Come on," Ellie urged. "There's a dry goods store just up the street a ways—see the sign? Maybe I can find a little lace to edge the baby's clothes."

Suddenly Susan began to have misgivings about their venture. She was shoved and jostled as she tried to follow Ellie through the crowds of people. Indians lounged in the doorways and some sprawled against buildings, their outflung legs or arms directly in her path. None of them moved as she skirted them with caution. She wondered if they were asleep or dead. Did anyone care?

She knew the Kansas Indians were said to be the dirtiest. She had no difficulty picking them out. They huddled beneath ragged blankets, their hair greased with a foul-smelling concoction that made her hold her breath as she passed. Then there were the Shawnee, a more civilized tribe, wearing clothes similar to those of the white man. The women wore calico dresses like hers and Ellie's. Some of the men had shaved heads and painted faces, unlike other Indians who wore feathered war bonnets.

Susan followed Ellie into the store. It was hot and even more crowded than the street. She shoved her way between two women who were arguing over the last bolt of muslin.

"Just look at this," Ellie called. "See? What did I tell you? They have enough lace to edge everything from here to Illinois."

Susan examined the display, but her attention wavered. The odor of unwashed bodies was overpowering and she lifted her face toward the ceiling in an effort to get a breath of fresh air.

"It's awfully crowded, isn't it?" she said.

"I expect everyplace in Independence is crowded these days. Here, look at this." A thin ribbon of lace slid between Ellie's fingers. "You won't find any better if you go clear to New York. Can you imagine it, in a little town like this?"

"Yes, it's nice." Susan swallowed hard and tried to shield her body from the pressing crowd.

"Now, if I could just decide which one to get.

How much do you think it'll take? And what's the price?" Ellie mumbled more to herself than to Susan as she twisted the spindle first one way and then another.

"If you don't mind, I think I'll go outside and wait."

"Huh?" Ellie regarded Susan with surprise. "Well, if you're not interested." She shrugged.

"It's not that. I just can't breathe in here."

"Well, all right. I'll be along directly." Ellie's attention returned to the lace edgings.

"Hey, take it easy," a man muttered as Susan stumbled against him. But she was beyond caring who or what stood in her way. She had to get out. She felt if she didn't escape she would suffocate.

At last she reached the door and burst into the street. The jostling crowd seemed a haven after the stifling interior of the dry goods store. She took deep breaths of the cooler air but the dust raised by the passing wagons choked her. Her eyes burned.

"I should have stayed in camp," she said aloud. No longer did she feel rebellious. George was welcome to this godforsaken town. All she wanted was fresh air and a drink of water.

She edged her way down the street. Ellie would catch up sooner or later. If she could just reach the edge of town where there was grass and shade, she knew she would feel better. Susan clutched at a post to steady herself and then pushed on. The end of the walkway shimmered in the heat like a mirage.

Three men lurched from the doorway of a nearby saloon. People sidestepped to make room for them and continued on their way, but Susan was slowed by her cumbersome body. As the crowd shifted, she was pushed off balance and stumbled to the edge of the boardwalk. Her arms flailed the air, vainly grasping for some support, as she felt herself falling toward the street. She saw a horse and wagon bearing down on her and knew she would fall in its path. Then, suddenly, someone grasped her arm and she was jerked back to safety.

Susan looked up into the gray eyes of her rescuer. In spite of his rough clothing, he had the authoritative air of a man used to command. His face was tanned and weathered, and his features were as sharp as though etched in granite. He was tall and slender and stood as if the ground was unfamiliar. Susan imagined he was more at home on horseback, riding across the prairie, his blue-black hair tousled by the wind. A small scar pulled the corner of his mouth into a cynical line and his eyes were hard and appraising. There was a coiled watchfulness about his face that Susan found forbidding. He reminded her of a mountain lion, lithe and powerful with an ability to strike with lethal speed. She withdrew her arm from his grip and smiled. There was no answering warmth in his expression.

"Thank you," she said. "I might have been killed."

"Yes, I expect you might have been."

She shifted awkwardly under his gaze.

"You ought to know better than to saunter down these streets like this was Philadelphia," he muttered.

Susan felt her face redden. "I have as much right to be here as anyone," she snapped. "I didn't know manners were left behind with everything else when people went west."

"You'd be surprised what's left behind and I'd advise you not to try to find out. Now, go find your husband, wherever he is, and see that he takes proper care of you."

He turned away abruptly and Susan watched him disappear into the crowd. She was still staring after him when Ellie joined her a few minutes later.

Chapter 2

Excitement crackled in the early morning air. This was the day they had waited for. Today they would leave Independence and begin the long journey to Oregon.

Susan stood beside the wagon and watched the others who would be part of their train. There would be a total of eighty wagons. All but twenty-four would head for California after they crossed the Rocky Mountains. Some had slogans and names painted on the canvas wagon covers. She could read a few of them from where she stood. "Gold Hunter." "See you at Sutter's Fort." "Enterprise."

The faces of the people who hurried by were filled with anticipation. They're all so sure they'll get rich in California, Susan thought. She shook her head. It was easy to feel the stirring of gold fever and she was surprised that George hadn't changed his mind and decided to head for California. Her father-in-law seemed to fit in better with the rough group of gold seekers than he did with the more serious settlers bound for Oregon. But his dream of free land had never wavered. Nearly a thousand acres were there for the asking if both families made claims.

This wasn't the first time George had been lured

by the land. Susan recalled Ellie's tales of how they had drifted west from Virginia after their marriage. Each new farm had promised better soil, a more bountiful harvest. But the dreams had never materialized and the farms grew smaller with every move. Not once had Ellie expressed any criticism of her husband in spite of his obvious aversion to physical labor and the numerous times he abused her.

"He's a good man," she had told Susan. "Things just never quite work out the way we plan, but someday they will. And they will for you and Adam. You just be a good wife and stand behind him and he'll take care of you."

At first Susan had admired Ellie's loyalty, telling herself she should be more like that. She had tried, but found it impossible to muster any enthusiastic support for Adam. Now she knew she never would.

As if it were yesterday, she recalled the day she had met Delia O'Connell and learned the real reason why Adam had married her so hastily.

Delia was strikingly attractive, tall and slender with long black hair and dark eyes that had flashed hatred at Susan. Their meeting in the general store had left Susan shaken and curious. She had confronted Adam as soon as she returned home.

She had found him chopping wood behind the house, the back of his shirt blotched with perspiration. Sunlight glinted from the axe blade as she shifted impatiently and waited for him to pause in his work. At last she cleared her throat.

"Adam?"

"Back already?" He didn't glance up.

"Yes. It didn't take long."

The axe lodged in a piece of wood and he pounded

13

it against the ground until the wood split, then hurled the pieces into the pile against the house.

"Adam . . ."

"What is it?"

"I . . . uh, I met a girl in town today."

There was no response.

"She said to give you a message."

She had his attention at last. He leaned on the axe handle and turned to face her.

"Well, go on."

"She said to send you her love—that her brothers would think of you come springtime and that marrying me wouldn't make any difference." Susan stumbled through the message. "She said her name was Delia."

She waited, searching Adam's face for a reaction. His eyes were cold and watchful.

"Is that all?"

"Yes."

He turned and resumed his work.

"Adam!" Her voice was sharp.

He stopped chopping, but didn't face her.

"What is that girl to you?"

"What makes you think she's anything?"

"Adam, she hated me. I could see it in her eyes. And I think she hates you too. Why?"

"Because she's no-account half-breed trash, that's why."

"That's no reason. I need to know. I was frightened—embarrassed. It's my right to know."

"Your *right!*" He laughed as he turned to look at her. "What makes you think you have rights?"

"I'm your wife."

He shrugged. "If you must know, she says I'm the

father of the child she's expecting. Now are you satisfied?"

Susan was stunned. She stared into his icy blue eyes, searching for any trace of feeling.

"And are you?" she choked out at last.

"Hell, any man could be the father. Bet there isn't a man in town who hasn't bedded her at one time or another."

"But Adam, if she—"

"That's enough. I don't want to hear any more about it."

"What did she mean about her brothers?" Susan persisted.

Adam glared at her in annoyance.

"She's got herself two no-good brothers, half-breeds, just like her. They rode out here one night thinkin' they could make me marry her, but I showed them."

"What do you mean?"

"I mean I wasn't here for them to threaten with their shotguns. Nobody makes me do anything I don't want to do. And I sure wasn't about to saddle myself with some trashy squaw and God knows whose bastard. I lit out of here long before they ever showed up. And now I'm married there ain't a damn thing they can do about it."

"But Delia said—"

"Delia said, Delia said," he mocked. "Ain't nothin' but idle threats and she knows it."

He struck viciously at a log with the axe, as Susan fled into the house.

As she paced the floor, all the little details that had bothered her about Adam's courtship came back to her. They were all beginning to fall into place now: his insistence that she marry him, his failure to tell her he loved her, his unwillingness to wait until his parents could attend the wedding, the too-big ring he had brought with him to Parsonville.

He had planned to marry someone all along. It hadn't mattered who, just someone to save him from an "unsuitable" marriage. She had been nothing more than a convenient way to escape.

In her hurt and shock she had gone to Ellie, thinking that surely another woman would sympathize. But she had reckoned without Ellie's strong sense of loyalty. Ellie had listened to Susan's jumbled outpourings with an expression of cold distaste.

"I can't see as any of that should make a difference," she had said when Susan finally paused. "You're the one he married and you owe it to him to be a proper wife."

"But don't you see that's impossible after what he's done? I thought at least he loved me!"

Ellie turned her back.

"I don't want to hear another word. Adam's a good boy, just a little wild sometimes like his Pa. You'll learn there's a heap more to life than *love*." She spat the last word as if it had an unpleasant taste.

Susan didn't bring up the subject again. At times when she failed to act her role of dutiful wife, she was aware of Ellie's unspoken disapproval, but little was said.

Susan shivered now as she remembered the day Delia's brothers had come to the house the second time looking for Adam. Delia had died giving life to Adam's child. Her brothers had sworn to find him, even if it meant following Adam to California. Somehow Susan believed they would find him. She didn't want to be there when they did.

"Whoa there, damn you." George's harsh voice broke into her thoughts. He had been attempting to harness the oxen for more than an hour now but had made little progress. The animals seemed to react with deliberate stubbornness, rolling their eyes in alarm. Other wagons were having similar difficulties and Susan wondered if every morning would begin this way. At this rate they would never reach Oregon.

Ellie clambered down from the back of the wagon.

"Everything's packed and tied down," she said. "Do you think George will ever get those ornery animals hitched up?"

"They just need to get used to him." Susan tried to be fair even though she felt a lot of the delay was caused by George's shouts and inept handling.

"If he don't get them hitched up pretty soon, we'll be last in line to start."

"It doesn't matter where we start—we'll move up one place every day."

"I know," Ellie replied. "But I'd sooner not start at the rear and eat everyone else's dust."

At last the four oxen were hitched. George paced back and forth, his hand curled around the black whip he swung at his side.

A heavyset man rode up. His beard was speckled with gray and his eyes squinted in the glaring sun.

"All set, Baker?"

"Yup."

"Good. You follow that wagon there." The man

turned in his saddle to point. "You'll be about midway in line today. We'll pull out in a few minutes."

He swung his horse around and rode toward the next wagon.

"That must be Mr. Taggerty," Ellie commented. "He's the one who put this train together. Guess he'll be in charge."

"Has he been to Oregon before?" Susan asked.

"Nope," George said from behind her. "We got a scout to lead us. Taggerty makes the decisions according to what Morgan tells him. Morgan's led three other wagon trains through."

"They're moving out, George." Ellie shaded her eyes.

Puffs of dust billowed into the air as each wagon creaked slowly into line amid the shouts of drivers and the crack of bullwhips.

"You women get up on the seat now," George ordered. "Time to go."

Susan whistled to Sam. "You stay close," she murmured as she bent to scratch the dog's ears.

She clambered over the front wheel to join Ellie, who was already perched on the hard wooden seat. The long line of wagons stretched into the distance. They were leaving at last. Susan glanced around the encampment that had been home for the last few weeks. Clusters of people watched the wagons lurch forward. Riders whirled past, shouting, waving their hats in the air.

"At last. We're finally leaving." Ellie's words were nearly lost beneath the uproar.

Susan felt a stirring of excitement as she took a last

look at Independence. It would be months before they saw anything that resembled civilization.

Oregon, here we come, she thought.

For the first time a sense of adventure lightened her heart. Who knew what would happen? It was too late to turn back. Nothing could change what destiny had in store for her and her fellow travelers. Together they would face what was to come.

They made little progress the first day. There were constant halts along the trail while oxen were untangled from poorly fastened harnesses. Taggerty seemed to be everywhere, shouting instructions and giving assistance. When they camped for the night word was passed that they had traveled eight miles.

"Eight miles." George was disgusted. "We should have made ten or twelve. We'll never get through the mountains before the snows if this keeps up."

"It'll get better, George," Ellie assured him. "Just natural to have delays the first day or so."

He grumbled something about women not knowing anything and stomped off toward the group of men gathered near Taggerty's wagon.

"We *will* do better tomorrow, won't we, Susan?"

"Of course."

Susan heard the doubt and worry in Ellie's voice and knew she was thinking of the Donner party. It had been more than a year since news of the Donners had reached the East. Susan could picture all too vividly the group huddled in the snow-filled mountain pass without enough food or supplies to last the winter. There had been gruesome tales of starvation, death, even cannibalism. Only forty-five people had survived—a few more than half. She shivered. They had to make it over the mountains before the snow.

The last of the daylight was snuffed out by dark clouds on the western horizon, and Susan studied them with a worried frown.

Ellie threw bacon into a pan and handed it to Susan, then lowered the tailboard of the wagon to mix corn bread.

"Sure ain't like cookin' in your own kitchen," she remarked as she tried to arrange utensils on the narrow plank.

Susan straightened from the fire and put her hands on the small of her back. It would feel good to go to bed tonight. She ached all over and perspiration made her clothes cling to her body. The air was heavy and oppressive as the clouds drew closer.

Flames from other campfires flickered around the circle of wagons. Music drifted through the night air and one thin voice began to sing. Soon the song was picked up by other voices. Susan hummed as she turned the bacon. The tune was "Oh, Susannah," but the words were different. She had heard it sung in Independence and she joined the chorus as she cooked.

Oh, California, that's the land for me.
I'm bound for San Francisco with a washbowl on my knee.

"Silly song, isn't it?"

The soft voice startled Susan and she swung

around quickly. In the firelight it was difficult to see the girl clearly, but Susan thought she was quite young. Her slender body was silhouetted against the wagon and her long hair hung straight to her waist.

"I'm Mercy Laughlin."

"Susan Baker."

"Glad to meet you." The girl extended a soft white hand. "My brother, Neal, and I are in the wagon ahead of yours."

"Are you going to California?"

"No—Oregon. How about you?"

"We're headed for Oregon, too."

"Good. Neal says Oregon will be good for me. He worries a lot." Mercy's smile was shy.

"Are you and your brother traveling alone?"

"Yes. Mama and Papa died in the cholera epidemic last summer. Neal says there isn't any cholera in Oregon."

"I'm sorry—about your parents, I mean."

Mercy nodded and smiled, displaying a row of perfect white teeth. The shadows played over her delicate features. What a pretty girl, Susan thought, and unconsciously smoothed her dress with her hands.

"When's your baby due?" Mercy asked.

"Two months."

"Oh, aren't you excited? I just love babies."

"Yes, I guess so. I wish I didn't have to have it like this, though." Susan made a sweeping gesture that took in the campground and the wagons.

"It won't be so bad. I've helped birth lots of babies back home. When your time comes, you just call."

Susan regarded the girl with surprise. She seemed so young to be giving Susan reassurance about the birth of her baby.

"Thank you. Where are you from?"

"We're from Missouri. Neal taught school in a little town east of Independence. I know he hated to leave, even though he never said it, but when I got sick last winter he said there was nothing else to do but go west. The doctor said I might not make it through another winter. I think it's silly. I'm stronger than they think, but you can't tell men anything." Her laughter tinkled like tiny bells in the wind.

A flash of lightning lit the sky followed by a peal of thunder and Susan jumped.

"Looks like we're in for a storm," Mercy commented.

"Yes, I'm afraid so."

"I'd better get back to the wagon or Neal will be worried. I'll see you tomorrow though. It's nice to have a friend."

After Mercy left Susan returned to the cooking with a slight smile on her face.

Yes, it would be good to have a friend. The last year had made her feel old beyond her eighteen years. She had forgotten what it was like to have the friendship of another girl. Maybe the trip wouldn't be so bad after all.

Chapter 3

The storm had left rivulets of water running through the campsite. It was impossible to start a fire with the wet wood, so for breakfast they ate leftover corn bread and cold bacon. Some of the stock had strayed during the night and had to be rounded up, delaying their departure for several hours. Finally the wagons started rolling out.

"Keep your wagons moving," Taggerty shouted as he rode down the line. "Gotta make up what time we lost."

George plodded along beside the oxen, his whip slashing the air more often than necessary.

"Haw! Get on there, you lazy animals!" he shouted.

Susan clung to her seat as the wagon swayed through a series of potholes. At least the storm had laid the choking dust of the day before. The wagon train stretched for nearly a mile and Susan could see laboring oxen and wagons in both directions as they moved on steadily.

The scruffy trees became fewer and fewer until at last there were none at all. Men shouted and chains rattled as the oxen strained against their wooden yokes.

The sun had nearly reached the peak of its arc when the approach of a rider from the head of the train was heralded by shouts. As he came into view Susan peered at him, expecting to see Mr. Taggerty, but then she felt her pulse quicken. Could it be? No, impossible. But as he pulled his horse up next to George she knew she had been correct. It was the man from Independence who had saved her from tumbling into the street.

He wore a red shirt with a neckerchief tied loosely about his throat and his face was shaded by a large felt hat. From where she sat, Susan could see only the jut of his nose and his clean-shaven jawline, but there was no mistaking the arrogant way he sat his horse or the cynical curve of his mouth.

His gray eyes met hers as he wheeled his horse. He reined in for a moment as though about to speak, surprise crossing his face. Then, with the briefest of nods, he urged his mount toward the rear of the train.

"Who was that, George?" Ellie called.

"That's Ross Morgan—the scout. Says we'll be stopping for the noonin' shortly."

"Good." Ellie sighed and leaned back against the seat. "I sure could use a rest from all this jolting. How do you feel, Susan?"

"I'm fine."

It wasn't true, but why bother to list her aches and pains? The question had only been a formality anyway.

Susan's feelings were in a turmoil as she thought of the scout who would accompany them to Oregon. There was a magnetism about him that went beyond his dark handsomeness. He made her uncomfortable, aware of her awkward body, in a way she had never felt before. What's the matter with me? she wondered. I'm acting like a schoolgirl, not a wife and mother.

But the image of Morgan's sardonic face stayed in her mind as the wagons pulled up four abreast for the nooning, and she found herself watching for a glimpse of his red shirt.

Susan had no sooner lowered herself to the ground than Mercy was beside her. In daylight the girl's slender figure seemed almost brittle, her skin so translucent Susan could see tiny blue veins in her neck and hands. Her white-blond hair only added to the ethereal quality of her beauty.

"Neal says we'll be stopped for a couple hours. Can you come meet him?"

"I should help with the meal."

"Oh, please. It'll only take a minute. I told him about you and I do so want you to meet him."

"All right then, but only for a minute."

Susan allowed herself to be led toward the Laughlin wagon.

"Neal, this is Susan Baker, the girl I told you about."

He towered over her, his shoulders blotting out the sunlight. He reminded her of a huge bear—a bear with red hair and brown eyes, she thought as she returned his warm smile.

"Pleased to meet you, ma'am." His voice was a low growl. His hand encircled hers in a gentle grip and she noticed the reddish gold hairs on his arm as they caught the sunlight.

"I'm pleased to meet you too, Mr. Laughlin."

"Please, call me Neal."

"All right, Neal. Mercy says you taught school in Missouri."

"That's right."

"My father taught school, too, years ago. Are you planning to teach in Oregon?"

"If they'll have me. Guess it kind of gets in your blood—teaching, I mean."

Mercy's coughing interrupted their conversation. The spasms that shuddered through her slender frame made Susan look at her with quick concern. Neal was at his sister's side at once.

"Are you all right?" he asked as Mercy caught her breath with a visible effort.

"Of course I'm all right. Just the dust." Mercy's smile was weak and she leaned against her brother for a moment. "Silly cough. It'll go away when we get to the mountains. You'll see."

"Of course it will." Neal's look demanded Susan's agreement.

"Yes, this dust is enough to make anyone cough," she said, but she frowned as she studied Mercy's pale face. Did Neal really believe that those wracking coughs were caused only by the dust, or that they would be cured by mountain air? His worried gaze met hers and she realized he wasn't fooling himself.

"Susan's going to have a baby in a couple of months."

Susan flushed at Mercy's outspokenness. It was obvious to all that she was expecting, but she wasn't used to discussing it with men she hardly knew.

"Maybe someday he'll be in one of my classes," Neal said, and Susan sensed that he understood her embarrassment. "Have I met your husband, Mrs. Baker?"

26

"No, he's not with us."

"Not with you?" Mercy's voice rose in astonishment. "You mean he let you make this trip alone? I don't understand. Oh—" She stopped in sudden confusion. A red flush stained her pale cheeks. "He's not . . . I mean, is he . . ."

"He went to California last winter by ship."

"Oh. I was afraid maybe he was dead."

"No." Susan's answer carried a finality that forbade any further questions on that subject.

"Are those your folks, then?" Mercy motioned toward the other wagon.

"They're my husband's parents."

"Oh."

Mercy appeared to be at a loss for words as she puzzled over Susan's situation. Neal broke the silence.

"I imagine you're anxious to get to Oregon."

"Yes, I suppose so."

"Well, I know we are. I can't wait!" Enthusiasm had returned to Mercy's voice.

"I'd better get back and help Ellie. It's been nice meeting you, Mr. Laughlin."

"Neal," he said again and they both laughed. "It's been nice meeting you too."

A wave of homesickness hit Susan with unexpected force as she trudged back toward her own wagon. She stopped and surveyed the busy scene about her. She felt as if she were invisible, locked away from the concerns of her fellow travelers. How I wish I were back with Pa and the boys, she thought.

The warmth between Mercy and her brother had served to remind her just how alone she was. In spite of the girl's frail health, Susan envied Mercy her

27

enthusiasm and Neal's concern. If only someone cared that much about me, she thought.

Then she felt a twinge of guilt. She knew her father and brothers cared about her. She had never questioned their love. It was just that things were different now that Pa had remarried so many years after their mother's death. It had been a surprise to all of them when he announced his intention to marry Martha Brown. The boys had adapted quickly, but Susan couldn't help feeling that she was being replaced. They had all relied upon her to run the house, but now she was no longer needed. No, things were not the same, so she had listened to Adam's urgings and married him. She could never go home to face her family with the admission that she had failed in her marriage. Much as they loved her, they wouldn't understand.

With a sigh, Susan returned to the wagon and was soon caught up in the chores that awaited her.

The afternoon ride seemed much longer than the morning's had been, and by midafternoon Susan yearned for a halt. When the scout appeared for the second time that day she welcomed his arrival. Perhaps it meant they would stop soon.

He walked his horse beside George for a few minutes, but their conversation was too low for Susan to hear. At last Morgan turned his horse and approached the side of the wagon.

"Afternoon, ladies." He touched the brim of his hat with one finger.

"Good afternoon, Mr. Morgan," Ellie replied in her very best southern accent. Susan couldn't help thinking that she sounded like she was attending a garden party.

"I was just talking to Mr. Baker about the oxen. They have a heavy load to pull." He paused and his eyes skimmed across Susan's face. "I've been telling most folks to walk as much as they can—spare the oxen some that way. We have a lot of miles ahead."

"You mean you expect us to *walk?*" Ellie asked, incredulous.

"That's right, ma'am." His voice hardened. "Ain't no other way, not if you expect these animals to make it to Oregon."

"Well, I never," Ellie spluttered. "I never heard tell of a thing like that. Expectin' ladies to walk."

Susan spoke up. "I imagine it would be a nice change from the jolting we've been taking on this wagon."

"*You* can't walk!" Ellie's tone was scandalized. "Not in your condition. Surely you don't expect *her* to walk, do you?"

Before Morgan could respond, Susan answered, "Of course I can. And so can you. If it's necessary to spare the animals, then we'll do it. Tell George to stop."

"I'll do no such thing. If you want to walk all day in that dust and blazing sun, you go right ahead. Probably lose the baby, too. I'm stayin' here, like a lady should."

Morgan gave Ellie a look of disgust. "It's your choice, ma'am. I'm just warning you. The train can't wait up if your team wears out. You can't expect everyone else to take on your hardship if you won't help yourselves."

"You mean you'd leave us?" Ellie's voice was shrill now. "In the middle of the wilderness?"

"Not if we can help it, but you'd be wise to think on it. Good day, ladies."

He spun his horse away from the wagon and Susan watched him ride off.

"The nerve of that man!"

"He must know what he's talking about," Susan defended him. "After all, he's done this before."

"Makes no difference. He obviously doesn't know a lady from a horse. No lady's gonna walk all the way to Oregon."

"I'm going to try."

Ellie watched openmouthed as Susan called to George to stop and then scrambled down from the wagon. It felt good to straighten her back and she took her place beside the team as they resumed their plodding.

It was hard going in spots. The side of the trail was rocky and uneven, but it was better than the wagon seat. Sam trotted at her heels. At least the dog was happy with her company.

When Morgan passed on his way back to the head of the train, Susan thought she saw a glint of approval in his eyes, but he didn't speak. She wondered if he really would have asked her to walk had she not made the decision herself. She thought not. He was a strange man, she decided.

Ahead Susan saw other women trudging beside the trail. She quickened her pace to catch up with the Laughlin wagon and fell into step beside Mercy.

"Do you think you should be walking?" she asked the girl.

"Why not? You sound just like Neal. If you can walk, I don't know why I can't."

"Well, I'm sure it wouldn't hurt any if you rode."

"That's what Mr. Morgan told Neal when he heard I'd been sick. But if it helps our oxen, then I'll do it."

Susan thought of Ellie, stubbornly ensconced on the wagon seat, and her hands clenched in anger.

"Poor things," Mercy remarked as she looked fondly at the oxen. "They all have names, you know."

"Oh? What are they?"

"That one's Sue, and the one on the off side is Joe. Behind him is Betsy and that one is Ike. I named them myself. It makes them seem like part of the family," Mercy explained. "Do you think that's silly?"

"Of course not."

"That Mr. Morgan sure is a good-looking man, isn't he?" Mercy asked.

"The scout?"

"Yes. I bet he turns all the ladies' heads."

"I suppose."

"Oh, Susan, you must have noticed him." Mercy's laugh tinkled.

Susan tried to ignore Mercy's comments. She had no right to notice another man. And she had no desire to gossip about their scout. Or did she?

Her curiosity was aroused more than she cared to admit. What kind of life was it leading wagon trains across the continent? What made him do it? Why wasn't he married? Maybe he was. She lost step with Mercy for a moment, then hurried to catch up.

"Is he married?"

"See there, I knew you'd noticed him," Mercy teased. Then her expression became serious. "I heard Neal and a couple of the men talking. I guess he was married but his wife died. No one seemed to know much more. I guess he isn't the kind to talk about himself."

Susan couldn't help but speculate about Ross Morgan. What little Mercy had said merely added to his aura of mystery. Then she shrugged her shoulders, impatient with herself. It wasn't any concern of hers.

"What's your husband like?" Mercy's question took her by surprise.

"Like?"

"You know—what does he look like, what sort of a person is he, things like that?"

She couldn't snub Mercy's innocent question.

"He's tall, with light hair and blue eyes." Susan remembered how she had once thought his hair the color of corn silk and how she had failed to notice the coldness of his blue eyes.

"Did you grow up together?"

"No. No, I met him in Indiana. He was visiting relatives."

"And he swept you off your feet, just like in the books?"

Susan couldn't suppress a bitter smile. "Yes, I guess you could say he did."

"How exciting!" Mercy's eyes shone with pleasure. "I wish something like that would happen to me."

Susan bit back the words that crowded into her mind. It seemed so long ago that she had had romantic dreams like Mercy's. She had been so sure that Adam would be the man she could love for the rest of her life. She would escape the hard farm life and the presence of a stepmother she couldn't accept. Adam would take care of her, shower her with attention, and she'd never have to worry again.

Her lip curled in a scornful smile as she remembered her first sight of his home. The estate Adam had so grandly alluded to had amounted to five hundred rock-infested acres, only a third of it tillable, and a house that was little more than a rundown shack. She shuddered at the memory of her arrival. No bride had ever faced a more disappointing homecoming. Her body had been bruised from three days of unaccustomed riding, and Adam's savage assault on their wedding night had only made her more vulnerable. Her reasons had seemed so good at the time she agreed to marry him. Even when she had been so rudely forced to face reality she had vowed she would learn to tolerate the nights and try to be a good wife. But her resolution had crumbled in the face of Adam's behavior and Delia's revelation.

Susan shook her head, trying to banish the wave of unpleasant memories.

"You should always be careful what you wish for," she told Mercy soberly. "Sometimes you get it."

Chapter 4

They had been on the trail five days when they camped at Lone Elm. There wasn't another tree or bush for miles around, just the one mighty elm that stood on a rise near a small creek.

Susan and Ellie carried buckets of water back to the wagon and washed the dust from their hair and skin. Susan brushed her long hair dry in the sun. It felt brittle to her touch and she sighed as she thought of how soft and lustrous it had once been. She pulled it back into a bun and hesitated a moment before picking up a carved ivory hairpin. It was one of her few ornaments and she still cherished it in spite of the fact it had been a present from Adam during their brief courtship.

She tried not to think of the day she had met him while admiring the pin in Spencer's General Store. How different her life would be now if she hadn't paused to gaze wistfully at jewelry she couldn't afford. The next day he had insisted she accept it as a gift. She should have known even then that things weren't quite right, but she had been impressed with his charm and generosity, not knowing how false they were. How easily she had been fooled!

Resolutely she pushed the memories from her mind as she left the wagon. The campfires flickered invitingly, but Susan felt the need to be alone. She slipped between the wagons and lifted her face to the evening breeze. The last streaks of orange and red sunlight filtered across the prairie grasses as she wandered to the banks of the little stream. The sound of the water was pleasant. She blocked out the sound of the shouts and laughter behind her and pretended she was alone, miles away from anyone.

She stooped to pick one of the prairie pinks that grew in abundance in the rich black soil and held it to her nose to breathe in its fragrance.

Something moved to her left. Susan froze. At first she thought it was an animal. Then, in the gathering twilight, she saw a tall form unbend itself from the grassy bank and recognized Ross Morgan. She relaxed once more.

"Where do you think you're going?" His voice was abrupt.

"Just for a stroll."

"The prairie isn't the place to 'stroll.'" He covered the distance between them in a few long strides.

"I don't see that it's any business of yours."

She bristled with annoyance at his high-handed attitude. Why did this man antagonize her so?

"Everything is my business on this train. It's my job to see that all you fools make it to Oregon safe and sound. I don't need some addle-headed woman getting lost."

"If you think so little of us, why bother?" Susan snapped.

"It's a job."

"Seems you could find something to suit you better. Besides, no one could get lost out here. You can see for miles."

"The prairie fools you. You can walk into gullies and valleys and never find your way back. What's your husband thinking of, letting you wander off alone like this?"

"My husband's in California, and I'm quite sure he wouldn't care what I did." The bitterness in her voice seemed to surprise him.

"Well, no one should leave camp, especially at night. Now, shall I take you back?"

"I'm not a child. I can find my own way."

Her head high, her back rigid, Susan turned and flounced toward the wagons.

Arrogant man, she thought, her mind seething with anger. What makes him think he's always right? Her foot caught in the hem of her skirt, and she stumbled and ran a few paces before she regained her balance. She heard a snort of laughter and turned to retort angrily, but he was lost in the darkness. Only his hearty, mocking laughter rang out in the night air.

Her cheeks burning with anger and embarrassment, Susan stomped back to the circle of wagons. From now on she would avoid Ross Morgan at all costs.

A week later Susan stood on a high river bank, watching the water flow past. Trees and shrubs reached out from the banks on either side.

"Awful steep, isn't it?" Mercy asked.

"Yes. I don't see how we'll ever get the wagons across."

"They're going to lower them with ropes. They're starting to hitch up the first one now."

A group of men had gathered around the lead wagon. Susan watched them lock the wheels in place and fasten a heavy rope to the rear axle, then twist the rope around a sturdy tree. Ross Morgan took his place with two other men at the back of the wagon. They pushed until the front wheels tilted over the edge and the wagon began to slide.

Susan held her breath as the men let the rope out, steadily easing the wagon down the slope until it came to rest beside the stream.

"Now they'll float it across," Mercy told her. "We're lucky the river's so low this year. Ross Morgan says sometimes you can't ford the Wakarusa."

The two girls watched as the process was repeated several times. Some of the men removed their shirts and sweat glistened on their bare backs as they struggled with the heavy wagons.

"It makes me hot just to watch," Susan sighed. "It'll be hours before it's our turn. I think I'll go sit in the shade."

The heat was oppressive. Susan wiped a damp curl off her forehead and tucked it under her sunbonnet. The bonnet kept the worst of the sun from her face, but her nose had already burned and peeled. It was almost two weeks now since they had left Independence. How many more to go?

Her body was heavy and listless, but she forced her feet to keep plodding until at last she reached a tree and sank to the ground in its welcome shade. Sam flopped at her side, his head in her lap, and begged for attention.

"Not now, Sam," she murmured and gently pushed the dog aside. The added weight was too much to bear. She fell into a fitful doze.

Susan awoke to the touch of Ellie's hand on her shoulder.

"It's our turn, Susan. Come on."

Still drowsy, Susan stumbled to her feet and followed Ellie to the river. Already thirty or more wagons stood on the other side, and she watched George bring their own up to the edge of the bank.

"As soon as they get it down, we'll follow and ride on it across the river," Ellie said.

Susan nodded and watched the men fasten the rope to the axle. Her head felt light and she clutched Ellie's arm.

"Are you all right?"

"Yes, I'm fine. Just not awake yet." She shook her head and blinked her eyes in an attempt to clear her blurred vision.

"There it goes," Ellie cried. "Oh my, I do hope they'll be careful."

Susan watched the wagon bump and jolt down the nearly perpendicular slope. It seemed about to overturn at any moment, but at last it was safely at the bottom.

"Come on," Ellie called and Susan followed her.

The bank was slippery and uneven and she clutched at outcroppings of rock and small bushes to keep her balance.

"There's a rock you can step on," Ellie shouted from below.

Susan paused in her scramble to look down. Ellie had reached the wagon and was watching her descend. She pointed to where Susan should put her foot.

Susan's vision blurred again and she rubbed her eyes with her free hand. Where' was it? Oh yes, there, just a little to the left.

She clutched the root of a tree that protruded from the bank and placed her foot cautiously on the rock. Just as she started to swing her weight from one foot to the other the root gave way with a loud snap. As she fought to regain her balance, she heard Ellie's cry of alarm.

Susan teetered there for a moment. Then she lost her balance and was tumbling down the riverbank. She clutched at roots and bushes in a frantic effort to stop her fall, but they came away in her hands. Clods of earth tumbled around her. A sharp, searing pain shot through her body as she rolled to a halt in the rocky stream bed.

Oh God, the baby, she thought, just before she lapsed into unconsciousness.

Chapter 5

"Susan!" A voice called her name. Was it Papa?

"Papa, here I am." She tried to force the words through her cracked lips. Someone pressed a damp cloth to her face. She let the darkness smother her.

Relentless pain dragged her back from unconsciousness. It wouldn't let her go. It held her like a vise, a band around her waist, cutting her in half. She moaned.

"It's all right, Susan. Just lie still."

The woman's voice was soft. Who was it? She fought to remember, but the pain fogged her mind—the terrible, white-hot torment that slashed through her each time she moved.

"It hurts." Was that her voice? It was the cracked voice of an old woman.

"I know."

Again the damp cloth. She tried to open her eyes but the effort was too great. Dimly she realized she was in the wagon, but she couldn't recall how she came to be there.

She sighed and the pain rushed at her again. This time she screamed. It was a moment before she realized the terrible cry had come from her own lips. Then she screamed again.

"Hush now." It was a man's voice this time. It commanded obedience. Was it Adam? Oh, dear God, no, don't let it be Adam. She writhed on the bed. She had to get away.

"Hold still. Here, hold my hands."

No, it wasn't Adam. She didn't know who it was, but the voice held reassurance. Her hands were clasped by two large calloused ones. She clung to those strong hands desperately, her fingernails digging into the skin. The hands didn't flinch. Gradually the pain subsided into a dark ache somewhere deep inside her, and she took a short, shallow breath. She tried to prepare herself for the next spasm.

"How is she?" Another voice, one she knew. Ellie.

"As well as can be expected." The man's voice again.

"You shouldn't be here. We can take care of our own."

Susan struggled to speak. She didn't want him to leave. Those strong hands were her only anchor in this sea of agony.

"No . . ." The sound was weak.

"What, dear?"

She felt rather than saw Ellie bend over her. Susan clamped her lips together as the pain threatened to wash over her.

"She'd be upset if she knew a stranger was here. Ain't no place for a man."

"It doesn't look to me like you were doing her much good. Heard her screaming all over camp."

"What do you expect—havin' a baby and all?"

Baby—oh God, the baby. That's why it hurt so much. Susan struggled to sit up, but hands reached out to gently push her back against the bed. It was too soon. She couldn't have the baby yet. She had to tell them, make it stop. Another wave of pain crashed over her and she groped blindly for support. His hands grasped hers tightly, pulling her through as they had before. She held her breath, using every ounce of will not to scream again. It was wrong to scream. Hadn't he said so?

This time there was no relief. It was a long continuous struggle against the torment that spiraled within her. She tossed her head back and forth against the pillow and clenched her teeth together.

"There now, Susan, it'll be all right," the voice whispered to her over and over until it became a meaningless phrase like the words of a nonsense song.

It was difficult to breathe. The pain burned her, engulfed her, and she lost all contact with what was happening. The steady hands that held her own and kept her from drowning in this agony were the only reality.

She heard the rush of water, the bellow of oxen, the shouts of men. Her eyelids flickered, then opened. Where was she?

The wagon was empty. She heard sounds from outside. They seemed to be moving, but the wagon didn't jolt. It was like floating on a cloud. Through the canvas opening she could see white, feathery clouds drifting against the blue sky.

I'm on a cloud, she thought, and then she smiled. How could a wagon get on a cloud?

Was she dead? The thought was an idle one,

neither alarming nor comforting, just something to think about. She looked down at her body. She could see her feet. It had been a long time since she could see her feet. She wiggled her toes.

Then she realized what it meant. The baby. The baby had come. She struggled to sit up, but the effort exhausted her and she fell back.

"Ellie." Her voice was cracked from disuse. She cleared her throat and tried again. "Ellie."

She heard shoes against wood planking, then the canvas flap was pulled aside and Ellie looked in.

"Did you call, Susan?"

"Where's the baby?"

"Shhh, dear. It's all right."

"Where's my baby?" Susan's voice rose in alarm. Why was the woman standing there staring at her? Didn't she understand? "I want my baby," she cried.

"Just a minute, dear."

Susan sank back against her pillow. At last Ellie had understood. She would bring the baby. Susan's baby. Not Adam's, but hers, her very own child. Her arms ached with the need to hold it. Everything would be all right now. She would have someone to lavish her love upon, someone who needed it and who would love her in return. Her mouth trembled into a smile.

She heard whispers outside the wagon, the shuffling of feet. What was taking so long? At last the canvas parted and Mercy pulled herself into the wagon.

"How are you, Susan?" She took Susan's hand in her own soft one. "We were so worried about you."

"Oh, Mercy, thank goodness you're here. I can't

make her understand. I want my baby. Where's my baby?"

"I know." The girl brushed a strand of hair away from Susan's feverish forehead.

"Is it a boy or a girl?"

"A little girl."

Susan smiled. "A girl. I'll call her Sarah. I knew it would be a girl. They all tried to tell me it would be a boy, but I knew it would be a girl. Can I see her?"

She looked into Mercy's gentle face. There was something wrong. Mercy wasn't smiling. Alarm quickened her heartbeat. She was afraid to ask, but she knew—deep inside she knew. The smile faded from her lips and she clutched Mercy's hand desperately.

"What is it?" Her voice was barely a whisper.

"The baby . . . Susan . . ."

"Yes, go on."

"The baby's dead."

Mercy lowered her head and her shoulders shook. She wiped tears from her eyes before she raised her face to Susan's.

"I'm sorry," she said simply.

Susan's hand dropped limply from Mercy's. She stared at the other girl, willing it to be a mistake. A terrible joke. Not her baby, not her daughter. She couldn't be dead.

"Where is she? I want to see her. She can't be dead. Let me see her." Susan's voice rose hysterically. "You have to let me see her."

"You can't, Susan."

"Why not? She's mine. I want to see her."

"We had to bury her." Mercy's voice choked on a sob. "It was the only thing to do. It's been four days since we left the Wakarusa. We couldn't wait any longer."

"You buried her?" Susan's voice rose in disbelief. "You buried her in that godforsaken place? How could you let them do it, Mercy? How could you?"

"There wasn't anything else to do, Susan. You must understand. She came early. She was too tiny to live. We did everything we could, please believe that." Mercy's blue eyes glistened with tears as she studied Susan's white face. "I said a special prayer for her."

Susan turned her head away.

Mercy hesitated, then patted her shoulder. "I'll come back later."

Susan didn't reply. She heard Mercy swing herself down from the wagon, an exchange of voices, Mercy's and Ellie's, then footsteps as the two women moved away.

My baby, she thought. My baby's dead. Dead before she could live. Oh God, how could you be so cruel? Anger filled her, anger at God, at Adam, at this whole crazy trip. If Adam had let her go by boat this never would have happened. She had tried to tell him. Now they could all see how wrong they'd been.

What good does it do? she thought. Now that it's too late, what good does it do? Her anger fled as swiftly as it had come and she was overcome by a cold, empty desolation. She envisioned a tiny marker beside the trail, like so many she had seen, only this one was different. This one didn't have a name. Her daughter hadn't even had a name. Somehow that was the worst part, knowing that somewhere behind them was a nameless marker over the body of her child. Susan turned her face into the pillow so no one would hear her cries.

Chapter 6

Day after day Susan lay on her makeshift bed as the wagon lurched westward. Mercy was constantly at her side, bringing broth, a cup of tea, anything to boost Susan's strength and spirits, but Susan remained lethargic. She couldn't bear to make polite conversation so she retreated into a brooding silence.

For hours she thought of the daughter she had lost. She wondered what would have happened if the baby had lived. Would she have been pretty? Happy? Susan knew this brooding was bad for her, that it was probably the worst thing she could do, but she couldn't resist the tormenting thoughts. Her only escape was when she managed to fall into a fitful sleep, but even then she dreamt of a crying baby she could never find.

"Why not try to walk a little today," Mercy coaxed. "It would do you good to get out in the sunshine and it's quite lovely—not too warm."

"I don't think so."

"You can't lie here day after day. You'll never get better."

"What makes you think I *want* to get better?"

"Of course you do. Don't talk nonsense." Mercy was vehement.

"Maybe tomorrow I'll get up." Susan turned her back to Mercy. She heard the younger girl sigh and leave the wagon, and felt a moment of remorse. Mercy tried so hard to make her feel better and take an interest in things. She wasn't being fair to her.

But it's not fair to me either, Susan thought fretfully. Why should I care if I ever get well? What's left to live for? Why can't they just leave me alone?

She dozed off and was awakened by the sound of boots against the wagon floorboards. Her eyes opened wide when she saw Ross Morgan's stern, unsmiling face.

"What are you doing here?" she gasped, jerking the bedclothes up to her chin.

"Mercy says you're feeling better."

"A little." Her answer was guarded.

"I thought you'd be out getting some fresh air."

"I haven't felt up to it."

"Oh? Makes it hard on everyone else, doesn't it?"

"What do you mean? I'm not bothering anyone. I just want to be left alone."

"Maybe so, but Mercy Laughlin is in and out of here every few minutes and she's wearing herself down. She worries about you, and it looks to me like you're so busy feeling sorry for yourself you can't see what you're doing to others."

"I didn't ask her to do anything."

"No, but Mercy cares about you. She's that kind of person—selfless." His mouth curled scornfully and she flashed him a look of resentment. What business was it of his if she wanted to spend the rest of her life in bed?

"You have no right to barge in here and start lecturing me," she retorted. "How would *you* know how I feel? You've never lost a baby. How could *you* understand?"

She recoiled from the suddenly violent expression in his eyes.

"I understand more than you think."

"Well, you can just tell Mercy and anyone else who's interested that I'll come out when I'm ready," Susan responded pettishly.

He turned to leave, but as he lowered himself to the ground he gave her one last look, his eyes hard as granite.

"No matter what you tell Mercy, she'll keep caring for you until you're on your feet or she collapses. I guess I was wrong. I thought you were a brave woman. But you're a child, a spoiled coward, afraid to face life as it comes."

Susan snatched up a hairbrush and hurled it at him, but he had vanished and the brush clattered into a corner of the wagon.

"Damn him," she muttered under her breath. "Damn, damn." Somehow the unaccustomed profanity made her feel better—alive for the first time in days.

I'll show him, she vowed. Coward, indeed.

She swung her legs over the side of the bed and struggled into a dress. The effort weakened her and she fell back, panting. The dress, which had been let out during her pregnancy, hung shapeless from her slender shoulders. Susan looped a length of rope around her waist.

There was talk and laughter outside the wagon. It must be time for the nooning, yet no one had brought her food. She wondered if they had given up on her and fought a wave of self-pity. She clambered shakily over boxes to the rear of the wagon.

When she lowered herself slowly to the ground, no one seemed to notice her. George and Ellie sat at a little distance, eating their noon meal. They were in the midst of a discussion and Susan felt no desire to attract their attention. She slipped around the wagon, and, with one hand against its side, walked on trembling legs toward the Laughlin wagon.

Sam loped up to greet her. His tongue hung from the side of his mouth and his tail wagged exuberantly.

Mercy's face brightened as she saw Susan. She immediately dropped what she was doing and hurried to her side.

"You should have called me. I was just going to bring you something to eat. I'm sorry if I took too long. You shouldn't be up without anyone to help you." Mercy put one arm around Susan's waist and led her toward Neal.

"You've done far too much for me as it is, Mercy. I'll never be able to repay you."

"Oh, hush now. What are friends for? Repay!" She shook her head.

"Hello, Susan." Neal's voice was grave. Does he think I've been selfish too, she wondered. But he seemed concerned only about her well-being.

"It's good to see you up again," he said. "We've missed you."

Susan felt tears burn her eyes at his concern and blinked them back. She wouldn't act like a coward.

"You shouldn't try to do too much right at first,"

Mercy fussed. "Why don't I take you back to the wagon, and then tonight when we stop you can get out again."

In spite of her resolution to be brave, Susan felt weak-kneed and light-headed.

"Yes, I think you're right," she said, and allowed Mercy to lead her back toward the wagon. "How long have I been in bed?"

"Let's see, it was four days until we crossed the Kansas—that was when you woke up the first time. And it's been five days since then."

"No wonder I feel so shaky."

"It's lucky you're alive."

"You said we crossed the Kansas."

"Yes. We were on the barge when you woke up."

Susan remembered the floating sensation, her fantasy that they were on a cloud. That explained it. It hadn't been a dream.

"Mercy, I remember, or I think I remember . . . when I was having the pains. Was there a man there?"

"Why, yes, but I didn't think you realized."

"Who was it?"

"Ross Morgan. He sat with you for hours."

Susan was stunned. She couldn't imagine Morgan caring enough about anyone to sit and hold their hands through such an ordeal. And yet Mercy said he had. She remembered his strong grip, her only support through those long hours. She suddenly regretted the way she had acted when he came to see her.

"He was very concerned about you," Mercy said.

"I suppose he was angry because I delayed the wagon train."

"Oh no. He was the one who talked Mr. Taggerty into waiting until . . . until the baby was born."

Susan shook her head in bewilderment. It didn't fit with what she'd seen of Ross Morgan. He always berated her, nettled her into doing things she didn't want to do, told her how wrong she was.

"I guess you just never know about people," she murmured as Mercy helped her into the wagon.

"You rest now," Mercy directed. "I'll tell Mr. Morgan you've been up a little. He'll be pleased to hear it."

A small smile curled Susan's lip as Mercy left the wagon.

"I just bet he'll be," she murmured.

Chapter 7

The wagon train had veered north again, and the days took on a sameness for Susan as she recovered her strength. But now she had company in her misfortune.

Cholera had swept the train. First a couple cases were reported, then a few more, and then it seemed that everywhere people were tending the ill and dying. During the sultry nights Susan lay awake and listened to the whimpers of the sick. The accepted remedies of laudanum, cholera clyster and mustard poultices were dutifully applied, and still the victims died. An unpleasant odor hung over the camp, like a smothering blanket—the smell of death.

Each day graves were dug beside the trail, and Susan watched parents, wives and husbands kneel beside the pitiful mounds of earth to bid farewell to loved ones. Every new grave reminded her of the baby she had lost.

They crossed the Big Vermillion River and found signs of other trains that had gone before. She counted more than a hundred graves as the train pushed on toward the Big Blue.

Their arrival in the Little Blue Valley was a happy

one. The cholera had finally subsided. They found grass for the stock, clear pure water and ample firewood. For the first time in days there was singing and dancing around the campfires and Taggerty passed the word they would spend the next day resting the stock and repairing the wagons. An air of celebration hovered over the camp.

Since her recovery, Susan had seen Ross Morgan only from a distance. She had expected him to make some sign, to acknowledge the fact that his words had had their intended effect, but he had merely glanced in her direction as she trudged beside the wagon. She was stung by his disinterest and wondered if he really could be the same man who had helped her through the birth of her baby. If Mercy had not told her it was true, she wouldn't have believed it.

"Susan, isn't it wonderful to have a day to rest?" Mercy almost skipped as the two girls made their way to the stream to fill their buckets.

"Yes," Susan agreed. "George even caught some fish for supper last night. It was a welcome change from salt pork."

"I know. Ross brought us some fish last night, too."

Susan felt an unexpected pang of envy and quickly pushed it from her mind. Ross Morgan seemed to be in Mercy's talk daily. She constantly reported little acts of kindness he performed for them, but her naive manner failed to indicate whether she thought she was receiving any special treatment or that it could have any particular meaning. Susan would allow her thoughts to go no further. It was none of her business if Morgan took a special interest in Mercy. The girl deserved all the happiness she could get, and it was wrong to feel this pang of jealousy every time Mercy spoke his name.

"That was nice of him."

"Don't you like him, Susan?" Mercy regarded her with serious eyes. "I would think you, of all people . . ." She paused. "Every time you see him you walk in the opposite direction. I'm sure it hurts him when you avoid him like that."

"Don't be ridiculous. He couldn't be hurt by anything I do. Besides, every time we do talk it's only to argue over something."

Mercy sighed. "You're wrong about him, you know."

Susan refused to discuss the matter further. They filled their buckets and returned to the wagons.

It was late afternoon before Susan finished her chores. She had laundered her clothes and bathed and washed her hair, and for the first time in months she felt attractive as she studied her reflection in the mirror. Auburn streaks glinted in the long hair that framed her oval face. The sun had tanned her skin to a golden honey tone that set off her dark-lashed amber eyes.

When she had married Adam it had seemed to turn her into an old woman overnight, and this was the first time she had begun to feel young once more. There was no reason for the light-heartedness she felt this afternoon, except that the sun was shining, the grass was green and she felt healthy and alive.

"I think I'll take a walk before dinner," she told Ellie, who merely nodded.

Only once had Ellie mentioned the baby.

"It's always a shame losin' a baby. Many's the one I lost myself," she'd said in an awkward attempt at conversation.

Susan had only nodded. Ellie could never have experienced the waves of despair she had felt at losing her daughter.

"I expect Adam'll be disappointed when he finds out," Ellie continued.

"Why should he be?" Susan couldn't resist the bitterness she felt. Ellie looked astonished.

"Why, it's only natural," she replied. "Even though he wanted a son."

"Adam never cared about our child. If he had, he wouldn't have forced me to make this trip."

Ellie's mouth thinned to a line of disapproval. "Don't you go blamin' Adam," she snapped. "Chances are you brought it on yourself, refusin' to ride in the wagon like any lady should. The good Lord knows Adam never expected you to walk to Oregon. Other women have healthy babies on the trail. Maybe *you* didn't really want Adam's child at all."

Susan knew it was useless to argue with Ellie, and such talk only revived her own grief. But the exchange further strained the atmosphere between them.

Now, as Susan strolled toward the river, she relished her solitude. The sun felt good against her skin, not scorching and punishing as it so often did. A bobolink sang in the currant bushes that lined the stream as she paused to examine wild-flowers and toss pebbles into the water.

"Out for another of your 'strolls'?" The voice startled her, but she knew before she turned to face him that Ross Morgan had deliberately followed her.

"I'm not going far."

"Peaceful here, isn't it?" he asked.

"Yes—yes, it is."

"Have you been to see the springs?"

"No."

"Come with me then. I'll show you."

She hesitated for a moment, then shrugged. Why not? It was the first time she could recall him ever being civil to her. She fell into step beside him, two of hers needed to match his one. He grinned and slowed his pace.

"It's good to see you up and around. Feeling better?" he asked.

"Yes, thank you." They fell silent.

The spring was lovely. It gushed from a ledge of rocks, fell into a basin and then fell another ten or twelve feet to a second pool.

"Come here." Ross motioned her to the left and she clambered after him. There, above the falling water, was a smooth stone with carved letters.

"'Alcove Spring,'" she read. "Who named it?"

"Don't know. Someone from an early wagon train, I suppose."

"It's a pretty name."

Susan idly traced the letters with her finger and then moved to others carved in the rock. She spelled them to herself, then stopped short.

"George Donner. He carved his name right here —here in this rock."

"Yes, I know," Ross said. "And so did James Reed. Look here."

Susan saw the words, "J. Reed, 26 May 1846." She stared silently at the names of the Donner party members for several moments, then shivered.

"Cold?"

"No. It just gives me a funny feeling, sitting here where they must have sat, knowing they felt just like we do. They were so sure they'd make it to California."

"Some of them did," Ross said.

"Yes, I know. But it was awful, even for the ones who survived."

"Life doesn't always turn out the way we plan."

"Oh, I know that. Look at me. A year ago I never expected to be here. I wasn't even married."

A closed look came over Ross's face. What had she said to offend him? She continued to trace letters on the warm rock as she gazed at the cascading water.

"Thank you for showing me," she said at last. "I . . . I want to thank you too for what you did when I . . . when I had the baby. Mercy told me. It was—"

"Forget it." His voice was abrupt. He looked away.

Susan remembered the story Mercy had told her of his wife.

"Do you have children?" she asked. For a moment she thought he hadn't heard her question.

"No, I don't have children," he said at last.

For some reason she was afraid to ask any more questions. His attitude clearly forbade it and told her she was trespassing. She sat awkwardly and waited for him to make some move, but he continued to gaze off to the west as though she were not there, his profile as stolid as though it, too, had been carved in rock.

At last she shifted, and he turned to look at her. His eyes narrowed and seemed to hold an odd warmth and Susan felt a tremulous stirring. Her own eyes widened as she stared into his for a long moment. She leaned toward him.

In one quick movement he rose and offered his hand to help her up. The spell was broken—if in fact it had been there at all.

"We'd better get back to the wagons," he said. "People will wonder what we've been up to. Not much else to talk about on the trail."

She followed him to the foot of the springs. Campfire smoke floated over the wagons. She knew it was time to return, but she was reluctant to leave. She felt strongly drawn to Morgan even though he maintained a careful distance from her.

"I'm quite sure you can find your own way back," he said and turned and strode off in the opposite direction. She watched him walk away, his step purposeful. Where was he off to now? She wished she were going with him.

She shook herself and turned to face the wagons. If only things were different. If only I'd had the sense not to marry Adam. Would Ross Morgan find me attractive then?

She forced the thought from her mind. It was all nonsense. If it weren't for Adam she wouldn't be here in the first place. All her resolutions to be a proper wife were hopeless. Maybe, if she were married to a man like Ross Morgan, things would be different.

I'll never know that now, she thought, and as she returned to the wagon the day's brightness seemed tarnished.

Chapter 8

The broad, glassy waters of the Platte shimmered silver in the sunlight. A few grassy islets in the river were the only green spots in a brown landscape.

"I always thought rivers had trees and shade," Mercy said.

"So did I."

"The poor animals. Neal says if we have much more of this heat they'll drop over dead."

Susan agreed as she watched the oxen strain against the heavy sand. It seemed as though they traveled through a nightmare. Every day there were frequent stops to tighten the steel rims of the wagon wheels and rest the weary oxen. Billows of dust hung above the train and a layer of grime clung to them all. The wagons blended with the countryside, their canvas tops no longer white. Susan longed for an end to the monotony and knew the others shared her feelings. Tempers were short and arguments flared for no apparent reason.

"Ross says we should spot buffalo any day now," Mercy said.

Game had been scarce. Although they had seen a few antelope in the distance, even skilled hunters like Morgan had been unable to bring one down.

"I wonder what buffalo meat tastes like," Susan said.

"Like beef. At least that's what Neal says, but the old ones are tough."

"Couldn't be much worse than what we've been eating."

"No, and we can use buffalo chips for fuel."

"Buffalo chips?" Susan was constantly surprised by the amount of information Mercy gathered.

"It's like cow pies." Mercy flushed. "But when it dries you can use it in place of wood."

Susan wrinkled her nose in disgust. "Ugh!"

"I know." Mercy's laughter tinkled. "I never thought I'd be building fires with animal droppings, did you?"

"I've done a lot of things I never thought I'd do."

"Can't you just see some of those uppity eastern ladies gathering buffalo chips?"

Mercy laughed again, but the laughter suddenly turned to choking coughs and she clutched Susan's arm as the spasms made her double over, her handkerchief held to her lips. Susan tried to shield her from the worst of the dust as the heavy wagons lumbered past.

At last the coughing ceased and Mercy straightened weakly, still clinging to Susan's arm. Susan glanced at the handkerchief clutched in the girl's hand. It was spotted with red flecks.

"Mercy!"

The girl quickly stuffed the cloth in her pocket and met Susan's worried gaze.

"Don't tell Neal," she whispered urgently.

"But Mercy, you should be in the wagon out of this dust. How long have you—"

"Only a couple days. It's just that the dust makes me cough so." Mercy smiled and began to walk again. "Come on, let's catch up with the wagon."

"But you must tell Neal. He'd want to know."

Mercy shook her head firmly. "What could he do? He'd only worry and he has enough to worry about as it is." She clasped Susan's hand, her face earnest. "Susan, you must promise not to tell him."

Susan hesitated.

"Please."

Bright splotches of color flared in Mercy's pale cheeks, and Susan realized it wouldn't help to argue with her.

"If you're truly my friend, you won't tell him," Mercy persisted. "Believe me, I know what I'm doing."

"All right," Susan agreed reluctantly. "But you must promise to ride in the wagon more. Stay out of the sun and the dust. It can't go on like this much longer."

"I will, Susan. Really, it isn't so bad except in the afternoons."

"It won't help Neal if you collapse." Susan heard the sharpness in her voice and tried to soften her words. "Please be sensible." She squeezed the girl's hand.

"I will, but don't forget—not a word to Neal. Once we get out of this dust I'll be fine. You'll see."

Susan nodded, but she knew that even Mercy must realize her condition had a more serious cause than the heavy dust. She vowed to watch the girl more closely. If only there were some shade.

* * *

That afternoon Ross Morgan reported a large herd of buffalo to the north and recruited half a dozen men to accompany him on the hunt. George immediately volunteered.

"You can tend the team," he told Susan. "If they get out of line, just give 'em a taste of this." He handed her his whip. "They're just like women—you gotta let 'em know who's boss." He laughed as he strode off to saddle a horse.

Susan watched the men ride into the distance and wished she could go with them. It would be wonderful to gallop across the plains and feel the wind in her face, free of the constraints of the trail. She sighed as she plodded along beside the wagon. At least there might be fresh meat for dinner.

The oxen were obedient and well used to working as a team. Susan found that they needed little encouragement to follow the tracks of those ahead. Ellie had retreated to the back of the wagon. Since they had reached the Platte she rested every afternoon. The dust and heat were too much for her, she explained, and even the seat was too uncomfortable during the heat of the day. Susan hoped Mercy was following Ellie's example. She was the one who needed rest.

The wagons halted for the night before riders appeared to the north. Susan peered through the gathering dusk trying to see if they had been successful, but it was impossible to tell from that distance. She turned back to the fire. There was little wood and she used it sparingly. No one knew when they would find more.

She heard voices near Taggerty's wagon as the

men reached the circle and she waited for George to appear.

"Are the men back yet?" Ellie asked, climbing down from the wagon.

"They just came in. They're over by Taggerty's wagon now."

"I wish George would hurry up. I'm mighty hungry."

"There's some corn bread left from yesterday."

Ellie wrinkled her nose. "I declare, I'm so sick of corn bread I don't think I could eat one more bite. I do hope they brought back some meat. What's takin' that man so long?" She glanced impatiently across the campground. "Don't he know we're waitin' on him?"

A figure detached itself from the group of men and strode toward them. Susan recognized Taggerty and felt a small pang of unease. He paused beside their campfire and removed his hat.

"Mrs. Baker, ma'am." It was obvious he spoke to Ellie.

"Good evenin', Mr. Taggerty."

"I have some news for you, ma'am. Maybe you'd best come sit here by the fire."

Ellie frowned, but did as he asked.

"It's about your husband, ma'am. There's been an accident."

"Accident?" Ellie half rose to her feet, but Taggerty stopped her.

"Is he hurt bad?" she whispered.

Taggerty cleared his throat and looked away. "I'm afraid it's worse than that, ma'am. You see, your husband was determined to kill the first buffalo we seen. When we came up on the herd he shot one big bull—not much good for eatin', but I guess he didn't think about that. Anyway, the buffalo fell and your husband, he rode up to make sure it was dead. Well, he no sooner got off his horse than that big bull got to his feet and charged. There weren't a thing anyone could do, it all happened so fast. He was trampled to death before we could kill the brute."

"Dead? You're sayin' George is dead?"

"'Fraid so, ma'am. Like I said, there was nothin' anyone could do. It all happened so fast-like. Morgan brought in his body, along with the horse."

"But he can't be dead," Ellie protested, her face wrinkled in despair as she looked from Taggerty to Susan. "He's bringin' meat home for dinner."

She turned and clutched Susan's hand, her eyes pleading for a denial of what she had just been told.

"It ain't so," she whispered. "He's not dead."

Susan held Ellie's hand and looked at Taggerty for assistance. He stood awkwardly, turning his hat in his hands.

"We'll see to the buryin' in the morning, I reckon," he said. "If there's anything I can do, just let me know."

Ellie watched him leave, her eyes vacant and her skin bleached of color.

"I don't believe it," she mumbled. "I just don't believe it."

"Why don't you lie down for a while?" Susan suggested sympathetically.

"What?"

"Why don't you rest?"

She helped Ellie to her feet and led her toward the wagon while Ellie continued to mutter to herself.

She allowed Susan to help her out of her dress and slipped under the quilt.

"I'll be back in a few minutes," Susan reassured her. "You just lie there and I'll tend to everything."

Susan left the wagon and made her way across the campground to talk to Taggerty about the burial preparations. She felt no real sorrow. Unease flickered in her mind, but she refused to speculate on what would become of them now that George was dead.

Chapter 9

The first clod of dirt fell into the grave just as the sun cleared the eastern horizon. The somber finality of the thud of earth made Susan glance at Ellie, who stood beside her.

Ellie had said nothing all morning. She had pulled a black dress from the depths of a trunk and donned it in silence. She nodded when Susan told her what arrangements had been made for the burial, but her eyes were lifeless. It was as though she, too, were dead. Now she stood motionless beside the grave as the men filled the shallow hole.

Susan was unable to feel sorrow. She had never liked George. His coarse manner and vulgar comments had repelled her. Still, the circumstances of his death were hideous and she could too easily envision the scene Taggerty had described.

The men piled rocks over the grave to discourage scavenging animals, and those in attendance filed past Ellie. She didn't respond to their murmurs of sympathy, but continued to gaze straight ahead. When they were alone, Susan touched Ellie's arm and the woman turned as though surprised to find anyone there.

"We have to go now, Ellie."

Ellie stared at her with vacant eyes.

"Please," Susan insisted. "We have to be ready to move out."

"I can't leave." Ellie looked surprised. "I can't go without George."

"We must."

"No, Susan. You go if you want. I'll stay here."

"You *can't* stay. George is dead."

"Oh no, dear. He'll be back. I'll just wait here for him."

Her words startled Susan. This was far worse than the tears and the rush of emotion she had expected —the normal reaction of a woman whose husband had met a violent death. Susan didn't know how to handle this blank refusal to face reality. She glanced over her shoulder toward camp. The usual morning activities were under way and some wagons were already hitched, waiting for the call to pull out. What should she do? She had to get Ellie back to the wagon, but short of using physical force, how could she do it?

"Ellie," she tried once more. "You must listen to me. George is dead. He's buried right here. We can't stay. I know how you must feel, but he'd understand. He'd want you to go on."

Ellie turned her face away. "I'll wait for George," she said quietly.

Susan twisted her hands. It was useless to try to reason with the woman, but something had to be done.

"Almost time to head out." Ross Morgan spoke behind her and Susan turned to him with a feeling of relief.

"I know, but she won't come." She nodded toward Ellie. "She says she has to wait for George. She won't believe he's dead. I don't know what to do."

Morgan studied Ellie, who didn't acknowledge his presence, but continued to stare across the plains. He moved to her side.

"Good morning, Mrs. Baker." His tone was casual.

There was no answer.

"I have a message for you—from your husband."

Susan stared at him. What was he doing? This would only make matters worse. But Ellie turned her face up to his, a slight smile on her lips.

"Why, good mornin', Mr. Morgan."

"Your husband sent word he's been delayed. He said you should go on ahead."

Ellie frowned for a moment, then her face cleared.

"That was right nice of you to bring me the message. I knew somethin' must have kept him."

Ross offered his arm and she delicately placed her hand on his sleeve.

"I was just thinkin' about when I was a girl," she confided as they moved slowly away from the grave. "George was such a gentleman. Why, all the girls in Richmond were jealous when he proposed." She fluttered her lashes at Ross. "'Course he always said there was never any question once he laid eyes on me. Isn't that the sweetest thing?"

"I'm sure he meant it, ma'am."

As they approached the wagons, Ellie continued to chatter about her days as a southern belle and Ross responded gallantly. Susan shook her head.

She was grateful for his deft handling of a difficult situation, but his gentle understanding of Ellie surprised her. This was the man who had snapped orders at her and scorned her as a coward. Where was his understanding where she was concerned? Then she remembered how he had helped her when the baby was born and felt ashamed.

Ross helped Ellie into the wagon and Susan knew there was nothing more she could do. It was time to get the oxen hitched—past time by the look of things. Ross set to work.

Soon the animals stood before the wagon and all that remained was to attach the harness chains. His back was turned to her when he spoke.

"As soon as we reach Fort Laramie we'll find someone to send you back with."

"Send us back? We can't go back—there's nothing to go back *to*."

He turned to face her, a look of irritation on his face.

"I can't help that. With George dead, you don't have a man to take care of you. I can't have you holding up the train."

"We won't hold anyone up. You can't send us back."

"I can and I will. It's up to me what happens on this train, and two lone women can't make it across the mountains. You'll go back or stay at Laramie. The choice is yours."

"Mr. Taggerty's in charge of the train. He won't make us turn back—not when we've come nearly six hundred miles."

"He'll do as I suggest."

Susan glared at him in defiance. "We'll see about that. Mr. Taggerty's a gentleman. He won't leave us stranded."

"And neither will I. We'll see you safely to the fort. After that it's up to you."

Angry and stunned, Susan gazed at him as he began to chain the oxen to the wagon. She would see Taggerty. Surely he'd understand that they couldn't go back now. Just because she was a woman didn't mean she couldn't do as well or even better than George had. She'd show Ross Morgan a thing or two about women. She thrust her chin up and marched to the head of the team.

"I can do without your help," she said stiffly. "I'm perfectly capable of hitching the oxen."

He shrugged. "Suit yourself."

She watched him walk away before she started to struggle with the harness chains. What had looked easy proved to be far more difficult in practice. Tears of frustration burned her eyes as the animals shifted restlessly away from her. Wagons began to pull into line and several men offered assistance. She rejected each offer as she remembered Morgan's words. She'd show him she could do it on her own.

At last the oxen were hitched to the wagon. She had lost her place in line and now they would have to bring up the rear. One fingernail had been torn to the quick on the heavy harness and her dress was ripped where it had caught on the chain, but she had succeeded in doing what she had set out to do. She clenched her teeth and narrowed her eyes against the billowing dust and cracked the whip over the heads of the lead animals.

"Get up there, now," she shouted.

The wagon creaked forward and they fell into line behind the rest. She had done it once. Tomorrow it would be easier. She would talk to Taggerty. She was sure she could make him see her point of view. Ross Morgan didn't know everything.

Chapter 10

By nightfall Susan was exhausted. After she tended to the animals she longed to collapse and sleep, but there were still chores to be done. She cast a resentful glance at the wagon where Ellie sat in calm solitude. Not once during the long day had she offered to help. At the nooning she had even complained about the food Susan had provided.

I've half a mind to let her starve, Susan reflected as she struggled to build a fire. She was so tired that the thought of food nauseated her. What if I get sick? Then they'll leave us behind for sure.

With renewed vigor Susan began to fix the evening meal.

"Susan." Ellie's voice was fretful and Susan was tempted to ignore her. What now? she wondered mutinously as she stomped toward the wagon.

"Yes?" Her voice was sharp, but she didn't care. There was nothing wrong with Ellie and no reason why she couldn't help.

"Is supper almost ready?"

"No, it's not. I had to tend to the animals first."

"Oh my, isn't George back yet?"

"No." How long would she have to play this

game? She wished she had Morgan's patience, but it was beyond her. She went back to the fire.

"Susan, I brought you some rabbit." Mercy's voice startled Susan from her reflections. The meat lay crisp and brown in the pan Mercy held and suddenly Susan was ravenous.

"Oh, Mercy, you're an angel."

"I thought maybe Ellie would feel more like eating if she had some fresh meat. Neal killed two jackrabbits this morning so we have more than enough."

Susan kissed the girl impulsively. "Thank you. I know Ellie will enjoy it."

Why tell Mercy that Ellie's appetite hadn't suffered in the least? How could she explain her mother-in-law's strange behavior?

"I haven't seen you all day," Susan said after she had delivered a plate of food to Ellie. "How have you been?" She studied Mercy closely.

"Fine. I took your advice and rode in the wagon. I've hardly coughed all day."

"Good." Susan took a bite of the juicy meat. It tasted wonderful. Grease ran down her chin and onto her dress, but she didn't care.

"You're the one who has it hard," Mercy said sympathetically. "How can you manage to do everything?"

"I don't know," Susan sighed. It was a relief to talk to someone. With Mercy she didn't have to pretend to be stronger than she was. "I thought the day would never end."

"Can Neal do some of the hard chores for you? I'm sure he wouldn't mind."

"No, Mercy. I have to do it myself."

"But why?"

"If Neal helps, Ross Morgan will say I'm holding you up and that's all the excuse he needs to send us back."

"Send you back! Oh, Susan, I'm sure Ross wouldn't do that. Not when you've come so far."

Susan's laughter sounded harsh even to her own ears.

"You think not? He promised to do that very thing."

Susan finished the last of the meat and wiped her face with a soiled handkerchief.

"Would you like me to talk to him?"

"No." Susan knew Mercy was only trying to help, but she couldn't let anyone else intercede for her. She tried to soften her refusal. "Thank you, anyway. I'll talk to Mr. Taggerty. If I can show them I don't need help, they can't make us turn back."

"You could go to your parents, couldn't you? Until your husband sends for you?"

"I don't think that would work, Mercy. My mother's dead and my father's new wife would hardly welcome me. Besides, what would I do with Ellie?"

"Poor Susan. This has really been an awful ordeal for you, hasn't it?"

Susan felt tears of self-pity sting her eyes. Yes, it had been an ordeal. It seemed as if nothing had gone right—not since she married Adam. Things have to get better, she told herself. What more can go wrong?

Mercy picked up the empty pan. "I'd better get back. We'd be happy to share our meals with you. At least let us do that much."

"Thank you, Mercy. That would help."

"Just come on over in the morning and if Ellie doesn't feel up to it, we'll send her back a plate of food."

As Susan watched her disappear into the deepening darkness, she thought of the days to come. They would be difficult. She prayed they wouldn't be impossible.

I'll make it, she vowed, and I won't let anything or anyone stand in my way.

The crack of the sentry's rifle woke Susan. For once she had slept soundly, untroubled by dreams. She watched the gathering daylight creep through the canvas and planned what she would do today.

She must speak to Taggerty this morning. She rehearsed in her mind all the arguments and pleas she would use. He didn't seem like the sort of man to refuse a woman, and she would present her case as persuasively as possible.

Ellie still slept as Susan splashed tepid water on her face and arms. Mosquitoes and other bugs floated on top of the pail of water, but she had learned to ignore them.

She pulled on a dress of green patterned muslin, brushed her hair carefully and allowed it to hang free. The reflection in her mirror gave her assurance. How could Taggerty refuse?

She roused Ellie and told her they would eat breakfast at the Laughlins' wagon.

"Do you want to go or shall I bring some food back for you?"

"Oh, I'll go, dear. It's so nice to visit with people."

Susan began to lower herself from the wagon.

"But where are you going now?" Ellie asked.

"I have some business to take care of. I won't be long."

"See if there's any word from George, will you?"

Susan nodded, but her brow wrinkled as she crossed the encampment. When would Ellie realize that George was gone? This situation just wasn't healthy.

Mrs. Taggerty, a large, rawboned woman, stood over the cook fire stirring oatmeal, while two plump children clung to her skirt. She looked up as Susan approached and pushed a lock of black hair back from her plain face.

"Mornin'," she called.

"Good morning. I wonder if I might speak to Mr. Taggerty."

"Surely. He was here just a minute ago." She looked around, then called to a gangly youth who had appeared beside the wagon, a bucket in each hand.

"Willy, you seen your pa?"

The boy placed the buckets on the ground and water sloshed over the sides.

"Seen him with Mr. Morgan awhile back. They was doctorin' one of the cows."

"Well, run fetch him. Tell him Miz Baker wants to see him."

The boy loped off toward the livestock and Susan shifted her weight from one foot to the other. The smell of oatmeal filled the air and she sniffed hungrily.

"Can I get you a cup of coffee?" Mrs. Taggerty offered.

"Please."

Mrs. Taggerty twitched the two children from her skirt much as a horse might switch off flies. The children gazed at Susan with round eyes. The boy scuffed one toe in the dust while his sister twisted a strand of her black hair around one finger.

"Hello." Susan smiled tentatively. Neither child answered, and when their mother returned with Susan's coffee they attached themselves to her skirt once more.

"Tad and Cassie ain't much for strangers," their mother commented as she dished up two bowls of steaming mush. "There now, you two. Go and eat afore it gets cold."

After one more shy glance at Susan the children scampered off.

"You'd never believe how them two chatter once they get to know you."

Susan nodded. She felt awkward and wished Taggerty would hurry. But what if Morgan returned with him? Her heart lurched. She would never be able to deliver her carefully prepared speech if Ross Morgan was there with his cynical smile and his determination to be rid of her.

At last Susan spotted Taggerty striding toward them alone, but her assurance suddenly vanished. What could she say? The future of everyone in the train rested on him and here she stood ready to add to his load. She squared her shoulders and took a deep breath. There was nothing to do now but see it through.

"Miz Baker, good mornin', ma'am. Willy said you were lookin' for me."

"Yes, Mr. Taggerty. I wondered if I might discuss something with you."

"Why, sure thing, ma'am."

"You eat your breakfast while you talk," his wife interrupted. "It's near ruined now." She shoved a bowl into his hands before disappearing behind the wagon. He settled himself on the tailboard and began to eat.

"Well now, what can I do for you?"

"It's about the rest of the trip. Mr. Morgan said I'd have to turn back at Fort Laramie since we don't have a man with us."

Taggerty studied his bowl. "Yes, that's what he told me, too," he said at last.

"But we can't turn back. We sold the farm for the money to come west. My husband's already in California. He's to meet us in Oregon City."

"Well now, I agree you have a problem, but surely you could find some place to stay till your husband sends for you. We can leave word for him in Oregon City."

"But we have no one to stay with—and no money."

She wondered if Adam *would* send for them. If he struck it rich in California, he'd have little need for either her or his mother. With enough money he'd be certain to find other women. Women anxious to please him, as she had never been.

"I'm sorry," Taggerty said. "But once we pass Laramie the going gets rough. Morgan doesn't think you can make it. Now, if you was to leave your wagon behind and go on with someone else, that'd be different. Why don't you ask around? Someone might have room for the two of you."

"I don't want to be beholden to anyone else. I know we can make it alone, if you'd just give me a chance to prove it."

Taggerty scratched his bearded chin and studied her face.

"I'd like to, Miz Baker, I really would. But it's not just me. I gotta think of the others. Morgan's made this trip enough times to know what it's like, and if he says you can't make it on your own, then I reckon I have to take his word for it."

Susan felt tears spring to her eyes. She was afraid to speak for fear her voice would break. Taggerty scraped the last of the oatmeal from his bowl and stood up. He patted her shoulder.

"I expect you'll find it's all for the best. Oregon ain't no place for two women alone."

"My husband will be there."

"You talk to Morgan again, if you like. If he agrees, it's all right by me. Either that or team up with someone else. But like I said, I think it's best you go back. We have a long journey ahead and it won't be easy—'specially not for a slip of a girl like you."

It was hopeless. She would never be able to persuade him to change his mind. Morgan had already convinced him that his way of thinking was right, and what chance did she have to sway Morgan? None.

"Thank you for your time, Mr. Taggerty. I'm sorry to have bothered you."

"No bother 'tall. I'm truly sorry I couldn't be more help. If there's anything else I can do, just holler."

Susan turned and walked toward the Laughlin

81

wagon. She could go to them for help. She knew that Neal and Mercy would quickly offer to share their wagon if it meant the difference between turning back or staying with the train.

For a moment she was tempted. How good it would feel to let Neal shoulder her burdens. Then she envisioned Morgan and his superior smile.

Susan held her head high and pushed her shoulders back. She wouldn't do it. Not if there was any other way. Somehow she'd show him—him and everyone else. She wouldn't give in to their misconceived notions. She'd get that wagon across the mountains and on to Oregon if it was the last thing she did.

Chapter 11

Susan woke to the acrid smell of smoke. For a moment she was disoriented. Had she missed the morning signal? But no, the light that filled the wagon wasn't that of early dawn. It flickered on the canvas walls and glowed reddish-orange.

Fire! The word burst into her brain. Now she became aware of the shouts of men, the frenzied screams of horses and the cries of women. She threw back the quilt and grabbed her clothes. She shook Ellie's shoulder.

"Wake up!" she cried. "There's a fire."

"What?" Ellie's eyes were narrow slits.

"A fire. Get dressed and wait here. I'm going to see what's happening."

Still fastening her dress, Susan jumped from the wagon. Dark shapes of men hurried past. To the east of the wagons rose a towering cloud of smoke licked by tongues of flame.

"What's happening?" she called to a man nearby.

"Fire near the horses," he shouted and hurried on.

Now that she was clear of the wagon Susan saw the fire was at a little distance. She stumbled toward it and smoke stung her eyes.

"What are you doing here?" Ross Morgan grasped her arm roughly. "Get back to your wagon. There's nothing you can do."

Susan watched him rush toward the flames, but she didn't heed his warning. Their own livestock were in that herd.

Animal screams filled the night air. A man ran past, a burning torch in his hand, and halted between the wagons and the milling stock. He was soon joined by more torch bearers. Susan realized they were attempting to keep the frightened horses from stampeding through the camp. Other men beat the smoldering grass with blankets and buffalo robes. She saw Ross Morgan's tall figure appear and disappear as he gave orders she couldn't hear.

She lowered her head against the billowing smoke and hurried on. She passed groups of women who clutched children close to their sides at each new burst of flame. Some called out to her, but she ignored them. She wouldn't stand aside and watch. There must be something she could do.

She reached the line of torch bearers. In the wavering light she saw the shadowy figures of horses and cattle milling about. Their heads were high, eyes wide in alarm and nostrils flared. Each time one of them neared the line someone thrust a torch forward and the terror-stricken animal retreated to the herd.

"Here," she shouted to one of the men. "I can do that."

He gave her a startled glance and she realized how she must look, her dress half fastened, her hair streaming down her back, but she put her hand out for the torch and after a moment's hesitation he gave it to her.

In the dim light Susan could scarcely see the men on either side of her. Only their torch flames were visible through the heavy smoke.

She spread her feet apart and hefted the burning stick with both hands. It was heavier than she had expected and soon the muscles across her shoulders began to ache. Time and again the horses edged toward them, only to be turned back by shouts and brandished torches. Susan wanted to watch the firefighters, but her own task required all her concentration.

Suddenly there was a shout to her left and, turning, she saw a canvas-covered wagon burst into flame. Men rushed toward the new threat. Oh God, she thought, the whole train will go soon.

Dark figures pushed the burning wagon out of the circle. Its dry frame crackled as the hungry flames ate at the wood. Susan glanced again at the milling stock. She no longer saw the torches of the men around her. Had they left to help with the wagon?

An explosion ripped the air as the flames found a keg of gunpowder. Suddenly the frightened animals bolted in a lunging mass.

Susan saw them coming but she was powerless to move. Fear held her paralyzed as she felt the ground tremble beneath her feet. Her torch was as useless as a twig and it fell from her nerveless fingers. Run! her mind commanded, but her feet refused to obey. The animals thundered toward her.

Strong arms suddenly encircled her waist, pulling her off her feet and dragging her beneath a wagon. Ross Morgan fell on top of her. Hooves drummed past, drowning out every other sound. She still expected to be trampled at any moment.

Finally the herd pounded away into the distance and the sounds of shouts and the crackle of flames filtered through her numbed senses. She became aware of the man above her. He smelled of smoke and sweat. Susan began to tremble.

He raised himself on one arm and looked down at her. His eyes were shadowed in the shelter of the wagon. She was painfully aware of his body next to hers and knew her trembling was not from fear alone. Her treacherous senses responded eagerly to the hard, lean maleness of him. She didn't move as his hand touched her hair. His fingers were gentle as they smoothed snarled ringlets away from her face, but his eyes remained dark and unreadable.

Her lips parted slightly as his face neared hers. Now, she thought, now he'll kiss me.

His lips were only a fraction of an inch from her own when he jerked away, and she lay there stunned and bewildered.

"What the hell were you doing out here?" he stormed. "Didn't I tell you to stay in your wagon?"

"I wanted to help."

His rough words startled her back to reality. Had she really been about to let him kiss her? Her cheeks burned with shame.

"This is no place for a woman. Why can't you follow orders? You could have been killed."

"That would have saved you a lot of trouble, wouldn't it?"

He glared at her. "Don't be childish."

Stung by his words, Susan rolled from beneath the wagon and scrambled to her feet. She slapped dust from her skirt, keeping her face averted from him.

"You missed a spot." She glanced at him. In one

swift movement he rose to his feet and put a hand under her chin.

"Right there." He rubbed her cheek and she jerked away from his touch. He was laughing at her. She stifled the childish urge to stamp her foot in anger and stiffened her body.

"Thank you, Mr. Morgan." Her voice was arctic as she turned on her heel to stalk back to the wagon.

The fire was almost out. Only a few smoldering embers resisted the firefighters.

As she neared the wagon her steps slowed and she thought of the brief interlude with Ross Morgan. Had she been mistaken, or had he really meant to kiss her? If so, why had he stopped? She was sure she had seen desire in his eyes.

An idea began to take form in Susan's mind. Perhaps he had a weak side after all. If so, she could put that knowledge to use. He was the only one who stood between her and her goal. There might be a way to persuade him to let her continue west.

For a moment she was ashamed of her thoughts. Then her lips thinned in determination. Because she was a woman he wanted her to turn back. But, at the same time, being a woman gave her the power to change his mind.

She smiled. War had been declared between them, but Ross Morgan need never know.

Chapter 12

Susan sat in the soft grass and leaned against a tree. It was wonderful to have time to herself, a few moments with no chores she had to do. Her eyes swept the wooded glen where they had been camped for two days. Wild roses bloomed among the ash trees that offered welcome shade to the travelers. Ash Hollow was aptly named.

It had taken a full day to round up the stampeded livestock, and several head of cattle had been lost. Although there was no proof, suspicion ran high that the blaze had been set by Indians to cut out some of the stock. If this were true, Susan reflected, those Indians were certainly eating well. Better than they were.

Her nose wrinkled in disgust as she remembered the stringy buffalo steak they had eaten the night before. Despite Mercy's best efforts it had been close to inedible, and Ellie had flatly refused to eat it.

Ellie, in fact, refused to do a great many things and Susan's patience was near the breaking point. Ellie still spent each day in the shelter of the wagon, preferring the bone-wrenching jolts to walking.

After crossing the South Platte, they had begun

climbing steadily uphill. They had crossed a water-less tableland, a long day's journey across deep gullies and arid plains, only to be faced with the steep descent of Windlass Hill. Fortunately there had been no mishaps. They had all agreed to rest the stock and repair the wagons before pushing on to Laramie. Tonight there would be music and dancing, a welcome relief from the tension of the last few days.

Susan's thoughts turned to Ross Morgan. Al-though her resolution to persuade him by any means available had not diminished, she had been unable to act. He seemed to avoid any contact with her and she wondered if he recognized the danger of his feelings. Perhaps tonight she would have a chance to put her plan into action. Even he would feel obliged to attend what had become a full-scale party. There were only a few days left before they reached Laramie. She must act soon.

A full moon hung overhead and the sound of fiddles and banjos drew people from their wagons into the center of the campground. Several large fires offered both light and warmth, for the night air was cool.

Susan watched her fellow travelers. They were all dressed as though for a gala occasion. Even Ellie had made an effort over her appearance.

"Susan—over here," Mercy called from where she and Neal stood beside one of the campfires. Mercy's face glowed with unusual vibrance. She wore a cream-colored shawl over a sky-blue dress, and her hair hung loose down her back.

"You look lovely, Mercy."

"You both do," Neal said. "I'm a lucky man to be graced with two such lovely ladies."

"Where's Ellie?" Mercy asked.

"She was here just a minute ago." Susan's eyes swept the crowd. "Oh, there she is—with the Taggertys."

She watched her mother-in-law for a moment, then turned her attention to the people who danced to the lively music provided by an impromptu band of musicians. The flounced skirts of the women swirled past and Susan tapped her foot to the beat of the music.

She caught sight of Ross Morgan and her pulse quickened. He was coming toward them. Would he ask her to dance? She kept her gaze fastened on the dancers and tried to blot out his image as he approached.

"Good evening." His greeting included them all.

"Oh, good evening, Ross." Mercy's eyes sparkled as she greeted the scout. "Isn't it a lovely party?"

"Yes, I expect it'll be some time before we see anything like this again." He shook his head as though marveling at the gaiety. "Would you care to dance, Miss Laughlin?"

Susan tried to hide her disappointment as Mercy and Ross joined the dancers. I should have known he wouldn't ask me, she told herself. She didn't blame him. Mercy looked like a fairy-tale princess as she dipped and spun to the music. Her blond hair shimmered in the firelight and her face was raised attentively to Morgan's. Even from a distance, Susan heard her tinkling laughter.

She looked away. Her plan to entice Morgan into

allowing them to stay with the train had been shaky at best. And wouldn't he have seen through it at once?

"Would you like to dance?" Neal put his hand on her arm. "I'm not much of a dancer, but I'll do my best not to step on your toes."

Susan smiled. "I'd love to."

Neal was surprisingly light on his feet and she was quick to compliment him. He flushed with pleasure at her words. Mercy and Ross whirled past and Neal skipped a step as his eyes followed them.

"I hope Mercy doesn't get too tired. She seems a little better lately and I hate to keep her from having fun." A worried frown lined his forehead.

"She seems fine," Susan reassured him. "I haven't heard her cough for several days."

"She coughs at night—she thinks I don't hear her."

Susan thought of the blood-specked handkerchief and longed to confide in Neal. But she had given her word.

Mercy waved gaily as they danced closer and Morgan nodded to them. Susan deliberately tossed her head and smiled at Neal. He looked surprised and she was filled with shame. She couldn't use Neal to strike back at Morgan. Besides, why would he care if she flirted with Neal?

When the music stopped Neal and Susan joined Mercy and Ross beside the fire. Mercy's face was flushed, her eyes shining, but her breath came in labored gasps.

"I don't know when I've enjoyed myself so much," she panted.

Neal's eyes were shadowed with concern. "I think you'd better rest a little." He put one arm around her shoulders.

"Oh Neal," Mercy protested, but Susan noticed that she leaned against her brother's encircling arm.

"If you'll excuse us, Susan, I think I'll find a place where Mercy can sit and catch her breath." Neal guided Mercy away from the campfire.

"Shall I come and keep you company?" Susan called.

"Don't be silly," Mercy laughed. "Neal has to play mother hen. You stay and have fun. Dance with Ross—he's a wonderful dancer."

Susan watched them walk away, Neal's red head bent toward his sister's blond one, conscious of Ross beside her. She was at a loss for words. Here was the opportunity she had waited for, but she felt awkward and tongue-tied.

"Shall we?" Ross put his hand out to her.

"You don't have to." Her tone was sharper than she had intended.

"Am I so terrible?"

"Of course not."

"Then since we've been directed to enjoy ourselves, I suggest we do just that."

Silently she put her hand in his and allowed him to lead her into the dance. At first her body was stiff and unyielding, but gradually she relaxed. Ross didn't speak as he led her through a series of dips and twirls. Deliberately she allowed her body to melt against his and felt his arm tighten around her waist. She raised her eyes, searching his for some clue to his feelings. His gaze was steady. She felt her pulse quicken as her eyes lingered on his. She forgot their surroundings. The other dancers faded into shadows in the background and the only reality was this man who held her close against him.

His hand moved lightly at her waist, his fingers almost caressing. It could have been her imagination, the movement was so slight, but she saw the darkening of his eyes and responded eagerly, moving closer, her lips parted. There was undisguised hunger in his face and his muscles tightened under her hands. His eyes held her spellbound as he guided her away from the crowd to the edge of the circle.

The music stopped, but still he held her as his eyes swept her face. She waited, motionless, holding her breath. She felt the pounding of his heart as it matched her own.

Abruptly he released her.

"You're an accomplished . . . dancer," he said and Susan felt her face burn. Had there been a deliberate pause between the last two words?

"Thank you, Mr. Morgan," she answered breathlessly.

"If you'll excuse me, I must do my duty by some of the other ladies." He nodded and turned away.

She watched him stride through the crowd, stopping now and then to exchange a word with someone. It was as if nothing had happened between them, but this time there was no doubt in her mind. Ross Morgan wanted her. Now it was up to her to bend that desire to her purposes.

Chapter 13

Although they had left Ash Hollow only two days before, that shaded oasis might never have been. Dirt from the sandy road covered everything. Even Susan's teeth felt gritty as she walked beside the oxen.

She gazed ahead at the huge pile of white rock they had sighted early this morning. This was Courthouse Rock, so named for its strong resemblance to a judicial building, complete with cupola. The mass of rock fascinated Susan, who had never seen anything like it. As they moved closer she imagined it took on other forms, at one time a storybook castle, at another a magnificent mansion.

Beyond it she saw the towering spire of Chimney Rock, a day's journey away, but appearing closer in the vast open space.

The wagons ahead ground to a halt and Susan sighed. At least two hours remained before they were supposed to stop for the night. What had caused the delay this time?

She pulled the brim of her sunbonnet lower, but it did little to keep the scorching sun from her face.

"Why are we stoppin'?" Ellie poked her head from the front of the wagon.

"I don't know."

Ellie shaded her eyes and peered ahead. "Can't see a thing," she complained.

Susan saw Neal striding toward them and went to meet him.

"Wheel came off Taggerty's wagon," he told her. "Reckon we'll be stopping here for the night."

"Was anyone hurt?"

"No. Lucky they weren't though."

The wagons began to pull out into a circle and Neal left to guide his own wagon into place. When Susan told Ellie what had caused the delay, the older woman rolled her eyes skyward.

"Might as well take a nap," she sighed. "No sense sittin' out in this blazing sun." She disappeared into the cavernous depths of the wagon and Susan knew she wouldn't see her again until hunger drove her out.

The unexpected delay left Susan with time to spare. Once the wagon was in place and the animals were unhitched there were no chores to attend to immediately and she was free to do as she wished.

The shape of Courthouse Rock beckoned and she decided to explore it more closely. Several other women and children had headed away from the wagons in the direction of the rocks and Susan realized she wasn't the only one drawn by the strange formation.

"Come on, Sam," she called to the dog. "Let's go for a walk."

She spotted Mrs. Taggerty ahead, Cassie and Tad clinging to her skirt on either side, and hastened her step.

"Hello, Mrs. Taggerty. How's your wagon?"

"Oh—Miz Baker. It'll be ready to go by mornin'. It's a darn nuisance though. I told Dave to check that there wheel when we was at Ash Hollow. But you can't tell a man nothin'." Her lips tightened in a thin line. "Now these two young 'uns have been yammerin' to go see the prairie dogs. They heard one of the men say there was a village of 'em halfway to the rocks. Don't know why I let 'em talk me into goin'. Say 'howdy' to Miz Baker," she prompted the children.

Two pair of eyes regarded Susan solemnly. "Howdy, Miz Baker," they chorused.

"Hello, Cassie, Tad. Have you ever seen a prairie dog?"

"I did onc't," Tad said proudly. "But Cassie ain't never."

"And why it has to be today I'll never know," Mrs. Taggerty grumbled. "I oughta be back there helpin' Dave and Willy, not out here huntin' wild animals."

"Ma, you promised," Cassie wailed, her bottom lip trembling. "I ain't never seed one afore. You promised."

"I know, I know." Mrs. Taggerty cast a helpless glance at Susan. "See how they are?"

"I'd be glad to take the children," Susan offered.

Mrs. Taggerty's face brightened. "Would you? That'd be right nice of you. Just bring 'em back to the wagon when you've had enough of 'em."

The woman hurried away and Susan smiled down at her two charges. "Well now, let's go find those prairie dogs, shall we?"

They walked for a while in silence.

"That your dog?" Tad asked, pointing at Sam.

"Yes."

"What's his name?"

"Sam."

"Sam?" Cassie joined the conversation. "If he was mine, I'd name him Goldie. He's too pretty to be a Sam."

Susan smiled. "That would be a good name for him, all right."

"You goin' to California to hunt for gold?" Tad asked.

"No—Oregon."

"So are we." His young face showed disgust. "Wish we was goin' to look for gold. Farmin' ain't no fun."

Cassie's steps began to lag and Susan shortened her own to allow the little girl to keep up.

"Look!" Tad cried. "Over there. I think I saw one."

Susan squinted. A small prairie dog stood on his haunches near a rock, his front legs curled up in front of him, his ears pricked forward. The animal sat still for a moment before it scurried out of sight.

"Come on," Cassie urged as she pulled Susan's hand. "Let's go see where he went." Susan allowed herself to be tugged toward the spot where the prairie dog had vanished.

"Look, there's his hole." Tad pointed at a mound of earth and the hole that led into the animal's burrow. There were other mounds with similar holes scattered beyond, and here and there a quick movement caught Susan's eye as the animals popped in and out of their burrows.

"If we're very still maybe he'll come back out," Susan cautioned and she knelt between the two children.

Sam growled deep in his throat.

"Hush, Sam," Susan murmured. But the hair bristled on the back of his neck and he growled again.

Susan shifted slightly to rest her hand on the ground. As she moved, she heard it—the sharp rattle that meant one thing. Her eyes darted toward the sound. Mere inches away from Cassie's chubby leg was a coiled rattlesnake, its tail erect.

"Cassie, hold perfectly still," Susan whispered.

The little girl hadn't seen or heard the snake, but Tad turned wide, scared eyes to Susan.

"Whatever you do, don't move," she warned, as she searched the ground with her eyes, looking for a weapon.

Cassie still stared at the prairie dog hole and Susan prayed that the little girl wouldn't lose interest. If she had just heeded Sam's warning growl. The dog crouched at her side, a low grumble in his throat.

Susan spied a rock only a few inches from her hand. If she could reach it and hurl it at the snake, maybe . . . She fastened her eyes on the coiled reptile as her hand crept toward the rock. It seemed like hours before her fingers curled around it. She closed her eyes for a moment, took a deep breath, opened her eyes and calculated the distance, then hurled the rock at the evil head of the snake with all her might.

At the same time with her other hand she yanked Cassie away from the snake that writhed in the dust. Susan stood watching in horror, her arms clasped tightly around Cassie. Sam barked furiously as he circled the snake. At last it lay still and Susan released a shuddering sigh.

"What'd you do that for?" Cassie questioned petulantly, still unaware of the danger that had threatened.

"She killed a snake, silly. Look." Tad's voice was shaky, but the color was returning to his face.

Cassie cried out when she saw the dead snake.

"It can't hurt you now," Tad blustered. "Miz Baker hit him with a rock. You sure throw good," he added with admiration. "Never seed a girl who could throw like that."

"Thanks, Tad. Now maybe we'd better get back to the wagons. Must be close to suppertime."

Susan tried to still the trembling in her legs as they started toward the wagons. She examined the ground carefully as they went, watchful for any movement. It had been so close. She said a silent prayer of thankfulness and squeezed Cassie's small hand.

Their arrival at the Taggerty wagon went almost unnoticed. Taggerty, Willy and Ross Morgan were struggling with the wheel as Mrs. Taggerty watched.

"Oh, good," she called. "You're back. Have a good time?"

"Miz Baker killed a snake," Tad announced with importance. "A big rattler. Musta been this long." He stretched his arms as far apart as they would go. "It near bit Cassie."

Mrs. Taggerty's face went pale and she rushed to gather Cassie into her arms. "Are you sure you weren't bit, Cassie? Are you all right?"

"'Course she is, Ma." Tad drew back as if afraid

he would be the next in line for his mother's attentions. "You shoulda seed Miz Baker throw that rock. That ole snake, he just twisted up and died."

Mrs. Taggerty's eyes met Susan's. "How can I ever thank you?"

Susan felt her face redden with embarrassment as she became the center of attention. "I'm just glad she's all right," she said, trying to avert their thanks.

"That was a mighty brave thing to do, ma'am." Dave Taggerty's face shone with gratitude. "It's lucky you was there."

Susan accepted their thanks as graciously as she could, conscious of Morgan's eyes on her. She'd done what she had to do. She wished they would stop fussing.

"I'd best get back to my wagon. It's time to get supper," she said at last.

"Can I come visit Goldie sometime?" Cassie called after her.

"Goldie? Oh—Sam. Why, I'm sure he'd like it if you did." Susan smiled at the little girl, a lump in her throat. To think what had almost happened. Thank God her aim had been good. As she walked back to the wagon Susan thought of the daughter she had lost. Would she have been like Cassie?

Chapter 14

Susan stood in the shadow of the wagon and surveyed the sleeping encampment. Her heartbeat quickened as she considered what she was about to do.

They had passed Chimney Rock and only two days remained before they reached Fort Laramie. She could delay no longer.

They had camped near Scott's Bluff, a picturesque valley surrounded by steep clay cliffs. Currants and chokecherries grew in profusion. The night air was mild, but she pulled her shawl more closely over the low-cut bodice of her dress.

Muted voices murmured in the stillness and she shifted. Thank goodness Ellie was asleep and wouldn't miss her. As she waited, Susan's mind was tormented with doubts. What if her plan should fail? If Ross Morgan suspected her motives, how would he react? She shied from the thought of his scornful expression and biting words. Worse yet, what if he made love to her and still refused to let her stay with the train? She wouldn't consider that possibility. This was her only chance—it had to work. She wished she had more time, more days in which to soften his resistance.

She heard the shuffling of the stock and the occasional cry of a night bird. Soon it would be time to change sentries. Then she would act.

How fortunate that Mercy had mentioned Morgan's sentry duty. It had been only a fleeting comment, but Susan had caught it. She knew it was likely to be her only opportunity to find him alone.

Someone moved past in the darkness and Susan flattened herself against the side of the wagon. She heard an exchange of voices in the distance, then the footsteps of the guard who had been relieved as he returned to his wagon.

She hesitated. Was it worth it? She thought of the animallike mating she had endured with Adam. She had sworn she would never again be degraded like that. How could she seek out Ross Morgan for that very purpose? What if she was unable to hide her revulsion? Everything would be ruined.

She drew in her breath and clenched her trembling fingers. Her body ached with tension. She took a faltering step away from the shelter of the wagon, then another. She wouldn't give up. Not yet.

She would have passed by him in the dim light if he hadn't called out. He stepped from the shadow of a tree, seeming to tower over her.

"I warned you once before about wandering away from the wagons."

"I wasn't going far. I couldn't sleep." Susan made her voice soft and soothing.

He studied her for a moment and she fought the urge to cringe from his observant eyes. Then he seemed to accept her answer. "If you insist on walking, you may as well join me. Then at least I won't need to worry about you getting lost."

Susan smiled and nodded, trying to hide the resentment she felt at the condescension in his voice. She allowed her shawl to slip down her back and was rewarded by a gleam of interest in his eyes. She matched her steps to his as he began a circling sweep around the cattle.

"It's quiet out here at night," she said.

"That's how I like it. Gives a man a chance to think."

"What do you think about?"

"Depends on my mood. Sometimes the past, more often what we'll face tomorrow and the day after that."

"What about the future? Beyond the next few days? Don't you ever think about that?"

"Sometimes."

He was in a gentle mood tonight. She seldom dared to question him, but he seemed to welcome her company. The air was free of the antagonism that usually crackled between them.

"Will you go back to Independence when we reach Oregon?" She forced herself not to hesitate over the word "we." "Will you bring another train out again in the spring?"

"No. I've had my fill of this life. It served its purpose for a while. Now it's time to start something new."

"Like what?"

He glanced down at her. "You wouldn't be interested."

"Yes, I would," she protested and found she meant it.

Encouraged, he continued. "What money I make from this trip'll be enough to finish paying off a saloon I intend to buy. I already have an option on it and when I get to Oregon it'll be mine, free and clear."

"A saloon?"

He laughed and Susan wished she had kept the surprise from her voice. "I guess that doesn't sound like much to you, does it? It's important to me, though. Just a beginning, but that's where the money's at. I figure I'll make enough in a couple years to invest in some solid holdings—a boardinghouse, a bank—things you'd approve of."

"I didn't mean—"

"I know." He cut across her apology. "I intend to be somebody one day. I don't aim to spend the rest of my life drifting or working for other men. The way I see it, Oregon's going to grow and I intend to grow with it."

There was enthusiasm in his voice, and Susan had no doubt he would accomplish what he set out to do. He was the kind of man she could have admired if she'd met him under other circumstances. Now, she reminded herself, there was no room for admiration. She glanced at him through lowered lashes and allowed the shawl to open at her throat. The evening breeze caught her loose hair and blew it against her throat. Morgan's eyes darkened.

"It's time you were getting back to the wagons," he said.

"I'd rather listen to you."

His gaze was hungry as it held hers and she glanced away in studied confusion.

"I've talked enough." His voice was harsh and Susan bit her lip in frustration. Had he seen through her act? Had she been too obvious?

He turned toward the wagons and she followed. She had to do something. She pretended to stumble on the uneven ground and clutched his arm. When he steadied her, she clung to him. Her shawl fell to the ground as she leaned against him. His arm tightened around her waist and Susan held her breath, not daring to move lest she break the spell. His other arm slowly encircled her waist and he turned her toward him. She raised her eyes hesitantly, but made no move to pull away. One corner of his mouth turned up. She couldn't tell if he smiled at her or himself.

His hand moved up her back to the base of her neck and he twined his fingers in her hair. Gently he rubbed her neck and Susan shivered. His hand moved to her throat and with one finger he drew a line from her chin to the neckline of her dress. His touch seemed to burn and she felt a quiver of apprehension, but she didn't move. She must do nothing to drive him away now that she was so close to her goal.

He cupped her chin in his hand and raised her face, and then his mouth covered hers. His kiss was soft and tender, but she sensed the power he restrained.

Deliberately she allowed her lips to part and his tongue lightly darted around the contours of her mouth. He drew her closer until she could feel the straining muscles of his chest and legs. His lips moved to her throat, the touch so light she strained to feel it. Warmth possessed her as she pressed against him, responding to him almost against her will, lifting her face to his caress. Her arms encircled his neck and her fingers stroked his hair.

With a groan, he pulled her to the ground and knelt beside her. She felt the scratch of dry grass against her back and fought the urge to scramble to her feet. For one long panicky moment she wished she had never come out into the night. His hands opened the fastenings of her dress and she tensed as he cupped her breast in his hand. But as his fingers stroked her, fire seemed to course through her. The world was reduced to the trembling she felt at his touch. Her planned responses were forgotten, lost in a surge of real passion as she lifted her face eagerly to his.

Susan hardly noticed when he slipped her dress off. She watched him fumble with his shirt and wanted to rip it from him, her pulse racing with a yearning to feel him beside her. Hurry, hurry, she thought.

When he reached for her she went to him gladly. His hand slid between her legs and her body strained to meet his. His fingers moved with velvety softness against the smooth inner flesh of her thighs. Each caress heightened the intensity of her passion until she was in a fever of desire. She whispered his name, fervently returning his caresses, and sensed a mounting urgency within him.

When at last he entered her she pulled his head down to kiss him with an ardor she had never known before. Together they climbed toward fulfillment, perfectly matched, moving together through a whirlwind of emotion.

A flood of warmth engulfed her and she clung to Morgan, her breath coming in gasps as she twined her legs around him to pull him even closer. He moaned and relaxed against her and she knew that he, too, had been satisfied.

. She curled her fingers through his hair and felt the damp warmth of his skin. Her fingers trailed lightly down the sinewy strength of his arms and he nuzzled his face against her neck. His warm breath tickled her skin and she wished she could lie there forever. She was filled with a sense of peace and satisfaction like nothing she had ever experienced.

Ross raised himself on one elbow but made no move to shift his weight from her. She gazed at him, fearless and secure in the afterglow of their lovemaking. Tenderly, he smoothed her hair back from her forehead and bent to kiss her ear.

"God, you're beautiful," he murmured, and she realized that these were the first words he had spoken since he had kissed her. She waited for him to say more, but he continued to study her face in silence. With one finger she traced the tiny scar at the edge of his mouth, her touch tender with a new awareness.

"How did you get this?" she asked. Suddenly it was imperative that she know everything about him.

He touched his cheek as though surprised to find the scar, then smiled and shook his head. "If I told you I got it in a duel, would you be suitably impressed?"

"Did you?"

"No, I was trying to break a new horse and like a fool greenhorn I didn't pay attention to what I was doing. He threw me and I landed on some rocks."

She traced the line again with her finger. He shivered.

"It's getting cold." He rolled to one side, stood up and began to pull on his scattered clothes. She watched him in the semidarkness. How could she ever have thought a man's body ugly? He was beautiful. Susan wanted to worship him with her hands and lips, but already he had drawn himself apart. Their time together was over.

"Here." His voice was gruff as he scooped up her clothes and tossed them to her.

As she dressed, Susan held her stomach muscles taut and arched her breasts forward, aware of him watching her. She fastened the last of the buttons on her dress and approached him. She ran one hand familiarly up his arm and stood on tiptoe to kiss him. He neither pulled away nor responded, and Susan began to feel uncertain. What was he thinking? She was afraid to ask.

"I'll see you back to the wagons." He pulled her arm through his, but there was no closeness in the gesture. It was as though by putting on their clothes they had become strangers again.

Still warmed by their lovemaking, she leaned against him, willing him to respond, but his stride didn't falter. She could have been a burr clinging to his sleeve for all the notice he gave her.

Stung by his indifference, she withdrew her arm and walked silently beside him. All too soon they reached the wagon.

"Good night," he murmured.

She raised her face to his, expecting a kiss, some acknowledgment, but he turned and strode back toward the livestock.

Susan watched him disappear into the night. The air had grown cold and she wrapped her arms around her body. She had left her shawl out there on the ground, but it scarcely mattered. She gazed up at the night sky, unwilling to enter the wagon.

Surprisingly, she felt no sense of victory. She had done what she had set out to do, but she felt only a lingering sadness and a desire to once again feel Ross Morgan's arms around her and his body next to hers. She had a strange premonition that she was not the victor in this battle. Indeed, she might have lost more than she had intended to wager.

Chapter 15

The adobe buildings of Fort Laramie were not what Susan had expected. She had come into the fort with Mercy but they had soon been separated by the milling mass of people. Two other wagon trains were camped outside the walls and hundreds of people seemed to be jammed within the narrow confines of the settlement.

"Susan!"

She turned to see Mercy struggling toward her through the crowd, an envelope clutched in her upraised hand.

"Look, there was a letter for you."

Susan took the wrinkled paper from Mercy's hand. It was from her brother, Michael, and she hesitated, almost unwilling to read it. Although she had written home to tell them she was going to Oregon, she had not expected a letter. She knew what a painful ordeal writing was for her brothers, and her father would be busy with Martha, his new wife. Susan turned the letter over in her hands.

"Aren't you going to read it?"

"What? Oh, yes—of course."

They edged away from the flow of people and took refuge against the flaking wall of an adobe building. Susan ripped open the letter. It was dated April 23, 1849.

Dear Susan,
We were told a letter might reach you at Fort Laramie and hope this finds you well. I wish I had a way with words like you and Pa always did, but I'm not much good at this sort of thing. I told you when I wrote last winter that Pa was sick. We thought he was getting better, but the fever seemed to settle in his lungs. He just got weaker every day. We did all we could for him, but he died last Thursday.

Susan clenched the letter in her hand as she reread the last sentence, then forced herself to continue.

If I'd known how to reach you, I'd have sent word, but we figured you'd already left for Oregon. Martha arranged the funeral right proper. Just about everyone was there. Don't know what we would have done without her these last few weeks. We've decided to sell the farm. Never has been much good—and with Pa gone, well, we just decided there wasn't any sense holding on to it. Reckon we'll get by all right, but it's strange not having Pa around. Send word when you reach Oregon. Someone will see we get your letter if we should be gone by then. Try not to grieve too much for Pa. He

*had a good life and I know he was happy the
last few months knowing you were taken care
of.*

> *Your loving brother,*
> *Michael*

As Susan stared at the paper, tears stung her eyes
and blurred Michael's awkward handwriting. Papa
was dead. She would never see him again.

She closed her eyes and imagined him as she had
seen him so often, seated behind his desk, thumbing
through scattered papers and books, his reading
glasses perched on the end of his nose. She remembered his blessing when she had left home with
Adam, and the sight of his slightly stooped figure
standing by Martha Brown's picket fence.

"Oh, Papa," she thought. "If only I hadn't left
you."

She felt a gentle hand on her arm and turned to
see Mercy's worried face. "Is it bad news?"

Susan tried to smile, but her lips trembled. "My
father's dead," she whispered.

"Oh, Susan, I'm so sorry!"

"He was dead before we left Independence,"
Susan cried. "If I'd known, if they'd told me how
sick he was, I could have gone to him. Somehow I
could have made it, Mercy."

"Shhh. There's no sense fretting over something
you can't help. He would have understood, Susan,
I'm sure of it."

"Yes, you're right. He would have. He always
understood everything."

"Would you like to come back to the wagon with
me? I'll fix you a cup of tea."

Susan shook her head. "If you don't mind, I think I'd like to be alone right now. Maybe later."

"Of course." Mercy squeezed Susan's arm and turned away.

Susan crumpled the letter and thrust it into her pocket. She wanted to escape from everything—from the noise and dust that engulfed the fort, from the hurrying men and women who passed her without a glance. With unseeing eyes, she pushed her way through the crowd, out of the fort and toward a clump of trees in the distance.

She sat a long time beneath the trees, her mind a careful blank against the pain that awaited her conscious thoughts. But that couldn't last. She knew she had to face the reality of her father's death. Now there was truly nowhere to go, no home to return to. Her family as she remembered it would soon be scattered, lost to her. She thrust the aching sorrow to the back of her mind. She couldn't afford to dwell on it, no matter how much it continued to hurt her. Now she had to make plans.

She had expected Ross to come to her the morning after they had made love, to tell her she could continue the journey, but instead she hadn't seen him at all. Her shawl, carefully folded, lay near the wagon when she awoke the next morning, but he didn't seek her out. The next day he had gone ahead to Fort Laramie, leaving the train to follow.

They had been here two days. Soon they must move on and still nothing was resolved. She knew she should go to Neal and ask for his help. It was better than turning back. In fact, it seemed to be the only choice left. But she knew it would require a sacrifice on the part of the Laughlins. How would they all fit in the wagon? Ellie's belongings would have to be cast aside or traded at the fort for more useful items, and Susan dreaded the scene she was sure that would cause.

But there was no alternative. She had tried to do it on her own, and she had failed. She felt a wave of humiliation as she remembered how she had thrown herself at Ross Morgan. And what good had it done? It had only driven him away. She had been wrong— to him she was just another woman, someone to satisfy his lust and nothing more. She should have realized. And now, to make matters worse, she found herself lying awake at night, reliving the feel of his hands against her bare skin, remembering the surge of passion he had awakened in her.

"Stop it!" she said aloud.

A startled crow rose from the branches of the tree and Susan watched him fly off with a raucous cry, envious of his freedom. If only she could run away from the heavy burden of the problems that plagued her, never have to worry about another thing.

Why did I ever agree to go to Oregon? If I'd been strong, I could have told them all to go without me, she thought. I would have made do somehow. Now I'm stranded in the middle of this wilderness and I can't go back, or forward either.

Susan rose to her feet and turned toward the wagons. She would have to set aside her pride and go to Neal. There was no other way. Will I ever be able to do anything on my own, she wondered as she moved slowly toward the wagons.

The feeling of defeat made her shoulders sag.

What sort of life was it when a woman must depend on a man for everything? It wasn't fair.

She caught sight of Morgan in the distance as she neared the wagons, and felt her pulse quicken. She expected that when he saw her he would vanish in the opposite direction; instead, he came to meet her.

"Good afternoon, Mr. Morgan." Her tone was carefully formal. She would never allow him to see how his nearness affected her. If he wanted to pretend nothing had happened between them, she would play the same game.

"Susan." He touched the brim of his hat. "I was looking for you."

"Oh? What was it you wanted?"

"Taggerty and I just had a meeting. We've decided to let you continue west. You haven't held up the train so far and Taggerty thinks you deserve the chance. That is, if you still want to. If not, I can make arrangements for your return."

"Thank you, Mr. Morgan. We intend to go on." She lowered her eyes to hide the triumph she felt. He might say Taggerty had made the decision, but she guessed differently. Ross didn't want to make her turn back.

"We'll be heading out in the morning," he continued. "I'd advise you to trade off anything heavy in your wagon for fresh oxen. You'll have need of them once we get into the mountains."

"Thank you for the advice." He stood awkwardly before her and Susan sensed he wanted to say something more. "Was there anything else, Mr. Morgan?"

"No, ma'am, I reckon there's nothing more I have

to say." His mouth curled cynically and his eyes were hard flint as they raked across her body. She met his gaze defiantly.

"Good day then, Mr. Morgan. I'll be ready in the morning."

She turned and walked toward the wagon, her back rigid with dignity. If he chose not to renew their relationship, that was fine with her. What need did she have for a man who thought so little of her? She refused to acknowledge the ache she felt. Her eyes burned with unshed tears and she knew that not all of them were for the loss of her father.

Chapter 16

Bloated carcasses lined the trail and circling buzzards waited for more oxen to drop beside the road. This was their third day of travel through a country of alkali and poisonous waterholes. They had camped at Willow Springs the night before. Belying its name, there had been no willow trees in sight, so they had burned sage for fuel. Today they had a long trip ahead to the Sweetwater. Grass was nonexistent. With dangerous frequency, axles and wagon wheels snapped as they traveled through the treacherous arroyos and ravines.

The train had been split into two parallel lines between which herders drove the loose livestock. At night the animals were crowded into the circled ring of wagons to keep them from the bad water. The dust was overpowering. It had even forced Ellie to leave the wagon and trudge beside the road, a handkerchief held over her face.

Susan wiped her forehead with the back of her hand. Sweat trickled into her eyes and the grit scratched her skin. She hoped Ellie would remember to watch for snakes. They seemed to be the only living creatures in this hateful country, and in Susan's opinion they were welcome to it. No one would want to stay long in this wasteland.

Susan lowered her head and studied the ground as she placed one foot before the other. Soon they would stop for the nooning and the day would be half over. At least she could rest for a few moments. There was a little water left and the thought of the liquid, warm and brackish as it was, raised her spirits. A small amount could be doled out to each of the thirsty animals and she would change the oxen so two others could rest. At Laramie she had traded Ellie's heavy cookstove for two fresh animals and now she was glad she had done so. They could take some of the strain off the rest of the team.

When the call came to stop, Susan leaned against the wagon in relief.

"I swear, I ache all over." Ellie's voice was high-pitched and whining. "I've just got to wash this dust off before I do another thing."

Susan snapped from her relaxed position. "We can't spare water for washing."

Ellie stared at her. "Why ever not? You can't expect me to eat like this." Her hands swept over her dusty garments and dirt-caked shoes.

"There's only enough to drink and some to give to the oxen."

"Give to the oxen! You must be crazy. Those animals don't need all that water. I intend to wash. I'm still a lady, and ladies don't eat with dirty hands. The oxen can have what's left."

Ellie marched to the back of the wagon where their small supply of water was kept. She dipped several cupfuls into a bowl and clambered into the wagon. Susan sighed. She would just have to do without a drink herself. She knew how much the animals needed it.

She began to release the two lead oxen from the yokes. She would let them rest and perhaps all six would make it to the Sweetwater.

Sunlight shimmered against the white landscape and in the distance she saw several pools of water. They were the color of black coffee and she saw the humped bodies of livestock that had died there. She averted her eyes and concentrated on her own team.

Released from their heavy burden, the oxen shook their heads back and forth, nostrils flaring. Susan was halfway to the milling herd to round up the two spare animals when a shout made her turn. She was in time to see the two unfettered beasts lumbering toward the alkali pools. How could she have forgotten to secure them?

She raced back to the wagon, snatched the bullwhip from the ground and ran after them, shouting. They only increased their speed. Even as she ran, Susan marveled that they had the energy to move so fast. She knew she must reach them before they got to the water. Her clinging skirts hampered her and she wrenched them up with her free hand.

The oxen reached the spring. They splashed through the pool and lowered their heads to the brown water that would kill them.

"No!" she screamed. "Don't drink that!" She was still fifty yards away and tears stung her eyes at the futility of her cries.

When at last she reached the edge of the pond she snapped the bullwhip over their heads, but they ignored her. Their long tongues lapped the water in eager gulps. Desperately Susan flicked the whip at the rump of the nearest ox. He raised a startled head at the lick of pain and began to plod toward the opposite side of the pool.

"Here, give me that." Ross Morgan's deep voice was urgent as he reached out a sun-browned hand to take the whip from her. She had no time to feel surprise at his presence.

"Get back to the wagon," he ordered. "Get two slabs of bacon, a prod, and as much vinegar as you can carry." Even as she turned to obey his terse commands, Susan heard the whip crack through the air as he attempted to force the two animals from the water.

She raced back to the wagon. Her sunbonnet fell unheeded to the ground, and she pulled her skirt up to her knees and ran through the blazing heat. Her breath came in labored gasps as she reached the wagon. Ellie poked a startled face through the canvas opening.

"Get me some vinegar, quick," Susan cried as she began to rummage for the bacon.

"Vinegar?" Ellie's eyes were blank. "What on earth do you want with vinegar?"

Susan's patience snapped. She had had all she could take of Ellie's simpering and whining. She glared at the woman with narrowed eyes and the venom in her voice made Ellie take a step back. "Just get it!"

Ellie's face paled and she retreated into the shadows of the wagon. Susan had no time to wonder whether the woman would obey her order. She pulled two large slabs of bacon from the box, grabbed the prod from the side of the wagon and yelled for Ellie.

"Where's the vinegar?"

Without a word Ellie handed her a jug. Susan grabbed it and turned to stumble back toward Ross.

Morgan had succeeded in getting the animals out of the water and he was urging them toward her. They walked slowly now, their sides heaving. Susan feared they would drop at any moment. At last she reached them, panting, and dumped her burden on the ground. Ross swiftly encircled the head of one ox with his arm and pried its mouth open.

"Quick!" he shouted. "Jam that bacon down his throat. Use the prod to make him swallow it."

Susan gaped at him for a moment, then flew to do his bidding. Her own stomach churned as she forced the bacon down the animal's throat, but at last he took it. Morgan still clung to the animal, although it had begun to twist in his grasp.

"Now the vinegar," he ordered. Susan grabbed the jug of vinegar and tugged the cork free.

"Pour some down its throat." She turned the jug upside down and vinegar gurgled into the ox's mouth.

"More," Morgan insisted. At last he released the beast. It made strange moaning sounds as it tossed its head back and forth and staggered away.

"Hurry up," Morgan called and Susan turned to see that he already had a grip on the second ox and was wrenching at its mouth. The huge animal shied and squirmed, but he couldn't elude Morgan's grim determination. This time Susan did her part without direction and soon Morgan released the second animal.

Susan's legs shook and she slumped to the ground beside the jug of vinegar as she watched the animals weave toward the herd. Morgan dropped his hand on her shoulder.

"Good girl," he said. "They should be all right now."

He turned toward the wagons and Susan sat huddled on the ground, watching his retreating figure in stunned surprise. If anything, she had expected blame for her carelessness. Now his words of praise, though brief, brought tears to her eyes.

What's wrong with me, she wondered. But she feared she knew what caused her weakness. There was no denying the sudden warmth she had felt when he touched her, even so slightly.

Susan watched the oxen rejoin the herd and hoped desperately that they would survive. She couldn't afford to lose two animals. She pushed her hair back from her face, rose to her feet and picked up the empty vinegar jug. Head down, she walked slowly back to the wagon.

Chapter 17

In the days that followed, Susan found little time to examine her feelings toward Ross Morgan. Miraculously, the oxen survived the poisonous water. Others were not so lucky and a dozen carcasses were left behind to feed the buzzards.

They reached the Sweetwater and Independence Rock. Every able person on the train scrambled up the sides of the huge rock to paint or scratch their names into its well-marked surface.

The train crept upstream through rugged terrain. They had to cross the river repeatedly as they traveled through a high-banked gorge. Everyone looked forward to the day they would reach South Pass and follow westward-flowing water for the first time. That goal lured them on and their pace quickened as the wagons lurched across steadily rising elevations.

"I expected it to be like the mountains," Mercy exclaimed when at last they reached the summit. "Something more dramatic."

Instead, grassy meadows rolled across the high tableland that was more like a flat plain, unexpected after the days of steady climbing.

Susan pointed to the mountains that towered to the north and south. "Just be glad we didn't have to cross those."

The snow-covered crags looked forbiddingly cold even in the warmth of the summer day. Mercy shivered.

"You're right, Susan. Isn't it silly to wish things were *more* difficult? It's been hard enough."

The Laughlins had been one of the families to lose livestock to the poisonous springs. Mercy cried when they left Ike's body behind and Susan had offered the use of one of her extra animals. Mercy promptly christened it Pacific, and vowed that the animal would live to see its namesake.

"Neal says tonight we'll see the first water that flows west," Mercy said. "It makes Oregon seem so much closer."

Susan nodded absently, but her thoughts were elsewhere. "I hear there'll be a council meeting tonight to decide whether or not to take Sublette's Cutoff. Which way does Neal want to go?"

"He says he'd rather go by way of Fort Bridger. There's more water and grass for the stock, and after losing Ike he's pretty cautious about taking on more desert. What do you think, Susan?"

"I don't know. We'd save sixty miles, but they say it's the driest stretch between Independence and Oregon."

Susan knew it made no difference what she thought. The men would decide which route to take and she could not voice her opinion. She wondered if the other women felt as helpless as she did. But at least most of them could try to influence their men.

Susan would be one of the few with no representation when the council met.

That night Susan sat with Ellie and Mercy while the men met at Taggerty's wagon. She heard the low rumble of their voices as they discussed the merits of the shortcut to the Green River. Occasionally one voice rose above the rest, but she was unable to hear what was being said.

"I'm tired of sitting here, not knowing what's happening," she said at last.

Mercy looked up in surprise. "We'll find out soon enough, Susan. There's nothing we can do. The men will decide."

"I know it." Susan paced back and forth. "That's what makes me so angry. We should all have a say. Why should they make every decision? I have a wagon to worry about and stock, just like the rest, but does anyone ask me which route to take?"

"That's the way it's meant to be." Ellie spoke from her place by the fire. "You let the men folk do the decidin'."

Susan scowled at her. "Well, at least I can listen to what they're saying." She turned her back on their protests and walked away.

The campfire cast flickering shadows across the faces of the men as Susan watched them from the shelter of a nearby wagon. Ross Morgan sat beside Taggerty, his face expressionless while one of the other men spoke.

"I say we go through Fort Bridger. We can stock up on food, rest the animals."

Susan saw Neal stand up. "I agree with Fletcher,"

he said. "Those headed for California can leave the train at Bridger and go on from there if they've a mind to. Taking shortcuts is too risky."

"'Tain't risky, not if you got a good team."

"Not everyone's got a good team."

"That ain't my fault."

"We could save a heap of time taking the Cutoff."

"Joe's right."

Finally one of the men asked, "What do you think, Morgan?"

Ross surveyed the faces of the waiting men before he spoke. At last he said, "I know the trip's been harder for some than others. Those who lost cattle or oxen don't want to risk losing more. I understand that." He glanced around the expectant circle. "What some of you are forgetting is time. It's the one thing we can't replace. We should have reached Independence Rock two weeks sooner than we did. There've been delays along the trail. Makes no difference who or what caused them, the fact is we're a good two weeks behind schedule. I say we'd best take Sublette's Cutoff and try to pick up some of that lost time."

There were a few mutterings among the men, but Morgan's word carried a lot of weight. Neal stood again and the men hushed expectantly.

"Ross, I figure you know what's best. You haven't led us wrong this far. But it's a hard crossing from what I hear, and some of us are weakened by the trip."

Although he didn't use her name, Susan knew he thought of Mercy. As he spoke, it was all she could do to keep from bursting into the group with pleas of her own.

A brief look of sympathy crossed Morgan's face and he waited until Neal sat down before he spoke.

"Mr. Laughlin has a point," Morgan said. "There are some of us who may not make it to Oregon. We knew that when we left. You were all warned of the dangers and difficulties of the trail. Those of us who have come this far have done so because we've been tough. We haven't let anything stop us and I don't believe we can start now. If we make exceptions for the few who are sick, *none* of us will make it. I still say we should take the Cutoff."

The men were silent. Susan bit her lip to keep from crying out. How could he be so heartless? He knew Mercy as well as any of them. He knew what the choking dust did to her, how she coughed as though she would never stop.

"I guess everyone's had his say," Taggerty said, his voice gruff. "Let's vote on it. Everyone who wants to go by way of Fort Bridger, raise your hand."

Neal's hand shot up, along with three or four others. Some men hesitated, moved their hands as if to vote with Neal, then were still. Morgan had won. They would take the Cutoff and damn the consequences.

Susan clenched her hands at her sides as she watched the men shuffle away toward their wagons. Morgan spoke briefly with Taggerty before he too drifted into the shadows. Susan hurried after him. She caught up to him at the edge of the encampment, his face turned toward the west.

"How could you?"

He spun around at the sound of her accusing voice.

"You know how sick Mercy is. Do you want to kill her? Don't you care about anyone?"

Morgan regarded her through narrowed eyes. "I can't risk the entire train for one person," he said at last.

"But you don't know how serious it is." Susan paused for an instant. She remembered her promise to Mercy, but she hadn't promised to keep it from Ross. "When she coughs, she spits blood. I've seen her handkerchief. The more dust there is, the worse she'll get. You must change your mind and tell the men we'll go the long way."

"I know she's sick, Susan. I've seen her when she gets one of those coughing spells. I'm not heartless, but I have to think of the good of the train." His voice held an unspoken plea for her understanding, but Susan refused to be swayed.

"I don't think you ever cared about anyone but yourself in your entire life," she blazed. "If you did, you wouldn't make this decision."

He shook his head, but remained silent.

"You use everyone," Susan continued, her anger not only on behalf of Mercy, but herself as well. All the days of frustration rose to the surface. He had treated her like a common squaw, taking her in the grass and dirt of the prairie and then ignoring her. She forgot how she had used every wile in her grasp to have him make love to her. All she thought of was how he had avoided her since that moment.

"No one's good enough for you," she shouted. "You think you can tell everyone what they should do and they'll follow you like a herd of sheep. If Mercy dies it'll be all your fault." She turned and started to run toward the camp, but he caught her arm and whirled her around to face him.

"You listen to me, and you listen good." He spoke through clenched teeth and Susan caught her breath at the cold fury in his voice. "You say I don't care about anyone, that I use people. I could say the same for you and with more reason. But I won't waste my time exchanging insults. I care about Mercy—just like I care about every living soul on this train—even you. But if we don't reach the mountains before October we're never going to make it to Oregon. Is that what you want?"

"No, of course not."

"I know this country, damn it. I know it better than you know your house back home. It's wild and dangerous and none of you seems to realize that. You act like you're on a damned picnic. I can't afford to be soft—I can't make allowances for people like Mercy, though God knows she deserves it. I just can't do it."

Her eyes widened as she saw the conflict in his face. She realized that he wanted to take the longer route, for Mercy's sake as well as for the others. But she also saw he was right. This was no place for the weak. It never would be.

Suddenly she was ashamed of her outburst, but she didn't know how to take back her words.

He released her arm and she rubbed the soft flesh where his fingers had bruised it. The rage had faded from his face, to be replaced by remorse and sadness. How lonely he suddenly seemed. The burden of every decision was on his shoulders, and if he was mistaken only once, the consequences would be his responsibility. If he allowed the others to persuade him to take the longer route and they were caught in the mountains, they would forget their earlier urgings for safety and remember only that it was *his* fault.

Susan placed one hand on his arm. "I'm sorry," she said softly. "I didn't understand."

He looked at her for a moment in silence, then drew her to him. She leaned against him. Her pulse quickened and she held her breath, waiting for him to kiss her. She didn't care that he had ignored her these past few weeks. Nothing mattered except the touch of his hand as he gently stroked her hair. She lifted her face to his, her lips parted. His eyes met hers and she saw the conflicting emotions within him. He put one finger against her eager lips and smiled sadly.

"No, Susan," he whispered. "Not again."

She wanted to cry out, to demand an explanation. She knew he wanted her, she saw it in his eyes, in the way the curve of his lips softened as he looked at her. But even as she noticed the softness, his chin firmed and he put her away from him.

"You'd best be getting back," he said. "The next two days will be difficult."

He turned her around as though she were a child and gave her a slight nudge toward the wagons. Susan thought she heard him call good night, but she was afraid if she turned he would see her tears.

Chapter 18

The next evening they camped at the edge of a desert that seemed to stretch on endlessly. Susan and Mercy strolled between the wagons, their faces lifted to the cool evening breeze.

"You should be sleeping," Susan said. "We'll be starting soon."

"I know, but it's so nice to be out in the night air. Doesn't it feel good after the sun?"

Susan glanced at Mercy. The girl had accepted the decision about the route without comment, but Susan knew she must be worried. Her face was pale and her hair hung to her shoulders in limp tendrils. The heat of the day had taken its toll on everyone, and in only a few hours the call would come to hitch up the teams to begin the long journey across this vast wasteland.

The two girls parted at the Laughlin wagon and Susan returned to her own. Her mounting apprehension made it impossible for her to sleep. Instead, she pulled her shawl closer around her shoulders and sat beside the wagon, her back against a wheel spoke.

She recalled her conversation with Morgan the night before and wondered if he slept. She wished she could go to him, feel the assurance of his arms around her, but she knew it was hopeless. Whatever it was that kept him away was stronger than his attraction to her.

She believed she had begun to understand him a little. At first she had thought him scornful of convention and personal attachments and their one night together had seemed to confirm that conviction. However, last night she had seen another side of him, a gentler side, and she wondered if he was really as tough as he appeared.

There was no denying the desire that sparked between them. Someday he would come back. She knew it as well as she knew she was sitting here. Whether they wished it or not, they were drawn to each other.

The crack of the sentry's rifle startled Susan from her thoughts. It was time to leave. She stood up and rubbed her shoulder where it had rested against the wagon wheel. She had been foolish not to take advantage of the few hours to sleep. Now it was too late. It was time to begin the long journey across the threatening desert.

Moonlight cast eerie shadows across the white alkali sands as the wagons moved forward like a ghost train. The normal sounds of their passage seemed muffled by the night and all Susan heard was the occasional crack of a whip and the constant creak of wheels. Shadowy forms first seen in the distance became the bleached bones of animals as they passed and she watched her own oxen anxiously. The night air was cool, but soon the punishing sun would clear the horizon and beat down on them as they struggled westward.

Taggerty and Morgan rode past, and Susan knew they were calculating how much more strain the oxen could bear. They didn't speak as they passed. It was as though they were creatures from another world. The whole scene had a dreamlike quality.

Gradually the darkness began to fade. The moon was no longer visible, but there was enough light to keep from stumbling on the gravelly rifts. The train moved at a steady pace, fleeing the sun that rose at their backs, a fiery orange ball on the horizon. Susan shaded her eyes from the glare of the white sand.

As the morning wore on Susan heard rasping coughs from the Laughlin wagon and wished there were something she could do to ease Mercy's ordeal. Would they ever reach the end of this desolate country? What if they had taken a wrong turn during the night? What would happen if they didn't reach water soon?

The thoughts preyed on her mind until she found she was clenching her hands in anxiety. Stop it, she told herself. This won't help anyone.

But as they continued to pass ravines and dried-up alkali lakes, she noticed the increasing number of carcasses. Many before them had failed to make it across the desert.

Ellie poked her head from the wagon only once. After a brief glimpse of the barren countryside, she quickly retreated.

It was an effort to put one foot in front of the other and Susan's legs shook with fatigue. Grit and dust enveloped her and she felt as if her clothes were rubbing her skin raw. She vowed to ignore the desert, to pretend today was like any other.

Suddenly the oxen lifted their heads and sniffed

the air. Susan saw nothing, but the animals seemed uneasy. The wagons ahead began to move faster and her own oxen broke into an awkward gallop.

"Whoa!" she cried in alarm, trotting beside the wagon, but the team continued their lumbering gait, hurtling the wagon across the rough terrain until Susan feared it would overturn.

"They've scented water," someone shouted and Susan felt her spirits lift. Soon they would be able to bathe and drink clear, sweet water. She broke into a run beside the animals.

We made it, she thought jubilantly. We made it.

Chapter 19

The Green River flowed crystal clear between banks lined with cottonwoods. A hundred yards wide and belly deep to the horses, it was the most beautiful sight Susan had ever seen.

She stood in the shade and watched the men water the livestock. Her own chores were done and now she could relax. They would spend the night here before crossing the Green. The charge for the crossing was two dollars and she wondered about their money. Ellie continued to dole out the necessary amounts at the various crossings and didn't seem concerned. Susan wished she knew exactly how much was left, but she hated to ask.

She shook the doubts from her mind. It was too beautiful here to let worry mar the perfection. The waters of the Green beckoned and she decided to take this opportunity to find a place to bathe. How good it would feel to be clean again.

She fetched a bar of lye soap and a towel from the wagon and was about to return to the riverbank when Mercy called to her.

"Oh, Susan, are you going to take a bath?"

"Yes, I'm sure there must be someplace where no one will see me."

"Do you think you should go alone?"

"Why ever not? There's no one around for miles."

"Let me go with you."

Susan hesitated. The icy water wouldn't be good for Mercy's delicate health. As if sensing Susan's concern, Mercy added quickly, "I won't bathe. I'll just sit on the bank and dip my feet."

"All right, come on then."

The two girls slipped through the cottonwoods and moved downstream from the wagons. Soon they could no longer hear the shouts and splashes from upriver and they approached a small cove where the water looked cool and inviting. Susan glanced in both directions and saw no one.

"This is perfect," she announced and began to undress.

Mercy perched on the edge of the bank, her bare feet churning the water.

"Oh, that feels so good. I wish I could jump right in, but I suppose I'd better not." She looked wistful as Susan eased herself into the water.

"Brrr, it's cold. No, you'd better stay right there."

Susan lay back and let the water cover her body, washing away the grime and dirt. She splashed playfully at a bug that swept past on the current and felt like a child again as she remembered all the times she had gone swimming with her brothers before Pa said she was getting too old for that sort of thing. The water rinsed away the indignities of the trail and she drifted on her back, dreamily gazing at the clouds in the blue sky overhead.

At last she roused herself, got the soap from the bank and began to work suds through her hair and over her body. As she rinsed off a call broke the solitude.

"Mercy!" It was Neal's voice.

"Oh, dear," Mercy cried. "I'd better go see what he wants. Shall I come back for you?"

"No, you go ahead. I'm almost ready to get out anyway."

Mercy fastened her shoes and hesitated. "You'll be right along, won't you?"

"Yes, don't worry. Go find Neal before he finds us."

This possibility made Mercy's face flush with embarrassment. "Oh, he mustn't do that."

Susan watched her disappear through the cotton-woods and sighed. She must get back soon, but it felt so good. The sun warmed her face and she closed her eyes for a moment, drifting.

A sound startled her and her eyes flew open. Had Mercy returned? She flipped over and gazed toward the bank. At first she saw no one, then she made out the figure of a man leading a horse through the trees. She couldn't tell who it was from this distance, but supposed it to be someone from the train. The men had assured them there weren't any Indians in this area and Susan had felt safe in that knowledge. But she didn't want to be seen like this, even by friendly eyes.

She lowered herself until she was almost sitting on the riverbed and waited for the man to pass out of sight. He turned his horse toward the bank a few yards upstream from where she sat and as he cleared the trees, she recognized Ross Morgan.

Her face was warm with embarrassment. Of all

people, he was the last one she wanted to find her here.

He hadn't seen her yet. He was merely watering his horse and quietly she moved closer to shore. She watched in dismay as he sat down and leaned against a tree.

Susan shivered. It was cold now that she wasn't moving. She edged as close to the bank as possible and watched Morgan. Would he never leave? She'd freeze to death if she had to stay here much longer. She glanced to where her clothes lay. They were much too far away for her to make a dash across the unprotected space unseen. She had no choice but to wait him out.

She shivered again and felt the tingling in her nose that preceded a sneeze. She pinched her nostrils together with water-wrinkled fingers. At last the feeling subsided and she moved her hand away cautiously. She sighed.

The sneeze came like an explosion in the quiet. Quickly she ducked her head beneath the water, but not before she saw Ross jerk upright and turn toward her.

Susan held her breath as long as she could, but at last she was forced to break the surface. She pushed her streaming hair back from her face and looked directly into Ross Morgan's slate-gray eyes as he stood on the bank above her.

"Oh." The small startled sound was all that came from her lips and she watched a smile spread across his face. He glanced from her to the clothes strewn across the riverbank, and the corner of his mouth twitched in amusement.

"How's the water?"

"Fine," Susan snapped and turned her head away.

"Maybe I'll join you."

"You'll do no such thing!" She turned to face him again, her eyes blazing. "If you were a gentleman you'd just go away and let me get dressed."

"But I'm not a gentleman, or have you forgotten?" His laughter infuriated her.

"You know what I mean." She watched in astonishment as he lowered himself to the ground beside her clothes.

"This is certainly a much nicer place to sit," he commented. "And the view is more interesting. Don't you agree?"

Susan glared at him in frustration. What would she do now? She couldn't stay here forever. Already her knees shook with combined anger and cold. But it was obvious he didn't intend to leave. He leaned on one elbow and idly picked at a few daisies that grew in the sparse grass.

"Please go away."

The lines of his face crinkled in laughter. "I must say you're not very friendly. I should think you'd welcome the company. Seems to me you were eager enough for it not too long ago."

Susan's face burned scarlet at his words, but she refused to be baited. She turned her back and sat shivering in the water. She would just wait until he tired of this game and left. Ross whistled a tune under his breath. It seemed to Susan that she'd sat there for hours, though it could only have been a few minutes. She heard a noise behind her and turned to watch him from the corner of her eye. Startled, she saw him remove his boots and then begin to slip off his pants.

He's really going to come in the water, she thought in fury. Oh! He's impossible!

She felt his eyes on her and knew he stood at the edge of the bank. She refused to acknowledge his presence, but when she heard his feet hit the water she quickly swam farther out into the river.

When she reached midstream, she turned to watch him.

"I must compliment you on your idea," he called. "It feels good." He splashed water over his back and shoulders and Susan felt a quickening of her heartbeat. His body was beautiful in the dappled sunlight that filtered through the leaves of the cottonwoods. He took her soap from the bank where she had left it and began to wash himself.

This was her chance.

As quietly as possible she paddled toward the shore, a little upstream from where he bathed. She glanced once in his direction and saw that his head was submerged. In one quick movement, Susan pulled herself onto the bank. She reached her clothes and had managed to struggle into her dress when he shouted.

Without waiting to fasten the dress, she clutched her undergarments and grabbed his clothing, which lay in a pile near her own. That would keep him from following, she thought, as she began to run through the trees toward the wagons. She stumbled on the uneven ground and winced as her bare feet struck rocks and prickly vines.

At last Susan paused to catch her breath. She

heard nothing behind her and grinned to herself as she envisioned Ross's consternation when he found his clothes gone. She placed his boots and clothing behind a tree and began to pull her dress together. She had outwitted him and she was pleased with herself.

She was reaching behind her waist to fasten her dress when a hand grasped her wrist and she was spun around to face Ross Morgan, wet and naked, his eyes shining with amusement.

"You didn't really think the lack of a few clothes would stop me, did you?" he asked as he took in her startled face. "I thought you knew what a savage I was."

"Let me go," Susan demanded. "Your clothes are over there." She motioned toward them.

"So I see, but I didn't come after my clothes."

His eyes were shadowy pools of light and Susan began to tremble. Wordlessly he drew her into his arms and she was intensely aware of his wet nakedness through the thin material of her dress. For a moment she struggled against him. Her mind protested that she no longer needed to let him make love to her, but her body had a will of its own. She sighed as she allowed desire to smother her thoughts.

She pressed against him and lifted her face for his kiss. She had known he would be back, but never had she imagined it would be like this. The sun warmed her skin as he gently slid her dress off and it fell to the ground. They stood together in the whispering cottonwoods, without pretense, each hungry for the other.

141

He took a step back and his gaze moved intimately over her body. Her face grew warm and she crossed her arms over her breasts.

"Don't." His voice was soft and it was as if he had touched her. Susan let her arms fall to her side.

"You have beautiful skin. Did you know that?"

Susan shook her head, aware of her growing need to touch him.

"Turn around."

She did as he asked, her back turned to him yet all her senses aware of his presence. His hands cupped her breasts as his lips burned a path along the back of her neck. She bowed her head and stared at his bronzed hands against the white flesh of her breasts. She covered his hands with her own and leaned back against him.

Gently he turned her to face him. He bent to kiss her breast and she sighed and pulled his head closer. She arched eagerly against him, her legs parted.

He eased her to the ground and his hands seemed to leave flaming trails on her body as he caressed her. He raised himself on one elbow and watched her face as his hand moved over her. She met his gaze through half-open eyes. His face was tender, yet strong. His eyes were dark with desire, his lips parted as he bent to kiss her once more.

Susan was lost in the thundering of her pulses as her passion rose to match his. She wrapped her arms around his waist and urged him toward her, her hips thrust upward, eager for the first contact with his body. But he held back, his hands caressing her and then his lips, until she moaned and lay still, allowing him to do what he wished with her.

As if by instinct he seemed to know how to bring

her pleasure. His touch was soft one moment, demanding the next. Her breathing quickened until it came in ragged gasps.

"Please," she whispered.

"Not yet." His voice was gruff with emotion. His lips made her tremble as they touched her breast and then her stomach. She quivered with expectancy as his hands and mouth explored her body. At last she could wait no longer.

"Please, Ross. Oh please, please love me."

He covered her body with his own and Susan lost all sense of reality as together they reached fulfillment.

Chapter 20

Her passion appeased, Susan snuggled against him. It felt good to lie next to Ross, to feel the beat of his heart. Idly she traced a pattern through the hair on his chest with one finger. She lifted her head to touch his lips lightly with her own.

His mouth covered hers and she felt him shudder as he drew her close once more. Quickly the flame that still smoldered within her grew to a fire to match his. She met his kisses hungrily, her lips moving beneath his to caress and torment. She moaned as once again he brought her to a shuddering climax.

Susan opened her eyes and gazed up at him. She didn't try to hide her feelings now, but let him see the warmth and satisfaction in her smile as she caressed the damp curls at the back of his neck. His face had resumed its expression of cool detachment. She stroked the side of his face, feeling the faint rough stubble of his beard.

"At least you could have shaved," she teased, willing him to respond, but his mouth was grim.

"I didn't mean ever to touch you again," he muttered as he drew away.

She rolled after him, unwilling to be separated even for a moment. She cradled his head in her arm and felt him relax. His arm encircled her waist and he held her close, his eyes shut. Susan sighed and nestled close to him. The rest of the world was forgotten. This was where she belonged.

Abruptly, Ross pulled away and sat up. She watched him, eyes widened with alarm.

"It's wrong, Susan. God knows, of all the people in the world, I know how wrong it is." His voice was soft, but beneath it was a hardening resolve that frightened her. She reached out and touched his arm.

"It's not wrong," she whispered. "How can it be?"

He sighed and drew away from her. This time she remained motionless.

"You belong to another man." His voice was cold.

"No," she cried. "Not now. Now I belong to you."

He smiled, but it was a smile tinged with sadness and wisdom. "No, Susan. However hard you try to convince yourself, you're still someone else's wife. I have no right to be here with you."

"But I don't love him," she cried. "I've never felt with him the way I do with you. Don't you see, that's what matters, not what it says on a piece of paper somewhere. I belong to you."

Ross shook his head and tenderly pushed a lock of hair from her face. "You know nothing about me, Susan. There are reasons—reasons I can't explain. But I could never take a woman who belonged to someone else."

"You were quick enough to do it before, when you thought I'd soon be out of your life." She fought to keep the bitterness from her voice.

145

"It was just as wrong then. I've thought about it—nights I've lain awake thinking about you, knowing I had to have you one more time. But it won't happen again. You must believe that. It's wrong—for both of us."

Susan rose on one elbow and studied his face. He couldn't mean what he said, not after what they had just shared. She knew he had experienced the same passion she had. Was he testing her? Was he teasing? She looked at him closely, but his expression was serious.

"You don't understand," she protested. She put out her hand to him, but he evaded her touch. "Adam means nothing to me—and I mean nothing to him. I never should have married him. But it's not too late. I'll leave him. You and I can start a new life together—a life of our own." Her voice was pleading and she bit her lip to control its trembling.

Ross's face was shadowed and she tried to see him clearly. His mouth seemed to curl cynically and for an instant she thought she saw hatred glitter in his eyes, but then it was gone. It must have been a mistake. She knew he didn't hate her.

Ross rose to his feet and began to pull on his clothes. Susan stood behind him, aching to put her arms around his lean waist, to have him tell her he understood, that they would do as she had suggested. But she held back, afraid of saying more.

He gathered her clothes and held them toward her. Tears stung her eyes as she hastily pulled on her undergarments and tugged the dress down over her head.

"Did you hear anything I said?" she asked.

"I heard you, Susan. But you didn't listen to me.

146

We'd both be miserable if we did what you suggest. You can't know how your husband really feels. How long has it been since you've seen him?"

"What difference does that make?" Her voice was defiant. "He'll never change. I know that. I hate him."

He shook his head. "Poor Susan." He spoke so softly she barely heard him.

"I don't want your pity," she snapped. If she stayed angry, perhaps she could hold back the tears. She blinked rapidly and glared at him.

"If you cared about me—really cared—nothing would stop you. Nothing would stand in the way, not a husband, not anything. It's just an excuse for putting an end to it—isn't that true?"

"If that's what you want to think, maybe it's best," he replied in a cool voice.

Susan felt as though he had hit her. She had expected denials, some sign that she really meant something to him, not this cold agreement.

"You give me no choice," she said icily. "And now, if you're finished with your dalliance, I'll get back to my wagon."

She turned and fled through the slender cottonwoods. As she ran they seemed to whisper her name mockingly. She thought she heard Ross call after her, but she didn't pause in her headlong flight until she had reached the encampment.

She came to a shuddering halt beside the Laughlin wagon and shook her head as if she could erase all remembrance of what had happened from her mind.

"Susan." The voice was deep and gentle, but she ignored it. She wanted everyone to go away, to leave her alone.

"Susan." The voice was more insistent and she turned reluctantly to find Neal Laughlin beside her, a worried frown on his face.

"What's wrong?" he asked.

As Susan looked into his soft brown eyes, the misery of the last few hours overwhelmed her. How could she tell him what was wrong? Her entire life was wrong. Nothing mattered to her anymore. She was alone and friendless except for Mercy and good, kind Neal who stood before her offering his understanding. He reminded her so much of her father. The memory of her father brought a new wave of grief and she threw herself into Neal's arms and sobbed against his shoulder.

"Hush, hush now," he whispered as he awkwardly drew her close and patted her shoulder. The fabric of his shirt under her cheek was soaked. Gradually her sobs subsided and with a shaking hand she clutched the handkerchief Neal offered.

"I . . . I'm sorry, Neal. I don't know what's wrong with me." She started to pull away, but he held her close. Like Papa used to do when I was a little girl, she thought, and leaned against him. It felt so good to have someone strong to lean on, if only for a moment.

"What happened, Susan? I saw you run out of the woods. Did something frighten you?"

"N—no . . . yes." The lie came quickly. "I thought I heard something in the bushes." How else could she explain her frantic race back to camp?

"It's all right," Neal comforted her. "It was probably just an animal."

"Yes . . . yes, I'm sure that's what it was. But I felt so alone."

"There, now. You know you're not alone. You always have us. Mercy and I would never let anything happen to you."

What would he say if he knew the truth? But he would never know. She'd forget Ross Morgan. She would pretend that nothing had ever happened between them. As far as she was concerned he no longer existed.

She squeezed Neal's hand and felt his arm tighten around her.

"Everything's all right now," he murmured, and she felt his lips brush her forehead. As she turned to smile at him she saw Ross leading his horse between the wagons. His face was a dark scowl and she knew he had seen them. Deliberately Susan rose on her toes to kiss Neal lightly.

"Thank you, Neal," she whispered.

Chapter 21

Fort Hall was another disappointment to the travelers. It was not a military fort, but was run as a trading post by the Hudson's Bay Company. For those planning to continue to Oregon, the word was discouraging. Everyone at Fort Hall told tales of impassable roads, treacherous mountain passes, coming winter storms and unfriendly Indians.

"Ye'll never make it," one bearded Scotsman informed Susan when she told him they were bound for Oregon. "Take my advice, lassie, and take the trail to California. A wee girl like yourself has no business tryin' to pull a wagon through those mountains. Why, there ain't even a proper road. You listen to me and go south with the others."

Susan nodded politely, made a few necessary purchases, and left the trading post, her spirits low. How will we make it, she wondered as she walked slowly toward the wagons. Is Morgan leading us into a wilderness we'll never get out of?

But it was senseless to consider the alternative. It was bad enough going to Oregon, but at least they were expected there. What would happen if she and Ellie changed direction for California? They'd never find Adam then, and she had vowed to deliver Ellie to Adam somehow, no matter what.

Susan blinked tears from her eyes as she stumbled over the uneven ground. She had worn one of her best dresses, hoping they had reached some outpost of civilization. But although the traders had been polite, it certainly was a long way from the life she had once known. If it was this bad here, what would it be like in Oregon?

"Let go, you varmint! Let go, I tell you!" Ellie's shrill voice pierced the stillness of the afternoon. Her heart pounding, Susan pulled up her skirts and raced toward the wagon. She rounded its end and came to an abrupt halt.

Ellie stood with her feet planted firmly in the dust. She held one end of George's tattered coat, while an Indian tugged at the other with dirty fingers. Taggerty had warned them that the Indians at the fort would steal anything, but what could he want with George's old coat? As Susan watched in amazement, he pulled harder and she heard the rip of fabric. Ellie lost her footing and tumbled to the ground, but kept her hold on the coat.

Susan was startled from her frozen stance. "Let go of that!" she shouted. He must be drunk, she thought, as she met the Indian's dull black eyes.

"Me take," he muttered and pulled again.

The garment tore still more and Ellie cried out, "Susan, make him let go of it. He'll ruin George's coat."

Susan glanced quickly around the encampment. There was no sign of life. Where was everyone? Even Sam had wandered off. She wished Ellie would let the Indian have the coat. It wasn't worth an argument. Warily Susan eyed his scrawny figure. His only clothing was a soiled loincloth, but a knife protruded from its waistband. As though sensing the direction of her gaze, the Indian dropped one hand to the knife.

"Me take," he said again and yanked at the coat. Ellie was pulled through the dirt toward the feet of the Indian. She shrieked and Susan snatched the rifle from the back of the wagon. With shaking hands, she leveled it at the intruder's chest.

"Drop it!" she commanded.

His eyes never blinked or left her face, although his hand curled around the handle of his knife. Oh God, she prayed, don't let him throw that knife. Please make him go.

At last the Indian's eyes dropped from hers and rested on Ellie. His hand tightened on the edge of the coat until Susan saw his knuckles whiten. Then, abruptly, he released it, spat on the ground and turned away.

Susan watched him walk slowly toward the fort, then she leaned against the wagon, the rifle held limply at her side. Her knees were weak and she put a shaking hand to her forehead. What a fool she had been. She should have let him take the silly coat. What good was it anyway? Ellie could have killed them with her foolishness.

Ellie sat in the dirt, the coat gathered into her lap as she examined the new tear in its shabby fabric. Tears streamed down her cheeks, but she didn't make a sound. She raised her head and looked at Susan for a long time. Then her gaze dropped back to her lap.

"He's dead, Susan." Her words were a whisper. "George is dead and he's left me all alone. A woman needs a man. Without a man she ain't nothin'. He was all I had and now he's gone."

Ellie buried her face in the dirty folds of the coat. Her shoulders shook as she rocked back and forth in the dust. Susan felt the sting of tears in her own eyes and bent to put an arm around Ellie's shoulders.

"It's all right. Everything will be all right, Ellie. You're not alone. You have me and . . . and Adam."

Ellie's tears made dirty rivulets down her face.

"Yes," she said at last. "I still have Adam, don't I? And you. Susan, don't leave me." Ellie's eyes were pleading. "Promise you won't leave me."

"I won't leave you. I'll see you get to Adam. I promise."

Ellie gave a ragged sigh. At last she got to her feet. The coat lay on the ground where it had fallen, unheeded.

"Not much sense keeping this old thing, is there?" she asked and Susan was unable to answer. She had risked her life for that "old thing," but it was worth it, she decided, if it had brought Ellie back to reality. With Ellie's help maybe, just maybe, they would be able to cross the barriers between Fort Hall and Oregon.

Chapter 22

The trail along the south bank of the Snake was narrow and treacherous. At times there was barely room for the wagons and each time the trail widened Susan sighed in relief. One slip and they would tumble hundreds of feet into the canyon below to be smashed against the jagged rocks that guarded the winding Snake.

Susan began to believe the trader at Fort Hall had told the truth when he said that no one could make it to Oregon by wagon. The few days since they had parted from the California group at the Raft River seemed like weeks. There were only eighteen dusty wagons now, slowly lurching toward Oregon.

Neal thought the trip wouldn't be as bad as the Hudson's Bay people had warned.

"They're only trying to keep settlers out of Oregon," he explained. "Morgan says they don't want more people. It makes the beaver scarce, and the furs brought out of Oregon Territory these last few years have made them rich. No wonder they want everyone to go to California."

Susan remained doubtful. The Scotsman had seemed sincere. And the longer they twisted and turned along this path that was little better than a goat track, the stronger her misgivings became. She had no reason to believe in Ross Morgan. Let the rest of them take his word as gospel. She had good reason to know that his word meant nothing and his actions even less.

Although the train had dwindled drastically in size, Morgan managed to avoid her. I'll forget he even exists, she vowed. If we ever get to Oregon I'll start a new life without Ross Morgan—and without Adam, too. This trip had proven she could survive without the overrated help of a man. She wouldn't slip back into dependency.

Susan glanced at the wagon seat where Ellie perched, her eyes wide with alarm at every lurch. Susan wished she could persuade her to walk beside the oxen, but even the threat of the sheer cliffs had failed to budge her. Lately Ellie's conversation was full of the future, when they would be reunited with Adam, and sometimes Susan almost wished for a return to the talk of the past.

Suffocating dust filled Susan's nostrils and she shook her head. Today they were to have been last, but instead the Jordans brought up the rear, their rickety wagon shuddering with each bump. She knew them only slightly, a family hard up on their luck, but she admired the plucky little man who was making a valiant effort to deal with a sickly wife and four children. They had been delayed by a sick child this morning and were still hitching their team when the call came to pull out. Susan had almost offered to trade positions with them, but decided it would make little difference. She hadn't wanted to be stranded behind them on the narrow trail. With constant stops to mend broken harness and tend to the children, the Jordan wagon was usually the last to pull into the evening encampment, no matter where they started.

Susan glanced over her shoulder and felt a pang of sympathy. Three of the towheaded children were squeezed onto the narrow front seat of the wagon and Susan guessed that the youngest rode in back. Mrs. Jordan walked behind, her head bowed, keeping up a steady pace that only changed when a child called for her attention. Mr. Jordan's wiry body seemed bent with care, but he never complained. No matter what misfortunes or delays descended on his family, he accepted them with resignation. Susan hoped he would be more fortunate in Oregon.

Ahead the Laughlin wagon slowed and Susan brought her own team to a halt. Mercy's head poked out.

"What's wrong?" Susan called.

"Just another narrow spot in the road. The men are trying to clear off a few fallen boulders before we pass through."

A large rock hurtled down the steep embankment and Susan watched it bounce to the bottom like a child's ball. It was a long way down. She gritted her teeth and looked away. There was no point thinking about it. There was only one way to go, and that was straight ahead.

In a few minutes the wagons began to inch forward again and Susan concentrated on keeping the oxen moving at an even pace. "Easy now," she cautioned in a low voice as they neared the narrow portion of the trail.

The animals plodded steadily after the tailboard of the Laughlin wagon and the trail began to widen.

Almost there, Susan sighed, and then she heard a low rumble behind her. As they gained firmer ground, Susan turned to look back.

The Jordan wagon was several yards behind her own. The rumble grew louder and Susan looked up. Large boulders cascaded down the hillside toward the frail wagon and its occupants.

"Look out!" she cried and Mr. Jordan raised his head.

Susan waved and pointed frantically at the avalanche of rocks and earth that plummeted toward the Jordans, but he seemed heedless of the sound above him.

"Hurry!" she shouted.

Mr. Jordan waved and smiled just as the first boulder hit the front wheel.

Susan watched, frozen with horror, as the wagon slowly tilted to one side and the children clutched at the seat. For a moment it seemed to hang suspended on the edge of the cliff. Then, as if in slow motion, the wagon and its occupants were swept over the side and disappeared. A few small pebbles bounced in the wake of their mighty brothers and Susan heard the echo of stone smashing against stone. She closed her eyes for a moment. It couldn't have happened, but it had. She heard Mrs. Jordan's shrill cry.

"My babies, my babies!" The woman rushed to the edge of the trail and Susan ran after her.

"Get back from there!" A rough hand pulled her aside and she looked at Ross Morgan with dazed eyes.

"The Jordans—" Susan caught her breath in a sob. "Mr. Jordan and the children . . . they're down there . . . all of them."

She began to tremble, and Ross put his hand out again to steady her. People clustered at the edge of the cliff, their voices hushed.

"Look," one of the women gasped. "Ain't that Melissa's little doll down there?"

Mrs. Jordan cried out and Ross turned to her. "Come away." He put a hand on her arm. "There's nothing you can do."

She let him lead her away from the precipice. Her eyes darted frantically among the crowd.

"My babies," she sobbed. "I want my babies. Andrew?" Her voice was shrill as she called her husband's name. "Andrew!"

"Hush." Ross urged her on, but her eyes fell on Susan.

"You!" she screeched and pulled away from Morgan's hand. "It's your fault. You killed them—my babies." She rushed at Susan, her hands clawing and scratching. "You made us be last. Couldn't wait a minute." Her words came in breathless gasps.

Susan threw her hands up to defend herself just as Ross succeeded in pulling the woman away.

"You'll pay for this," Mrs. Jordan cried. Then her face crumpled and she clung to Ross's arm for support. "Oh, my poor babies," she wailed.

He put one arm around her shoulders and motioned to Mrs. Taggerty. "See what you can do for her. We have to get these wagons out of here."

"We can't leave them there," Susan cried. "What if they're still alive?"

Ross studied her with silver-gray eyes void of any emotion. "No one survived that fall."

"You can't be sure. We have to find out."

There were murmurs of agreement from the crowd.

"And how would you suggest we do that?" Morgan's voice was cold.

"Why, go down and look, of course."

His lip curled into a sneer and Susan wished herself miles away from him and from this awful country, but she kept her gaze steady.

"And who, may I ask, is going to be foolhardy enough for that mission?"

"It seems to me that's your job, Mr. Morgan." Susan's voice was icy, but she was proud that she didn't sound as shaken as she felt.

"My job is to get this train to Oregon."

The group surrounding them shifted uncomfortably.

"If you were half a man, you wouldn't hesitate," Susan taunted.

"I'll do it."

Susan turned to see Neal, a coil of rope held in one hand, his dark brown eyes concerned.

"Don't be a fool, Laughlin," Ross snapped. "No one can make it down to the bottom of that gorge and back up in one piece."

"Someone has to try." Neal's voice was steady and assured.

Susan was alarmed. Neal mustn't risk his life. If anything happened to him, what would become of Mercy?

"No, Neal, you mustn't," she said. "Let someone else do it. You're needed here."

"Seems to me that others are needed more than I am—and besides, I'll make it." He smiled down at her. He tossed the end of the rope to Morgan.

"Can you fasten this?" he asked as he tied the other end around his waist.

"You're crazy," Morgan snapped, but he motioned Taggerty to his side. "Tie this to the oxen." He motioned to Susan's team. He raised his voice. "The rest of you, move these wagons out. That hillside could come down on us any minute."

As the crowd moved away, Neal walked to the edge of the trail. He glanced at Susan, smiled briefly, and began to lower himself over the side.

Susan heard a gasp beside her and turned to find Mercy, her face ashen as she watched her brother disappear from sight. I shouldn't have let him, Susan thought. Ross was right. No one could survive a fall like that. She clasped Mercy's hand.

The clatter of loose rocks made her jump, but Morgan and Taggerty continued to feed out the rope, little by little.

Please let him make it, she prayed. She watched the muscles of the two men strain from the weight of Neal's slowly descending body, then glanced at the rock-strewn slope above. So many things could happen. The rope could break, the men could slip, another rock slide could carry all of them to the bottom of the ravine. She held her breath.

After what seemed an eternity, the taut rope slackened in Morgan's hands.

"He's down," he muttered and glanced at Mercy. "He'll be all right. Don't worry."

Susan glared at his back. How dared he stand there and reassure Mercy about Neal's safety when he should have been the one to go below?

A faint shout brought Morgan and Taggerty back to attention. Ross stepped cautiously to the crumbling edge of the bank and shaded his eyes. "He's ready to come up," he announced and took his place beside Taggerty.

The return trip dislodged more loose stones than the trip down, and at each rattle of rocks Susan bit her lip. Slowly, steadily the two men pulled in the rope until at last Neal pulled himself onto the trail and lay there panting. When he stood up his face was pale. Susan didn't want to know what he had seen. No one said a word, but the same question was in everyone's mind. At last Neal shook his head slowly.

"They never had a chance," he said at last.

Only Mrs. Jordan's shrill wail broke the silence as she was led away by the wagon master's wife. Tears burned Susan's throat. Her last sight of Mr. Jordan was etched in her mind and she doubted she would ever forget it. If she had followed her impulse and changed places with them this morning, it could have been her body down there among the rocks.

She shivered as though a cloud had passed across the hot sun. As the train began to move she took her place beside the oxen. Would any of them make it to Oregon alive?

Chapter 23

That evening Taggerty led a short memorial service for the Jordans. Susan sat at the edge of the circle, her hands clenched in her lap. She barely heard the words Taggerty read from his well-worn Bible. Mrs. Jordan sat silent, her face pale, but her lips set in determined composure as she listened to the wagon master's words.

Susan thought of Neal's calm bravery, saw again his pale face as he hauled himself back onto the trail. If something had happened to him, it would have been her fault. In her anxiety, she had forced the issue. She remembered the words she had spat at Ross Morgan, foolishly accusing him of cowardice.

What if Morgan had gone over the side to check the shattered remains of the Jordan wagon and something had happened to him? The image of Ross's body at the bottom of the ravine made her shudder. Suddenly she knew that no matter how much she declared her hatred for him, her true feelings could not be denied. I love him, she realized.

Even that day by the Green River she hadn't put the thought into words. It had been there in her actions and her pleas, but she had never actually put it into words. Now the revelation made her catch her breath.

I must never let him know, she vowed. Let him think what he wants about me, but I must never show how much I care.

As the quiet group disbanded, Susan remained behind. The firelight began to fade and the only sound was that of the shifting livestock. Stiff and weary, she finally rose, made her way to the wagon and crawled into bed.

Although exhausted, she was unable to sleep. Images passed behind her closed eyelids—images of Morgan's face as he pulled her away from the cliff. Had he been concerned? There had been no tenderness in his expression, only anger. Would he have cared if it had been her wagon? I'll never know, she thought as the day's anxiety claimed its toll and at last she slept.

Day after day they twisted and turned along the Snake River until they reached Three Island Ford. The river was deep and swift. Morgan warned them that it would be a difficult crossing, but he promised that conditions would be better on the other side.

The crossing began easily enough. One by one the wagons sloshed through the swift flowing water. Occasionally they tipped precariously, but they were soon righted and splashed onto the opposite shore. Then Neal was ready to take his wagon across and Susan waved to Mercy, who peered from the back.

The Laughlins were halfway across when one of the lead oxen stumbled and fell to its knees. In the rapid current it struggled vainly to regain its footing. Neal scrambled from the seat and fought his way toward the thrashing animal. From the back of the wagon, Mercy craned her head around the side, but her view was blocked by the flapping canvas. She stood up, placed one foot on the tailboard, and grasped the bowed frame of the wagon top.

"Mercy!" Susan shouted. "Get back inside."

Instead, Mercy leaned out to watch Neal. At that moment Susan saw a log swirl around the bend of the river. It wasn't large, but its speed made it deadly.

"Mercy! Get back!" she screamed.

Mercy had seen it too, but instead of climbing back to the safety of the wagon, she leaned out still farther and shouted a warning to Neal just as the log struck the wagon wheel. The wagon lurched to one side and Mercy tumbled into the water.

"Mercy!" Susan screamed and jumped to the ground.

She saw Neal turn, but knew he was not aware of his sister's fall. A few yards downstream, Mercy clung to a rock and tried to stand up. Each time she gained her footing she slipped and splashed back into the water. Susan grabbed the long bullwhip from the seat of the wagon and sped downstream. Mercy couldn't hang on for long. Soon the weight of her petticoats would pull her under.

Standing on the shore, whip in hand, Susan called to Mercy. "Here, catch the end."

Mercy raised her hand in acknowledgment, but grabbed the rock again as she lost her balance.

Taking careful aim, Susan played the length of the

whip out across the water, upriver from the rock. The current carried the leather strip toward Mercy and the girl lunged at its end. For a moment she held it in her hand before it slipped away and she clutched at the rock once more.

Susan looked upstream. Men moved toward her, but they were still too far away to make it in time, and she didn't dare have Mercy let go of the rock a second time. Pulling her own petticoats from under her dress, Susan dropped them to the ground and rushed into the water. In most places it came only to her knees, but at times it reached her waist, and it was icy cold. Heedless of the chill, she splashed toward Mercy.

"Hang on!" she called.

The rocks of the riverbed shifted beneath her and she fell headlong into the water. The current tugged at her, but she scrambled to her feet and pushed her dripping hair from her eyes. She must reach Mercy before the girl was swept downstream.

Susan heard shouts from shore as she reached the rock. She braced herself against it and reached for Mercy, who gasped as Susan's fingers closed around her wrist. Her precarious hold on the moss-covered rock loosened.

"Oh, Susan, I thought you'd never get here," she sobbed.

We haven't made it yet, Susan thought. It had been difficult to reach midstream alone. It would be impossible to make the return trip with Mercy.

"Catch the rope," a voice called from the bank, and Susan saw a coil of hemp trailing through the water toward them.

Carefully she shifted her weight to free one hand. The end of the rope gathered momentum as it neared and Susan realized how difficult it must have been for Mercy to catch the end of her whip. Although the rope was heavier, it twisted and turned like an unruly eel, its movements unpredictable. She would have only one chance to catch it.

When the rope seemed near enough, Susan lunged for it. She grasped the end for an instant before the current twisted it from her numbed fingers and swept the rope downstream. Tears of frustration blurred her vision.

"It's all right," Ross Morgan shouted from the bank. "You'll get it next time."

His words reassured her and she dashed her tears away with the back of her hand. She couldn't weaken now.

Once more the rope was launched, this time farther into the stream. Susan bit her lower lip as the rope snaked toward her. If she missed it this time, there might not be another chance.

It came within inches of her hand and Susan grabbed it easily.

"Good girl," Morgan shouted. "Now, tie it around Mercy's waist and hold onto it yourself. We'll pull you in."

Susan did as she was told, fumbling with the wet rope. At last she looked toward the shore and called, "We're ready."

She clamped one hand on the rope in front of Mercy's waist and put her other arm around Mercy's shoulders as the rope tightened. Stones shifted beneath them and Susan feared they would both topple into the river, but inch by inch they neared the shore. At last they were there, and hands were reaching down to pull them out. Someone threw a blanket around her shoulders and Susan watched Neal lift Mercy into his arms and hurry to the nearest wagon. She started to follow, but Ross Morgan caught her arm.

"Get out of those wet clothes," he ordered.

"But Mercy—"

"Mrs. Taggerty and the others can see to Mercy. You won't help anyone if you stand around like that and catch your death of cold. Do as I say."

She knew he was right. Already her teeth chattered. Her skirt tangled around her legs as she staggered toward the wagon. Ellie helped her peel the wet garments from her body, and Susan felt a tingling in her numb feet and hands. She pulled on dry clothing and worried about Mercy. What would this do to her already weakened health? As she smoothed the skirt of her dress, Susan's fears grew. She had to see what she could do. Ignoring Ellie's protests, she swung to the ground and hurried toward Neal, who paced outside the Taggerty wagon. His worried frown eased slightly when he saw her.

"How is she, Neal?"

"Mrs. Taggerty is taking care of her. I only hope the shock won't be too much. That water's like ice." His eyes met hers. "How can I ever thank you?"

Susan blushed at the emotion in his voice. She had done what had to be done. She didn't expect thanks.

"If it hadn't been for you . . ." Neal shivered. "I hate to think what might have happened. And you—you could have been drowned trying to save her."

"Neal, it's all right. I'm fine—and Mercy will be, too. You'll see."

He grasped her hands in his and gazed into her face. "You're a brave woman, Susan. I'll never forget what you did—and neither will Mercy. I just wish I could tell you how grateful I am."

Mrs. Taggerty poked her head out of the wagon. "She wants to see you, Mr. Laughlin," she called. "You too, I reckon, Miz Baker."

Susan followed Neal into the wagon. A makeshift bed had been constructed over several packing boxes, and Mercy's slender form was buried beneath a pile of quilts and buffalo robes. Susan squinted in the dim light to see Mercy's face. Her lips were pinched and blue, her eyelids half closed. Neal gathered his sister into his arms and Susan blinked back tears as Mercy clutched him.

"Oh, Neal—it was so awful," she whispered. "I was so frightened. It was like the water was alive, tugging and pulling at me. I never would have made it if it hadn't been for Susan."

"It's all right now, honey," Neal crooned. "You just rest a spell and before you know it you'll be up and around, just like new."

Mercy smiled and relaxed against the pillow. She held out her hand to Susan, who took it in her own, appalled at how cold it felt.

"Don't let Neal worry," Mercy whispered. "I'll be fine." She smiled tremulously and Susan bent to kiss her forehead. Mercy sighed and her eyelids drooped. Susan carefully tucked her limp hand beneath the covers. Quietly she left the wagon, leaving Neal to watch over his sister.

Head bowed, Susan walked toward her own wagon. She was proud of what she had done. Although Neal's gratitude had embarrassed her, it had also warmed her. It had been a long time since someone had praised her. It seemed that lately all she heard were criticisms from Ross Morgan or Ellie.

As if her thoughts had made him appear, Ross stood in front of her. "How's Mercy?" he asked.

"She seems to be all right. She's so cold though."

He frowned. "It won't do her cough any good, that's for sure."

For the first time his gaze focused on her. Susan expected some acknowledgment of her rescue. Instead his frown deepened.

"That was a damn-fool thing to do," he snapped. "You could have killed yourself and not been one bit of help to Mercy."

Susan stared at him, speechless with surprise. How could he be angry with her? Hadn't Neal just said that if it wasn't for her, Mercy would have been lost?

"If you'd had more sense, you'd have waited for one of the men," Morgan continued. "We were right behind you. But no, you have to race to the rescue. Actions like that can endanger the entire train. From now on, think before you act and leave the rescue missions to those who know how to handle them." Not waiting for a reply, he turned on his heel and stalked away.

Tears burned Susan's eyes. How could he be so

cruel? She hadn't risked anyone on his precious wagon train except herself. He's just angry because *I* did it, she thought. He lost his chance to show what a great hero he can be.

She glared after his retreating back. Damn you, Ross Morgan, I hope someday you get what you deserve.

Chapter 24

For days Mercy lingered in a shadowy, fevered world, unable to recognize anyone. Susan observed Neal's worried face and wished there were some way she could ease his burden. Even Ellie spent hours trying to spoon broth between Mercy's trembling lips. All of them prayed.

Little by little Mercy seemed to improve. At times Susan thought it was only her imagination, but as the days passed her hope grew stronger.

"She's better, isn't she?" Neal asked each day, and she knew that he too feared it was only wishful thinking.

"Yes, I think she is," she reassured him. And at last it became a reality. The fever became sporadic and there were more frequent moments when Mercy could carry on short conversations. She remained dangerously weak, though, and her hacking cough frightened Susan. Try as they would, it was impossible to keep the billowing dust from sifting into the wagon. It covered everything. They were afraid to roll back the canvas cover of the wagon, yet at times the closed-off interior was like a furnace beneath the blistering sun.

They left the Snake at Farewell Bend and the train

wound between lofty, inaccessible mountains. There were numerous crossings of the Burnt River and the land was rough and stony. But the others seemed happier in spite of their surroundings.

"We're really in Oregon now," Ellie said one night as she and Susan sat by the campfire. "It won't be long before we reach the Dalles, and then we'll have an end to this constant bumping."

Susan wondered how it would feel to sleep in a real bed again, to have a solid floor beneath her feet and to eat something besides dried meat and fish. Her mouth watered as she thought of the vegetables and fruit long since vanished from their diet.

"Do you suppose Adam will be waiting when we get to Oregon City?" Ellie asked as she chewed a piece of jerky.

"I suppose it'll depend on how well he did in California."

"Oh, I do hope he'll be there. I'm so anxious to see him." Ellie gazed toward the horizon. "He'll be sorry about the baby, I expect. 'Course, you'll have lots more, but I know he set great store by that baby."

Susan didn't answer. If he had cared so much about his child, would he have sent her halfway across the world in this jolting wagon? And there wouldn't be any more children—at least not with Adam. She wouldn't let him near her when they met in Oregon. I don't care what he says or does, she vowed. Our marriage is over.

She wondered if she would ever have children of her own. What would Ross Morgan's children look like? Would they have his slate-colored eyes?

She shook her head. There was no sense day-dreaming about a man who had no use for her. Perhaps she would never have children. But if the price for having them was the bondage she had endured as Adam's wife, it was too high.

When the train crested the hill above the Grande Ronde Valley, Susan could scarcely believe her eyes. Below them lay a perfectly round valley, covered with lush grass and wild-flowers. It was the most beautiful sight she had seen since they left the prairies. Even the difficult descent failed to mar her enjoyment of this oasis. They would rest here for a few days before they continued through the Blue Mountains—the last mountains they would have to cross before they reached the Columbia. Susan wished they could stay here forever.

Neal carried Mercy to a sunlit patch of grass where he had spread a buffalo robe to guard against any dampness. Her cheeks were sunken and her skin looked gray, but her blue eyes sparkled with enjoyment as a light breeze riffled the grass.

"Oh, Susan, isn't it lovely?"

Neal brought them small bunches of wild-flowers, and Susan inhaled their delicate fragrance. How thoughtful he was. Had anyone ever picked flowers for her before? She couldn't remember.

Susan sighed and leaned back in the soft grass. The sun was gentle on her face. She listened absently to the conversation between Neal and his sister, her mind drifting.

She was awakened by the gentle tickling of a blade of grass across her face. Neal bent over her, smiling.

"I hated to wake you. You looked so happy. Were you dreaming?"

Susan stretched and sat up. "I don't need to dream here. This entire valley is like a dream after the last few weeks." She glanced around the deserted campsite.

"Where's Mercy?"

"Resting in the wagon. She seems so much better, Susan. If it hadn't been for you . . ." He stopped and Susan turned away from the warmth in his expression. The feelings openly displayed on his face embarrassed her. She and Neal had become close in these last few days. Like a brother, she told herself, and yet she had begun to wonder if his feelings were brotherly or more complex. She frowned.

"What's wrong, Susan?" Neal knelt beside her.

"Nothing." She smiled, forcing the frown from her face. She was imagining things again.

"I hate to see you troubled." He paused. "What will happen when we reach Oregon City?"

"Why, you and Mercy will go and start your school, and Ellie and I will meet Adam."

"But we'll keep in touch. We'll see you, won't we?"

"Of course."

He toyed with the blade of grass he held. "What will you do all alone there with no friends?"

"I'll have Ellie . . . and Adam. I'll be fine. I can take care of myself."

"I know. But you're so . . ." He paused, then rushed on. "You're so vulnerable. You need someone to take care of you when things get difficult. Will Adam do that?"

"Don't worry. I'll do just fine." She couldn't tell him she had no intention of relying on Adam for anything. That would only worry him more and she had no right to his concern. He had his own life to live and Mercy to care for.

"Maybe Mercy and I will stay in Oregon City. I could teach there just as well."

Susan smiled and touched his arm. "You know you wouldn't be happy with that. Mercy told me how you plan to start a school in one of the settlements. Don't even consider staying behind—not because of me."

"We'll let you know where we are, though, Susan. So if you need us, or we can help you, all you need to do is send word. Will you promise to do that?"

"Of course, Neal. But what could go wrong in a town like Oregon City? I hear more than eight hundred people live there. It'll certainly be an improvement from what we've been through."

He regarded her seriously for a moment. "I'll feel better if I know you can reach me."

"I will, Neal. I promise."

He patted her hand. "You mean a lot to us, Susan—to Mercy and to me."

She pulled her hand from his and scrambled to her feet. "I . . . I must go and . . . and help Ellie with supper."

She felt awkward and defenseless and wanted to put some distance between herself and Neal. There was really nothing in what he had said to disturb her, but there was something in the way he spoke that had made her uncomfortable. She knew that if she let him, Neal would assume too much responsibility for her, and it wouldn't be right. She would only make him unhappy.

It was Ross Morgan who filled her dreams at night—not Neal with his gentle manner and tender expression. She mustn't become too close to him.

Chapter 25

In spite of her resolution, Susan found it impossible to avoid Neal. The long months and shared crises had forged a strong bond between the two families. Ellie treated Mercy as if she were her own daughter, telling tales of her southern girlhood while Mercy listened patiently, even when the same story was retold for a second or third time.

Susan tried to act naturally toward Neal, but she couldn't regain the comfortable feeling they had once shared. She felt his eyes following her, and each time she started a chore he was there to help her lift, pull or harness. She wondered if Ellie noticed too, but nothing was said.

It's just me, Susan tried to persuade herself. But it did no good. She didn't want to hurt him, yet somehow he seemed to sense her withdrawal.

What kind of person am I, she wondered. I'm legally bound to Adam, yet all I can think of is Ross. And when I'm not thinking about him, I'm imagining Neal is in love with me. Other women don't have thoughts like that. What's wrong with me?

* * *

Once they crossed the Blue Mountains into the Umatilla Valley, the days seemed to fade into each other. Every night Susan felt she had only to turn and look back across the treeless meadow to see the place where they had camped the night before. Their progress seemed pitifully slow, although Neal said they were making good time. She watched for Ross, but she was certain he was avoiding her. Even Mercy remarked on it one night as they sat by the campfire after dinner.

"I haven't seen Ross for days now."

"He asks after you whenever I see him," Neal said. "Seems like he's busier than ever."

Mercy sighed. "I wish I didn't have to spend so much time in the wagon. I miss seeing him, and I miss being able to walk alongside the trail like I used to."

Neal smiled at her fondly. "You'll have lots of time for walking when we reach Oregon City. Right now you need rest."

"Oh, Neal, you fuss so." But even as she spoke, her words were broken by the ragged coughing that had become constant since her fall into the Snake. Neal rose to help her back to the wagon.

"This night air ain't good for you," Ellie fussed as she tagged along behind them. "You get back in the wagon and get covered up good. It's chilly tonight."

Susan stayed by the fire, poking at it idly with a stick. She saw two figures fade into the darkness at the edge of the campground and heard a muffled giggle. The young people had paired off on the trip. Two weddings were already planned for when they reached Oregon City.

Her limbs weakened as remembrance of Ross's embrace caught her unaware. How she yearned for him! If she could just be with him one more time, feel his hands against her skin, she would be happy. If just once more he would come to her.

She sighed. Even as she wished it, she knew she wouldn't be content with that. She would never have enough of him. She shifted uncomfortably and tried to think of something else.

She whirled at a sudden sound behind her. Even though his face was hidden by shadows she knew the figure there was Ross's. No one else stood so tall and proud. Still warm from the memory of his lovemaking, she moved toward him.

"Ross." Her voice was a whisper in the darkness, but she knew he heard her. He took a step forward.

"I came to see how Mercy was." His voice was toneless, unfeeling. It held nothing for Susan. Her hands, which had unconsciously been stretched out to him, fell limply at her sides. He hadn't wanted to see her at all.

"She's as well as we can expect." Her tone was abrupt to match his, but she longed to rush into his arms, to press her body against his. One sign was all she needed. She would fly to him if he would only put out his hand to her. But already he had turned away.

"Tell Mercy I asked after her," he mumbled before he faded into the darkness.

Susan stood alone, straining to hear the sound of his footsteps in the night. The silence was torn by a youthful giggle and a sob caught in her throat. Picking up her skirts, she ran heedlessly through the dark to the shelter of the wagon. She threw herself across her bed, the pillow clamped against her mouth, and tried to stifle the shuddering sobs that ripped through her body.

Chapter 26

At last the broad expanse of the Columbia glimmered before them in the sunlight as it wound between sage-covered hills. Each evening's conversation centered on their arrival at The Dalles. Soon their journey would be over.

The closer they came to Oregon City, the more Susan's apprehension grew. What would it be like? Could she find a way to support herself in a rough frontier town?

"I'll be so glad to leave this wagon," Ellie said repeatedly. "Maybe Adam will already have found us a place to live." She fell into verbal daydreams of neat clapboard houses with white lace curtains. Susan kept her thoughts to herself.

"I just don't understand you," Ellie complained. "You'd think after all these months you'd be more excited about seeing Adam again. I'm sure he's anxious to see you."

"Yes, I suppose so." Susan tried to sound enthusiastic.

"See," Ellie accused. "There you go again. Why, I believe you don't even *want* to see Adam."

Susan bit back a sharp reply. How could she show

excitement when she felt only dread? She didn't want to leave the trail behind. For the first time she had been independent. It was impossible to envision herself meekly obeying Adam's directions, answerable to him for all she did. And, she admitted, leaving the trail also meant leaving Ross.

Why did she fool herself? It wasn't so much her independence she hated to abandon, but the daily sight of Ross as he strode through the campground or rode beside the wagons. How could she spend the rest of her life not knowing what he was doing? Perhaps she would see him in Oregon City, but even if she did they would be like strangers—worse than strangers after all they had shared.

When at last they reached The Dalles, there were other wagons ahead of them. The town was little more than a few ramshackle buildings gathered together beside the trail, and they made camp along the riverbank some distance from the settlement.

A strong wind whipped Susan's skirt and flung her hair into her face. The river narrowed here as it rushed through a deep chasm. A few Indians stood silhouetted against the rocks, poised to spear the salmon that supplied their livelihood. Whitewater frothed across the surface of the pewter-colored river and leaden clouds hung in the sky. Barren brown hills lined the bank, bordered by terraced basalt cliffs. Susan shivered and turned away from the austere scene.

Their second day at The Dalles, Neal brought word of a change in plans. "Taggerty and the rest have decided to go by way of the Barlow Road."

"Barlow Road!" Ellie exclaimed. "What's that? I

thought we were going to get rid of these wagons and take to the water. Isn't that what everyone does?"

Neal nodded. "They used to. But with the weather what it is, there's no telling when we could start down the river. Taggerty says this new road's been open for two or three years now, and we can make it to Oregon City a lot sooner if we go that way."

"What do you think, Neal?" Susan asked. She tried to conceal her relief. She hadn't looked forward to traveling on the capricious Columbia.

Neal thought for a moment, then shrugged. "Morgan says the river can be treacherous. There've been a lot of people who lost everything in the rapids, and if a storm comes up, or a strong wind, we could be stranded for days. He's been over the mountains once before. Says it's a good road."

"Well, I for one have had enough of Ross Morgan telling us where we can go and what we can do." Ellie's voice was shrill. "I don't plan to go one more foot in that crazy wagon. The river's good enough for them other people, it'll be good enough for us. There's no law says we gotta stay with the rest of the train."

"But if they—"

Ellie cut off Susan's protest. "I say we're going by water and that's that. You can find someone who'll let us go along with them, Susan. We can pay our way."

"Oh, you can't," Mercy cried. "What will we do without you and Susan? We might never see you again."

Ellie shook her head. "I've made up my mind," she stated. "You and Neal, if you had any sense, would do the same as us. Ain't gonna do *you* no good traipsing over miles more of this desert."

Mercy turned to her brother. "Maybe Ellie's right. Maybe we should wait and go by boat."

Neal shook his head slowly and sighed. "I have to trust Taggerty and Morgan," he said at last. "They know what they're talking about." He turned to Susan and she saw his concern for them. "Don't you think you'd be better off to stay with the rest of us, Susan?" he asked.

Before she could reply, Ellie spoke again and Susan was surprised at the animosity in her voice.

"It's not up to Susan what we do," she snapped. "I'm the one who owns this here wagon—and I'm the one who's paying for the trip. If I decide we take the river, that's what we'll do. I haven't had much to say before now, but I know what makes good sense and what don't. Morgan and Taggerty can spend the rest of their lives crawlin' over mountains if they want to, but I don't plan to join them." Ellie folded her arms across her chest.

Susan felt her face burn with humiliation. What Ellie said was true. She had control of the money, and if she refused to take the Barlow Road, Susan could do nothing but accept her decision.

"It's all right, Mercy," Susan said, trying to ease the tension. "We'll see you in Oregon City. Who knows, we may be there in time to welcome you."

Mercy tried to smile, but her lips curved downward.

"I don't know what luck you'll have," Neal said, "but I'll be glad to ask around some for you tomorrow."

"That won't be necessary," Ellie said. "Susan can

find someone to take us, and she can do it now—
tonight."

Susan looked at Ellie in astonishment. Twilight
was gathering and soon it would be dark. Surely her
search for transportation could wait until morning.

"Don't you think—" Susan started to protest, but
Ellie interrupted.

"The sooner we get this settled, the better off we'll
be." Her eyes narrowed as she looked at Susan. "I
know *you're* in no hurry to reach Oregon City, but *I*
feel differently." Her tone was heavy with sarcasm,
and Susan could no longer sit there and tolerate
Ellie's criticism. Better to be away from all of them.
She stood up and brushed the skirt of her dress. The
wind whipped the fringe of her shawl against her arm
and she pulled it more closely around her shoulders.

"All right," she said. "I'll go now."

"Don't let them talk you into paying too dear a
price," Ellie cautioned. "We ain't rich, you know."

"Do you want me to go with you?" Neal offered
softly.

"No, Neal. Thanks, but you stay here. I won't be
long."

Chapter 27

As she walked slowly toward the meager buildings clustered near the riverbank, Susan began to wish she had accepted Neal's offer to accompany her. Boisterous voices rose from the encampments she passed and she kept her eyes focused straight ahead. She felt increasingly uncomfortable as daylight dwindled from the overcast sky.

On the streets of the settlement she was jostled and bumped, but no one apologized. There was an air of urgency about the people who passed her. She paused to watch a group of men intent on building a raft. It looked so frail. How would it ever survive the battering currents of the Columbia?

She made her way toward the largest building and pushed past a group of men standing in the doorway. Their dirty clothes reeked of grease and smoke.

"Hey, girlie," one of the men called. "What's your hurry?" His dirty, calloused hand clutched at her shawl, and Susan snatched it closer. He laughed as she crossed the room to the corner that had been set aside for trading.

Bags of flour, dried fish, stacks of animal pelts, and coils of rope were jumbled in confusion near the counter. The top was littered with newspapers, old posters and wrapping paper, all dotted with fly-specks and stained with water or spilled drinks. The man behind the counter worked at a frantic pace measuring flour into cloth bags. He kicked at a gray kitten that twined itself between his legs.

"Get out of here, you damned varmint," the man cussed at the scrawny animal. Then his eyes met Susan's and he blushed.

"Pardon me, ma'am. These damn—darned critters are thick as fleas on a dog. Folks cart 'em all the way from back East, then decide they can't take 'em no farther. The Dalles is gonna be a town of cats afore long."

He brushed his thinning hair back from his forehead and leaned against the counter. "Now then, what can I do for you?"

"I'm trying to find someone to take us to Oregon City." Susan spoke quickly. "It's just my mother-in-law and myself."

"What about the rest of your train?"

"They're going overland, but we'd rather go by boat if we can."

"Well, I reckon you have your reasons, but if you ain't got a man to build you a raft of your own, you're out of luck."

"Are you sure? Couldn't we pay someone to take us?"

The man laughed and glanced toward the group of men near the door. "I don't figure you've got enough money to buy space with them as you'd want to travel with, and you might not want to pay the price the rest would ask—if you get my meaning."

Susan glanced at the man who had grabbed at her shawl. No, she definitely wouldn't want to travel with someone like that. But surely there were those who could use the extra money.

"Aren't there families who are ready to leave who wouldn't mind two more people?"

"Two more men maybe, but I don't reckon anyone wants to take on two more women. Women ain't much help when the goin' gets rough, and it gets right rough between here and Oregon City—rapids, storms, portages. You ain't seen nothin' till you've seen the Columbia take it into her mind to kick up a fuss." He said the last proudly, as though the river's moods were his doing.

Susan was discouraged. She hadn't realized that the addition of two more women might be more responsibility than any traveler would want to assume.

"You can ask around," the man suggested. "But I figure you'll be wastin' your breath. They just ain't got time for anyone else's troubles. If I was you, I'd stick with your own train. You don't want to end up stranded here."

He glanced down at his feet, where the kitten had returned to bat his trouser leg. He scooped up the bundle of fur in one hand and held it over the counter. "Wouldn't like to adopt this here little bit of trouble, would you?"

Susan smiled and shook her head. The man absently scratched the kitten's ear. "Wish I could help you, ma'am, I surely do. But there ain't no sense givin' you false hope. You take my advice—pull out with the rest of your train."

Susan turned away from the counter. She hadn't wanted to travel the river in the first place. Now she could tell Ellie with a clear conscience that it would be impossible for them.

The streets were quieter now. Occasionally a group of men passed. Their eyes raked over her body, but she kept her head high and her gaze averted.

Campfires flickered along the riverbank. A night bird shrilled overhead, invisible in the darkness. The strains of fiddles and concertinas floated through the stillness and an occasional voice was lifted in song, but she couldn't hear the words.

Susan slowed her pace as she considered what she would tell Ellie. Once she had accepted the reality of George's death, Ellie had been easier to get along with. She had seemed to accept the need to rely on Susan's strength now that she no longer had a man to lean on. But her tirade at the campfire was far worse than any of her earlier defenses of Adam. What had changed her attitude?

The sound of footsteps behind her made Susan stop. She listened, but heard nothing more. But as she continued toward the wagons she heard the snap of a dried twig and turned to search the darkness. There was no one in sight. She quickened her steps, suddenly aware of the isolation of the spot.

"Well, will you lookey who's here." The voice rang out behind her and she whirled. A bulky form loomed out of the darkness and she recognized the man who had clutched at her shawl. He moved toward her slowly, as if he stalked a deer.

"Ain't no need to be a-scared of old Fred," he said as she backed away. "I ain't never hurt nothin' as purty as you."

Susan edged away.

"What's the matter, honey?" his voice rasped. "Ain't you got nothin' to say to old Fred? Just want a little company. A man gets tired of Injun squaws."

"Go away," Susan whispered. She tried to steady her voice. She mustn't let him see her fear. "Someone is coming to meet me," she said, louder this time.

He scanned the trail behind her. "Don't see nobody. Musta stood you up. That's a downright shame, a purty thing like you. But don't you worry none. Old Fred'll keep you company. Here, try some of this." He took a bottle from his pocket.

"No." Susan turned her head away.

"Hey now, that ain't no way to be. I was just bein' friendly." His voice took on a note of self-pity. He thrust the bottle toward her and she struck it from his hand. She heard it shatter.

"Now, that weren't very nice." All trace of joviality left his voice and he grabbed her arm. "I reckon you'll have to pay for that."

"Let me go!"

"Ain't likely," he muttered, groping around her waist with his other hand. Susan struggled but he was too strong. He pulled her close and his mouth clamped down on hers, hurting and demanding. The overwhelming odor of liquor gagged her. She bit his lip and he yelped and pulled his head back.

"You little bitch!" he gasped. "I'll show you!" His hand crashed against her cheek with a blow that brought tears to her eyes.

"You do that again and I'll break your neck." With one hand he ripped open the bodice of her dress. She snatched at it to hold it together, but he grasped her other hand and twisted it behind her back, forcing her arm up until she thought it would break. Then he pulled her against him.

"You know who's boss now?"

Susan bit her lip to keep from crying out as he gave her arm a vicious wrench.

"I asked you a question, Missy."

"Please," Susan cried. "Please leave me alone."

His laugh was a harsh animal sound. "That's better. A little bit of begging never hurt no woman." He pushed her to the ground and fell on top of her. His fingers clawed at her breasts. Once more his mouth clamped over hers and she wriggled beneath him, trying to force her knee between them. He ripped her dress from her shoulders and clutched at her breasts. Susan twisted her head away from his and sucked in air. Before she could scream, he was gone, his weight miraculously lifted from her.

She struggled to her knees in time to see Ross Morgan lift the man from his feet and hurl him to the ground. She heard the sound of knuckles against flesh and bone. Fred lay on the ground, cringing from the fists that battered him.

"That's enough, Mister," he wailed. "That's enough. Just wanted a little fun."

Morgan stood over him, his hands clenched at his sides. "Get up," he ordered.

"Didn't mean no harm, Mister. Ain't you never wanted to have a little fun?"

"I ought to break every bone in your weaselly little body!" Fred cowered. "Get up and get out of here before I change my mind," Morgan ordered.

Fred scrambled to his feet, half running as he gained his footing. Susan heard him stumble once, then he was gone.

Morgan turned to her, his eyes blazing with fury. "What the hell are you doing out here?"

"I went to . . . to town. To find so—someone to take Ellie and me on the river." Susan clutched her dress closer.

"And I suppose you tried to bargain with your body." His words were cold as his eyes took in every detail of her dishevelment.

"No," she gasped. "Of course not."

"'Of course not,'" he mimicked. "There's no of course not about it. You did it once with me, didn't you?"

She stared up at him silently from her crouched position.

"Didn't you?" he demanded.

Susan nodded, her eyes wet with tears. She should have known he had never been fooled. He had seen through her all along.

"Answer me," Ross prodded. "You thought you could barter your body so I would let you stay with the train, didn't you?"

"Yes," she whispered. "But it was—"

His laughter interrupted her words. "You little fool." His voice cut through her. "And did you think it would work again with someone else?"

"No, I never—he followed me. I never even talked to him. I went to find a family—someone who would let us pay for passage to Oregon City."

"Sure you did," he sneered. "Just like you came to me that night. You thought you changed my mind, didn't you? You thought I was taken in by the offer

192

of your body. Well, let me tell you, Susan, you have a long way to go before you'll understand men—and me in particular. It was Taggerty who changed my mind, him and his wife—after you saved their daughter from that rattler. They asked me to let you stay with the train, and like a fool I let them talk me into it."

Susan looked up at him. Yes, he told the truth. She should have known he wouldn't have changed his mind that easily. He hadn't allowed her to stay because he wanted her. She'd been a fool. He had only taken what she had been so quick to offer. His eyes blazed into hers and she turned away.

"Pull your dress together and get up," he ordered curtly. "Your friend won't be back, but someone else may come along the road. I'll see you back to the wagons."

Susan stumbled to her feet and pulled the shredded remains of her dress across her breasts. He snatched her shawl from the ground and put it roughly around her. She winced as he touched her bruised shoulders.

"Are you hurt?" His voice was gentler.

"I'm all right."

"Then let's get back."

Morgan halted at the fringe of the camp. "You'll be safe now."

"Thank you." She put her hand on his arm, but he jerked away from her touch. His face was shadowed.

"The train leaves day after tomorrow," he told her. "Did you find someone to take you down the river?"

She shook her head.

"If I were you, I'd be ready to leave with the train.

You'll reach Oregon City in a few days, then you can forget all this."

"All of it?" Her voice was so soft that she wondered if he had heard her.

"I'll be gone in the morning," he continued. "I won't see you again."

She stared at him in amazement. Gone? "But who will lead the train?"

"Friend of mine I ran into said he could use the work. He knows the trail as well as I do. You won't have any problems."

"But where are you going?"

"Oregon City for now. I can make better time alone. I'll be gone by the time you get there."

Tears stung her eyes. She would never see him again. But that was impossible. She loved him and she had never told him. He mustn't leave now, not without knowing.

"Ross." She put her hand on his arm again. This time he didn't move away.

"Don't, Susan. You'll only be sorry. It's best this way."

"No!" she cried. "It's not best. You can't deny you care, in spite of everything you've said. Please . . ." She swallowed the tears that threatened her voice. "Please take me with you."

He groaned and pulled her into his arms. She trembled at his touch. This was where she belonged —where she wanted to stay forever. She raised her face to his, her lips parted, anticipating his kiss. For a moment his eyes were soft, but then they hardened.

"Damn you, Susan," he muttered as he bent to kiss her. She clung to him, her arms wrapped around his waist, matching the contours of her body to his. She felt the hardness of him, drank in the smell of his skin. His arms tightened and she knew he wanted her.

Abruptly he thrust her away. She staggered and clutched at a wagon wheel to keep from falling.

"Something to remember me by," he said. "Good-bye, Susan."

She put her hand out to him beseechingly, but he was gone. She couldn't even hear his footsteps in the stillness. It was as if he had never been there.

Chapter 28

It seemed as if she had been away for an eternity, but there was still movement about the campground. As she made her way toward the wagon, Susan almost collided with Mrs. Jordan.

"Oh my." The woman stopped in surprise, her gaze sharp as she stared at Susan's torn dress. Her eyebrows arched questioningly, but Susan brushed past her without speaking. Let her think what she liked. All Susan wanted was to escape from prying eyes.

There was no sign of Neal or Mercy and she breathed a sigh of relief. If Ellie were asleep . . . But she was not so fortunate. She had just started to climb into the wagon when she heard Ellie behind her.

"Well, it took you long enough."

Susan tried to ignore her, but Ellie persisted.

"What did you find out?" she demanded. "Did you get us—" She stopped as she saw Susan's dress. "What on earth?"

"It's nothing." Susan turned away, but Ellie clutched her arm.

"Nothing! Look at you. Where have you been? What happened?"

"I . . . I fell into some bushes in the dark." Susan groped for words that might sound believable.

"Bushes, huh?" Ellie snorted. "Musta been some kind of bush to do all that."

Susan shrugged. "I have to change."

Ellie followed her into the wagon. "You haven't answered my question. Did you find someone to take us down the river?"

"No." Susan's voice was muffled as she pulled the ruined dress over her head. "We'll have to go on with the train."

Ellie was silent as Susan pulled on her nightgown. "I don't believe you," she said at last. "I don't believe you even asked." Her voice rose to a shout. "You don't want to ever get to Oregon City! I've seen you day after day, batting your eyes at that nice Mr. Laughlin, and him fool enough to do your bidding!"

"Shhh." Susan was sure Ellie could be heard all over the campground.

"Don't you shush me," Ellie screeched. "You think I'm blind! Well, I'm not, and I'll tell you this, if Adam takes you back, you'll be lucky. Believe me, I'll have a few things to tell him when we get to Oregon City. You may think you can twist every man around your little finger, but you'll find my son ain't no fool."

"And neither am I," Susan snapped. "We both know why Adam married me. Do you think I care whether or not he 'takes me back'?" Susan watched in satisfaction as Ellie's mouth gaped open.

"Well, I never . . ." she spluttered. "After all we've done for you—gave you a home, treated you like a daughter. Is this the thanks I get?"

"You gave me nothing I didn't already have when I met Adam. And you may as well know I have no intention of ever living with him again."

"We'll just see about that. There's laws about a wife and her duties to her husband. No one ever said Adam was perfect. Maybe he didn't marry you for the *right* reasons," she sneered, "but that don't give you a license to fall into bed with the first man who comes along."

"I don't know what you're talking about."

"Don't you? Well, I know all about you and that Ross Morgan. I've been talking to Mrs. Jordan. She told me all about seein' you and Morgan together. She didn't want to say nothin'—not at first. Then she figured it was her Christian duty to let me know, me bein' your mother-in-law and all." Ellie paused for breath, then rushed on. "And when Morgan had enough, you turned to Neal Laughlin, didn't you?"

"Leave me alone," Susan hissed through clenched teeth. She turned her back on Ellie and crawled into bed.

"I'll leave you alone, all right," Ellie shouted. "I'll be happy to leave you alone. But you remember this—I'll be watching you. Maybe we'll go with the train and maybe we won't. That's my decision. But from now on you're going to remember you're my son's wife, and you're going to act like it." Ellie threw the bedding back and climbed into her bed. The force of her motions made the wagon sway.

Susan squeezed her eyes shut. Ellie's words had been like physical blows against her already weakened defenses. Things had been bad before, but with

Ellie's accusations between them, how could she survive the next few weeks?

How foolish to have thought her actions had gone unnoticed. She should have realized there was a reason for Ellie's sudden change of attitude. How long had she known? Susan tried to remember the last time she had seen Ellie and Mrs. Jordan together, but there had never been a reason to notice.

She pulled the covers up around her chin, trying to forget the words Ellie had screeched at her. But they were the truth—twisted by Ellie's mind, but still the truth. That's how anyone would interpret her behavior with Ross, they would make it seem dirty and cheap. No one would understand how she felt.

She shifted uncomfortably and tossed her head against the pillow. There was no escape from the realization that she had let her emotions lead her into an affair that cheapened her even in her own eyes. Was that how Ross saw it? She remembered how his eyes had blazed with anger. He had thought the worst of her tonight. She could never face him again, knowing he had seen through her attempt to seduce him. How he must despise her!

Then she remembered. She would never have to face him again because in the morning he would be gone. Out of her life forever. Tears ran down her cheeks and her body shook with sobs as she remembered his good-bye. He had told her to forget all that had happened. Would he forget too? Would he ever think of her? And if he did, would it be with longing or with scorn?

She knew that no matter how humiliating it might be to face him, it was going to be far worse never to see him again. Her life stretched endlessly ahead, like the trail she had followed for so many months. But there was no end to the months she would have to spend without Ross.

Chapter 29

Oregon City.

Susan had lived with the name for more than a year. Half the conversations she had heard had begun, "When we reach Oregon City . . ." At times she had thought they would never arrive; at others she had nearly doubted its existence. Yet now, seventeen days after leaving The Dalles, it lay before them, a small, almost insignificant settlement to have held such importance in their lives.

Ellie had been forced to remain with the wagon train, but the last few days had been strained. Susan was aware of Ellie's constant watchful gaze and the woman's few comments were barbed with double meaning. Susan avoided her whenever possible.

The journey across the Cascades had been uneventful except for the loss of Sam. One day the dog had been there, loping by her side as usual, the next day he was gone. Although Susan had called him repeatedly, there was no joyful yelp, no flick of a yellow tail in the underbrush. She missed him more than she cared to admit.

It was raining as they neared the outskirts of Oregon City. Gray clouds hung in the tops of the lofty fir trees like dingy laundry spread out to dry. Susan's thin clothing was no protection against the damp cold, and she shivered as she struggled up a mired street beside the oxen. Mud oozed through the worn soles of her shoes and clung to the hem of her skirt.

When the wagons halted, Ellie scrambled to the ground, a look of distaste on her pinched features. Gingerly she approached Susan, testing the slippery ground with each step. She glanced up the street toward the cluster of buildings. "Not much of a town, is it?"

"I'm sure it's nicer when it isn't raining." Susan's defense sounded weak even to her own ears. At the moment there seemed little to commend the frontier town.

Ellie glanced at Susan's bedraggled skirts that hung heavy with mud. "You're a mess," she declared. "I don't see how any respectable establishment would let us in with you looking like that."

Susan glared at her mother-in-law. It was easy for Ellie to stay clean in the shelter of the wagon. "I expect they've seen worse," she snapped. "If you think I look so bad, *you* can find us a place to stay."

Ellie's thin lips parted to reply, then she pressed them together and glanced back at the wagon.

"I think I'll wait here," she announced. "When you find Adam you can come and get me. Don't forget we're supposed to meet him at the best hotel."

Ellie picked her way back to the wagon. Rage churned within Susan. Only a few more hours, she vowed, then she would be free of Ellie. She had never thought she would see the day when she would be anxious to see Adam.

It wasn't difficult to find the best hotel in Oregon City. The first person Susan approached was quick to direct her to the Main Street House.

"Best in the territory," the man told her. "Run by Colonel Richardson, and you won't find no bedbugs nor fleas neither. He runs a good, clean place."

Susan thanked him and picked her way down the narrow plank walkway that teetered precariously over the mud.

Although she had little desire to meet Adam alone, perhaps it would be best. After she told him she didn't intend to resume their life together, he could go and claim his mother and Susan would never have to see either of them again. She rehearsed the words she would use and vowed to remain calm and reasonable. When at last she reached the Main Street House Susan almost looked forward to her meeting with Adam.

The man at the front desk was busy, and a couple minutes passed before she caught his attention.

"Sorry to keep you waiting, ma'am, but this has been one of the busiest days I've seen this season, what with everyone on the wagon train wanting a room or a bath or both." He smiled at her encouragingly. "Now then, what can I do for you?"

"Is a Mr. Baker staying here? Mr. Adam Baker?" The man frowned and scratched behind his ear.

"Adam Baker," he muttered. "Adam Baker."

Susan waited impatiently for his answer. Her heart thudded painfully in her chest. At any moment Adam might come around a corner and she would be face to face with him.

"Nope," the man said at last. "Nobody here by that name."

"Are you sure?"

The man looked slightly offended for a moment, then pulled a leather-bound register across the desk.

"I reckon I'd know if he was, but I'll check the book. We run a proper hotel here, not like some folk. Everything right and proper."

He ran a finger down the list of scrawled signatures, then turned back to Susan. "Like I told you, ma'am, he ain't here. Are you sure it was the Main Street House where he was stayin'?"

"I'm not sure of anything," Susan replied. "My mother-in-law and I just arrived with the wagon train. We were supposed to meet my husband here— at least, he said at the largest hotel in Oregon City. This is the largest, isn't it?"

"It surely is. Not only the biggest, but the best."

"Has anyone been asking for us? My name is Susan Baker. My mother-in-law's name is Ellie. Or . . . or he might have asked for George Baker."

"No, ma'am, and I'da remembered for sure. Never forget a name—at least that's what people say, and I can't say I ever have. If someone had been askin' for a Mrs. Baker I'da known."

"Could they have asked someone else?"

"Might have, but it's a sure thing whoever they asked woulda checked with me. See, I'm sort of in charge here, even though it's Colonel Richardson's hotel. Everyone knows to ask me if anything comes up they can't handle. So you see, he ain't been around."

Susan turned away. They would just have to wait.

She tried to shake her feeling of disappointment. It would have been such a relief to have the meeting behind her. How long would it be until Adam arrived?

She was almost at the door before she remembered to ask for a room. She knew Ellie would refuse to spend one more night in the wagon.

"Sorry, ma'am, we're all full up. Maybe in a day or two. You might try down the street, though. Not as nice as here, but they probably have a room."

"Thank you. And if my—my husband should ask for us, please tell him where we are."

Reluctantly Susan left the dry sanctuary of the lobby and plodded toward the second hotel. Even from the street it appeared to be but a shabby cousin of the Main Street House, but she forced herself to walk up the front stairs and enter the lobby. Dishes and cutlery rattled in an adjoining room. Through dusty velvet curtains she glimpsed a long table set for dinner, and her stomach rumbled.

The man who greeted her was slender, with silver-gray hair and a military bearing. He bowed slightly over her hand when she introduced herself and explained her needs.

"Miz Baker, we'd be honored to have you stay here with us." Susan noticed that he spoke with a slight southern accent. "Can I send a buggy to get your mother-in-law? It's a shame to have you walking out in all this mud after your long journey."

"I—I don't mind." Susan stumbled over her rejection. She would have liked to accept his offer, but what would he charge for the service? She had no idea how much money was left in Ellie's carefully concealed pouch of coins, and now that Adam wasn't here to meet them, they must watch every expense.

As though reading her thoughts, the man put a hand on her arm. "There's no extra charge," he said. "It's a courtesy we offer our guests."

With relief, Susan accepted and stood quietly while he dispatched the carriage. "Maud!" he shouted toward the back room. "Come here."

A young girl appeared in the doorway, wiping red hands on a soiled apron. "Yes, sir, Mr. Wilton."

"Show Miz Baker to our best room, on the double, you hear?"

"Yes, sir."

"When you've had a chance to freshen up, ma'am, I'd be pleased if you and your mother-in-law would join me for dinner."

Susan smiled her thanks and followed Maud up the dark narrow stairs to the top floor of the building. The lone whale-oil lamp that burned on a hallway table cast little light. A threadbare carpet covered scuffed floorboards and the air smelled of unaired linen. At the end of the hall the girl threw open a door and stood to one side so Susan could enter.

Susan crossed the room and pulled back the dark curtains that hung limply at the window. It faced the back of the hotel, and over the roofs of nearby houses she saw the steep barrier of cliffs that bordered the town. She noticed that the windowsill was edged with mildew before she turned to survey the room.

A braided rug before a sooty fireplace provided

the only bit of color. The double bed was covered with a dun-colored bedspread that matched the curtains. A dark wardrobe stood in one corner and in the other was a washstand and a mirror. Above the bed was a painting, which upon closer examination proved to be a scene of buffalo being slaughtered by Indians. Susan quickly turned away.

"Is this the best room you have?"

"Oh yes, ma'am, the very best."

Susan's shoulders drooped with exhaustion. She hadn't expected luxury, but she wished it was more cheerful.

"Bring an extra lamp, then," she directed. "And water for a bath, please."

"Yes, ma'am." Maud nodded her head and disappeared into the gloom of the hallway.

The surroundings did not improve with the added light, which only revealed dirt and dust that Susan had failed to notice before. The furniture was as scratched and battered as though it had been dragged the length of the Oregon Trail by a team of flighty horses. She tested the bed gingerly as Maud hauled bathwater into the room. The straw mattress rustled when Susan moved and dust assailed her nostrils. Perhaps it would only be for a few days, she tried to reassure herself.

"Will that be all, ma'am?" the maid asked from the doorway. For the first time Susan noticed the girl's eyes were crossed. It was disconcerting to look at her and Susan glanced away.

"Yes, that'll be all for now. Thank you."

The door shut softly and Susan walked to the window. Ellie should arrive soon. Once their belongings were delivered, Susan could take a bath and change into clean clothes. What a luxury that would be!

Susan was surprised by Ellie's reaction to their lodgings. She had expected the older woman to be full of criticism, but Ellie had given the room only a cursory glance before she began to unpack her belongings and hang them in the wardrobe.

"Hurry up, Susan," she prodded as Susan bathed in the lukewarm water. "I declare, I'm so hungry I could eat a horse."

"We've been invited to eat with Mr. Wilton," Susan said as she donned the least wrinkled of her dresses.

"Yes, I know."

Susan watched Ellie pat her hair into place for the third time, then pinch bright spots of color into her cheeks.

"It's too bad Adam wasn't here to meet us," Susan said.

"Yes." Ellie's reply was absent as she tucked a handkerchief into the bodice of her dress. "There, how do I look?"

"You look fine," Susan replied, surprised that Ellie did not seem more disappointed. For weeks all the woman had talked of was meeting Adam in Oregon City. Yet now that they had arrived, it was as though his absence hardly mattered.

"Let's go downstairs then," Ellie said.

She sailed out of the room and Susan followed. Ellie carefully descended the narrow stairs to be greeted at the bottom by Mr. Wilton.

"Ma'am, it is indeed a pleasure to have you honor

my humble establishment." Mr. Wilton bent over Ellie's hand and kissed it. "To look at you, no one would ever believe you had just completed such an arduous journey. You will be like a flower gracing my table tonight."

Ellie fluttered her lashes coquettishly. "Why, Mr. Wilton, how gallant you are. Do I detect a trace of the South in your speech?"

"Yes, ma'am." His drawl became even more pronounced. "I'm from Charleston. And if I'm not mistaken, you too are from the South."

"Yes, though years ago now, I fear. I was raised near Richmond."

"A southerner is always a southerner, no matter where he goes," Mr. Wilton said as he placed Ellie's hand on his sleeve. "May I escort you in to dinner?"

Susan followed them into the dining room. Several guests sat at the long table, but Mr. Wilton steered them toward a small table in the corner. He held a chair for Ellie and then one for Susan.

"I can't tell you how pleased I am to meet someone from home," he murmured as he took his seat.

The meal, served on heavy crockery, was excellent. There were courses of venison and fish, baked with a light hint of herbs, and a salad of miner's lettuce. The biscuits were light and flaky. Susan wondered if the boarders who sat at the long center table were treated to such delectable fare, or if it was reserved for Mr. Wilton and his personal guests.

Ellie and Mr. Wilton dominated the conversation with reminiscences of their lives in the South. Susan watched in amazement as Ellie flirted all through dinner. This was a side of Ellie she had never seen before. The woman looked almost pretty in the dim light of the dining room, her cheeks flushed with excitement and her eyes glistening as she watched Mr. Wilton's face with rapt attention.

"May I offer you some tea, Mrs. Baker?" He held a cup toward Ellie.

She took a sip, then glanced at him, her face a mixture of curiosity and surprise. "I declare, I don't believe I've ever tasted tea quite like this before."

Wilton laughed and shook his head. "I expect not, ma'am. That's Oregon tea."

"Oregon tea? Whatever do you mean?"

"It's made from the leaves of the yerba buena. That's Spanish for 'the good herb.'"

"Well, if that don't beat all." Ellie took another sip, then smiled at their host. "I think it's downright clever of you all to think of making tea from a funny little bush. You must show me how it's done."

"I'd be delighted."

Susan sipped her tea and remained quiet.

At last Ellie patted her mouth daintily with her napkin and rose from her chair.

"It's been a lovely meal, Mr. Wilton," she said. "But Susan and I have had a hard day. We really must retire now. Thank you again. It's such a pleasure to find civilized company so far from home."

"My pleasure, ma'am. Perhaps tomorrow I might have the honor of escorting you through town—and your daughter, too, of course."

"Why, I'd love to, Mr. Wilton," Ellie gushed. "But I'm afraid Susan won't be able to join us. She'll be busy."

"Shall we say around one o'clock?"

"I'll look forward to it."

Mr. Wilton escorted them to the foot of the stairs.

"I'll see you tomorrow," Ellie said as she turned to extend her hand to Mr. Wilton. Once more he bent to kiss it delicately. Susan thought she would be sick if she had to watch one more flirtatious instant. She turned and hurried up the stairs.

Ellie flounced into the room a few minutes later.

"Well, I must say, you weren't very polite," she snapped. "You didn't even thank Mr. Wilton for the meal. I thought you had better manners than that."

"I hardly think he noticed."

"What do you mean?"

"I mean he only seemed to be interested in what *you* had to say, not in me."

Ellie's frown disappeared and a faint smile crept over her lips. "Yes, it did seem that way, didn't it?" She walked to the mirror and examined her face closely.

"You know, Susan, I'm not really all that old. I'll only be thirty-six my next birthday."

Susan did some mental arithmetic and decided that Ellie would have been twelve when Adam was born if she was only thirty-six now. Oh well, she shrugged, if it kept Ellie happy and out of the way, let her have her little flirtation.

Long after the lamps were snuffed out and Ellie was snoring peacefully on her side of the bed, Susan lay awake. She heard footsteps on the plank walkway outside their window and the plop of rain dripping from the eaves into wooden rain barrels. At last she rose and went to the window. Down the street she saw the lights of a saloon. Torches lit the front of the building and a group of men stood near the door.

Could that be the saloon Ross Morgan had planned to buy? The figures were indistinct in the flickering light. He could be among them and she would never know. He had said he'd be gone by the time she arrived in Oregon City, but Susan didn't want to believe it. It would be too unfair if she were never to see him again. He had to be out there somewhere, perhaps even now within sight of her window.

Chapter 30

It was by chance that Susan learned the whereabouts of Ross Morgan. Ellie insisted that Susan return to the Main Street House the next day to see if there had been any word from Adam. She made the visit with a mixture of dread and anticipation, but she knew that Ellie would not leave her alone until she had made her report.

The desk clerk greeted her by name. "Sorry, Miz Baker, no word from your husband yet." It was what she had expected, but as she turned away from the desk, the man called after her.

"Miz Baker, hold on a minute. We have a vacant room now. Had someone leave just this mornin'. If you'd like, I can show it to you."

"Yes—please." Susan felt relief as she followed him upstairs. How much more convenient it would be if she and Ellie could stay here where they were to meet Adam.

The clerk held a door open at the top of the stairs. The room was large and pleasant, with bright calico curtains at windows that faced the river. The furniture was of polished rosewood and an Oriental screen sectioned off one corner.

"It's lovely," Susan said eagerly. "I'm sure we'll take it, but I must check with my mother-in-law."

He nodded. "You'll like it here. Furniture came all the way around the Horn."

Susan took one last look before she followed him downstairs. As they reached the lobby they were approached by a man with thinning hair and a weathered face. He eyed Susan for a moment with obvious curiosity before turning to the clerk.

"Tom," he said, "is Morgan still here?"

The desk clerk shook his head. "Nope, left this mornin'. Surprised the hell outa me, too—thought he was figurin' to settle down."

Susan caught her breath at the mention of the name. Could it be Ross?

"Weren't he plannin' to buy you out, Mike?" the desk clerk asked.

Mike nodded. "Got a note this mornin'." He thrust a crumpled piece of paper toward the clerk. "Along with the rest of the money for the place. Says he wants me to watch the business for him. But not a word 'bout when he'll be back or where he's off to." He stuffed the paper back in the pocket of his jacket.

"I knew somethin' was wrong," Mike continued. "Acted real peculiar, if you know what I mean. But he never said a word. Did he tell you where he was off to?"

"Said he was headin' south."

Mike grunted. "There's a heap of country to the south. Can't figure it out—for months he's been talkin' about buyin' me out, and when he finally gets the money he up and takes off like a fool tomcat on the prowl."

"What you figure to do, Mike?"

"Hell, reckon I'll do like he asks, leastwise for a while. I got my price, but I can't see closin' the place down and havin' it fall apart. I owe him that much."

The man called Mike turned toward the door.

"I'll be back," Susan assured the desk clerk, and she hurried after the departing visitor. Thoughts whirled through her mind. Everything fit. It must have been Ross. Yet she must make sure. She caught up with the man just as he turned the corner.

"Excuse me." She faltered as he turned to face her. His skin was creased so deeply that his faded blue eyes seemed to peer at her through narrow slits.

"Ma'am." He touched his forehead as if to remove a nonexistent hat. "Somethin' I can do for you?"

"I . . . I heard your conversation back there in the hotel. I was wondering . . ." She felt her face redden as she paused to phrase the question, then hurried on before she lost her courage. "The man you mentioned, Morgan . . . is his first name Ross?"

Mike's face crinkled into more lines and furrows as he studied her. "I mighta known," he said at last, half to himself. "It had to be a woman."

His intent gaze made Susan shift uncomfortably. Finally he seemed to realize she still waited for his answer.

"Yup, it's Ross Morgan all right. Was it you he was runnin' from?"

"Running? I don't understand."

"No, I reckon you wouldn't. But I've known Ross Morgan for nigh on to five years now, and there ain't nothin' that'll make him edgy 'ceptin' maybe a woman, a pretty one like you." Mike stared past

215

Susan, his eyes focused on the distance. "I've seen him handle a bar full of rowdy trail hands, tame drunken Indians and ride out storms on the river what woulda killed half a dozen men, but women—" he halted in midsentence. "Where'd you happen to meet up with him?"

"He guided our wagon train."

"And you fell for him. Don't deny it," he added as Susan began to shake her head. "You wouldn't be the first one."

"I . . . I just wanted . . ."

"I know, I know." His smile was understanding and she felt suddenly comfortable with this stranger.

"But why?" she asked. "Why do you say he runs from women?"

"I guess he don't exactly run. Kind of shies off is more the way I'd put it." He rubbed his chin and regarded her for a moment. At last he extended his hand. "Seems we ain't been properly introduced. My name's Mike—Mike Chapman. I own the Tamarack—sort of half saloon and half boarding-house—or at least I did own it." His hand engulfed Susan's.

"I'm Susan Baker."

"Glad to meet you, ma'am." He paused and glanced up the street. "I ain't got a fittin' place to offer you no hospitality, but if you don't mind walkin' along with me, I'll tell you what I know of Ross Morgan."

Susan eagerly fell into step beside him.

"I met Morgan in '44," Mike began. "He came out with one of the first trains ever to make it all the way through to the Willamette. Had himself one of the prettiest wives I'd ever seen, long, black hair and green eyes—eyes the color of spring grass. And a little boy, the image of his mother he was. Ross set great store by that son of his, I can tell you."

"What was his name?"

Mike paused and regarded her with raised eyebrows.

"The little boy," Susan prompted. "What was he called?"

"Randal. Named after Morgan's wife's family back east. He was two, maybe three, the year they arrived. Anyhow, as I was sayin', they came west and right away Ross cut himself out a parcel of land up north. He built a cabin and had fields plowed and planted afore you could blink an eye. Seemed right happy too, least for a while. Then in '46 we had us a real humdinger of a winter. Folks were snowbound for weeks at a time and when the snow melted all the roads were washed out. Come spring Ross moved his family into town. Told me Julia—that was his wife—said Julia couldn't stand it no more out there, cut off from everything like she was."

Mike squinted toward the hills north of town.

"Gets mighty lonely out there in the winter. All you hear are the wolves howlin' and the wind ablowin' day after day. Couldn't say I blamed Julia none—a pretty thing like her. Just didn't seem right to keep her away out there with no other womenfolk for miles around."

He shook his head.

"Well, Ross weren't about to let that farm sit empty, so he spent most all his time out there during the spring and summer while Julia and Randal stayed here in town."

A sad expression crossed his face. "Never will

know what really went wrong. Thought on it a lot for a while, too. Guess Julia was just too pretty, too young to be content to sit at home and wait for Ross to come back to town. At any rate, there was a young lieutenant, name of Campbell, came to Oregon City that summer. He'd been commissioned to do some sketches of the territory. Had a fair amount of talent, too. Folks used to stand and watch him by the hour while he drew pictures of the town and the river, but he never seemed to mind them watchin' none. Well, pretty soon it seemed like everywhere you saw Campbell, there was Julia, too."

Mike glanced at Susan as if expecting her to question him, but she kept her eyes on his face, silently willing him to continue.

"I said something about it to Ross on one of his trips to town, but he couldn't never see no wrong in Julia. Told me I was a gossipy old woman and it did Julia good to have company, what with him havin' to be gone so much. Well, after that I never said no more, but it sure looked to me like there was more to it than company." Mike shrugged.

"Come September, Campbell was due to take a ship back east. There were farewell parties and a lot of get-togethers to send him off. Well, no sooner had Campbell left but Julia and Randal just dropped out of sight. Morgan was away up north and things were busy at the saloon, so I hardly took notice. But folks talk, and every now and then someone'd say they hadn't seen Julia for a spell. I kept meanin' to get over and see if she was sick or somethin', but what with one thing and another . . .

"I never will forget the night Ross came to the saloon. He looked like he was fit to kill a grizzly, but he never said a word, just took a bottle and went and sat at a table in the corner. Pretty soon I went over and sat with him.

"'Well, Ross,' I says, 'it's been a couple weeks since you've been around town.' He never said a word, just glared at that bottle like he wanted to smash it 'longside someone's head. I shoulda known right then, but I kept on talkin'.

"'How's Julie,' I says, 'and Randal? Haven't seen 'em lately.'

"'And you won't, Mike,' he says.

"All of a sudden my blood just froze. I remember thinkin', my God, they've got sick and died and I never went to see them. Then he turns those gray eyes on me and they was cold as gunmetal.

"'They've gone, Mike' he says. 'Julia's left—with Campbell.'

"Well, I guess I musta sat there with my mouth open like an idiot for nigh onto a full minute afore I could say anything.

"'And Randal?' I says at last.

"'She took him too. So help me, Mike,' he says, 'if I could find her I'd kill her with my bare hands, I swear I would. I'd tear her into pieces and throw her to those wolves she used to hate so much. I hope she rots in hell for what she's done.'"

Mike fell silent and Susan thought back over her encounters with Ross. She remembered the glimmer of hatred in his eyes when she had offered to leave Adam. Ross must have thought of Julia then and remembered how his wife had so easily deserted him for another man. The words he had spoken made sense to her now. Of course he could never have taken her with him—not while she was married to

Adam. Had he thought her as heartless and wanton as Julia had been? Susan squirmed inwardly as she heard her words and saw her actions as Ross must have. She couldn't have done anything to more effectively drive him away.

She became aware of the man at her side as he stopped at the corner.

"That there's the Tamarack." Mike pointed across the street. "I don't know if I've helped you understand Ross or not. I don't know that he ever wanted anyone to understand." Mike started across the street toward the saloon, but Susan called out.

"Wait—Julia and Randal . . . what happened to them? Where are they now?"

Mike was silent for a moment, then his gaze shifted from hers. "Their ship went down off the Horn," he said. "All aboard were lost."

Chapter 31

As she walked slowly back to the hotel Susan remembered the thoughtless remarks she had hurled at Ross. She recalled the words she had used when he tried to prod her from the wagon after her baby died.

"You've never lost a child," she had cried. "How could *you* understand?"

Now those words made her cringe. If only she had known. But she knew Ross was not the type to confide in anyone. His pain would stay buried beneath his surface calm, with only a flicker of an eye or a fleeting expression to betray its existence.

Ellie was still out with Mr. Wilton when Susan returned to their room. She paced the floor, longing to escape the tormenting memories. She yearned for activity, something to take her mind off the past. The move to the Main Street House would help.

But when Ellie returned she flatly rejected Susan's proposal.

"Move!" she exclaimed. "Why, what would Jesse think after all his kindness? We can't just up and leave."

Susan noticed the familiar use of Mr. Wilton's first name. Ellie wasn't wasting any time.

"Besides," Ellie continued, "this is quite satisfactory. If Jesse were a little more stern with that girl—what's her name? Mary? no, Maud—if he were more stern with Maud, the rooms would be perfect. But he's such a gentleman, you can see he hasn't the heart to scold the poor thing."

Susan sighed. It was obvious that Ellie would refuse to move until Adam arrived. She wondered if that day would ever come.

"Jesse knows everyone," Ellie told Susan later that evening as they prepared to go down to dinner. "Why, just today he introduced me to Dr. McLaughlin and Governor Lane."

Susan fought her feelings of resentment. What had Ellie done to deserve acceptance in this new society? I don't care, she argued with herself, but she couldn't erase the small feeling of envy as Ellie chattered on.

"Of course, it's not like back home," Ellie twittered, "but they're both such charming gentlemen." She shook out the folds of her tafetta dress. It was an elaborate style, although somewhat worn.

"I must see about some new clothes," Ellie murmured as she frowned over a small stain on the sleeve. "These old things just aren't in style anymore. Tomorrow I want you to see about selling the oxen, and the wagon, too," she instructed. "We needn't waste our money paying someone to feed those animals."

"But won't we need them—I mean if Adam decides to farm—"

"Farm!" Ellie's voice was scornful. "I never intend to farm again. That's for peasants. Adam will be rich. If he wants land, I'm sure he'll have people to work it for him and he certainly won't need those scrawny animals."

"But—"

"Don't argue, Susan."

"But animals are scarce," she persisted.

"I don't care to discuss it further." Ellie turned and headed for the door. "It's time we went down to dinner. We mustn't keep Jesse waiting too long."

It wasn't difficult to find a buyer for the oxen. Farm animals were in short supply and Susan got a good price for them. So good, in fact, that she decided to keep some of the money for herself. Ellie would never know the difference, and a few dollars could keep her from starving while she sought employment.

Susan felt a twinge of guilt as she tucked the money into the bodice of her dress. I earned it, she argued. If it hadn't been for me, neither Ellie nor the oxen would have made it to Oregon. She was so engrossed in silent argument with herself that she almost failed to notice Neal Laughlin approaching.

"Susan! I'm so glad I found you. I have wonderful news." He pulled her to the side of the walkway, his brown eyes sparkling with excitement.

"I've found a teaching job," he told her. "It's only two days upriver. I met a man at the hotel who's started a lumber mill. He says there are ten or twenty families there already, and there'll be more come spring. He's offered me a cabin, plus two dollars a quarter for each pupil, and he'll even provide the schoolhouse. Isn't it marvelous?"

"Yes, Neal. I'm so happy for you."

"I knew you would be. I can hardly wait."

"When do you leave?" Susan forced a smile and hoped that Neal wouldn't sense her unhappiness.

"Tomorrow. That's why I wanted to see you. I tried the hotel but you weren't there. Ellie told me your husband hasn't arrived yet."

"No, he must have been delayed."

"Will you be all right alone? I know Ellie's not much help. Can I do anything for you?"

Susan wanted to cry out, "Yes, take me with you," but she shook her head.

"No, Neal, I'll be fine. Adam should arrive any day. How's Mercy?"

"The doctor says she's as well as can be expected. I hope I did the right thing, bringing her out here." A frown furrowed his brow.

"Is it all right to move her?"

"He said it shouldn't hurt, so long as she doesn't get chilled."

"She'd probably get worse if she thought she were holding you back from what you wanted to do." Susan tried to ease some of the worry in Neal's face.

"Yes, I guess you're right. And it'll be wonderful once we're settled and I can start work. Oh Susan, you have no idea how I long to be back in a classroom."

Susan smiled and touched his arm. "I think I do," she said softly. "I wish you and Mercy all the luck in the world."

"We'll be back, Susan. It isn't far, and I'm sure we'll come to town often. When we do, we'll always be sure to visit you."

"Thank you, Neal. I'll stop and see Mercy on my way back to the hotel, but if I don't see you before you leave, have a safe journey."

"If you ever need me, Susan . . ." He didn't finish the sentence, but she knew what he meant to say.

"Good-bye, Neal." She turned away quickly before he could see the tears in her eyes.

Her farewell to Mercy was more emotional than Susan had expected. Mercy reclined on a settee in the room she and Neal had rented at the Main Street House, a robe thrown over her legs. The girl's slender figure seemed to have shriveled in the last few days and her skin had a translucent quality, although a faint blush of pink tinted her cheeks.

"Susan, I'm so glad you came." Her voice was so soft that Susan strained to hear the words.

"I met Neal just now. He said you were leaving in the morning."

"Yes, isn't it wonderful? Everything is working out just the way he wanted." She paused as a spasm of coughing shook her body.

Susan couldn't keep her eyes away from the handkerchief in Mercy's hand and what she saw made her glance sharply at the girl. Mercy crumpled the spotted linen and shook her head. "It's all right, Susan. Remember, it's our secret. Yours and mine."

"But . . ." Susan fought to find the right words.

Mercy smiled faintly and brushed a lock of hair from her face. "Neal believes I'll be better soon. He has to, don't you see? If he knew I was worse he would never take this job—and he must, for his sake. He's spent far too much time worrying about me, putting me first." Another coughing spasm shook her and she paused to catch her breath.

"But I know . . . and so did the doctor, Susan.

There's nothing anyone can do. The best I can do is to try to hide it from Neal as long as I can. I want to see him happy."

Tears burned Susan's eyes as she stretched out her hand to clasp Mercy's. "You're very brave," she whispered.

"Brave!" Mercy laughed. "If only you knew how frightened I really am. No," she shook her head, "I'm not brave, but maybe . . . maybe God will give me the time to see my brother settled and content in a world where he belongs. That's all I pray for now."

Susan wanted to deny what Mercy was telling her, but she couldn't meet the honesty in the girl's eyes with false assurances.

"Neal's a lucky man," Susan choked out at last.

"And you won't do or say anything to make him change his mind about the trip, will you, Susan?"

"No, if this is what you want, I won't do anything to stop you."

"Thank you. You're a wonderful friend. I knew I could count on you."

At last Susan rose to leave. There was nothing left to say. All the words that came to her mind sounded trite and foolish in the face of Mercy's determined bravery.

"I . . . I'd better be going, Mercy. Take care of yourself."

"I will. Good-bye, Susan."

At the door, Susan turned. Mercy looked so frail. Would she ever see her again? It was all she could do to keep from running to throw her arms around the slight figure, but there was nothing she could do to help Mercy now.

Susan closed the door softly behind her and leaned against the wall for a moment. She choked back the threatening tears and dashed a hand angrily across her face. How could she be so weak in the face of Mercy's strength?

Chapter 32

October drifted into November and still there was no word from Adam. Ellie didn't even seem concerned. She flitted through the town's limited social life on the arm of Jesse Wilton as if she hadn't a care in the world. Susan, however, was growing impatient, eager to turn Ellie over to Adam and begin a life of her own. She had offered to look for employment, but Ellie was quick to voice her disapproval.

"There's no need for you to work," she told Susan. "We have enough money to last until Adam comes. Besides, what would people think if you went to work? It's not ladylike."

Ellie's lips closed in a firm line, and Susan hadn't the will to fight her. When Adam arrived she'd be free.

At times the thought was exhilarating, but more often it frightened her. What could she do in this tiny town so far from civilization? The only single women were those who worked in the saloons or poor girls like the unfortunate Maud, too physically unappealing to attract the most anxious of men in this community where women were so scarce. Even Ellie had entrapped Jesse Wilton, who hovered over her constantly.

The first winter storm swept through the valley and Susan watched from the window as wind and lashing rain loosed the last brown and orange leaves from the trees, allowed them to whirl madly for a moment, then dashed them into the mud. Was that how her own independence would end, a brief flurry followed by disaster?

Tom, the desk clerk at the Main Street House, regarded her with sympathy as she made her daily pilgrimage. Each day he shook his head even before she reached the desk and vowed he would send word the moment Adam arrived. Still she went. It was something to do.

Occasionally she met Mike Chapman as she performed her errands. He always greeted her pleasantly and sometimes escorted her back to the hotel. He seemed to be the only person she could talk to now that the Laughlins had left Oregon City.

Sometimes she wished she had been closer to other people on the wagon train. Mrs. Jordan had come to call on Ellie several times, but Susan always tried to avoid the woman. When they did meet, Mrs. Jordan's eyes were speculative as they swept over Susan's figure and her mouth tightened in disapproving lines.

The waiting drew Susan's nerves tight. If Adam did not arrive soon, would he be able to make it over the winter roads or would they be forced to wait until spring? She wasn't sure she could wait that long, but she'd vowed she would stay until Ellie was reunited with her son. She couldn't explain even to herself why she continued to tolerate Ellie.

Susan thought of the money she had secreted in the lining of her valise. Perhaps the guilt she felt for taking money that lawfully belonged to Ellie was what made her stay.

As the days of November crept by, the weather bound Susan to the drab hotel room. Hardly a day passed that the skies did not spit out their allotment of rain. The streets were a quagmire and the narrow plank walkways were covered with thick oozing mud. She had ruined her last decent pair of shoes, but no amount of inclement weather could make her spend an entire day in their depressing room.

With the coming of winter, the crowd of loungers in the Main Street House lobby had grown. Susan began to feel uncomfortable when she made her daily trip to Tom's desk, conscious of the stares that followed her and the momentary lull in conversation. She was convinced that the men discussed her among themselves. At times she felt she was being followed when she left the hotel, but when she looked back she couldn't pick out a familiar face among the few stragglers who braved the weather. It's my imagination, she told herself, and tried to shrug off the feeling of watchful eyes.

One blustery day the prickling became a certainty. She was struggling against the wind, holding her cape closely over her dress to keep out the worst of the dampness, when she sensed a presence behind her. She stopped and turned.

This time she was startled to find a man close behind her. He was dressed in faded denim pants and a red flannel shirt. The wind whipped blotches of color across his unshaven face and his close-set eyes were bloodshot and watery. He cleared his throat and sidled closer.

"You Miz Baker?" His voice was dry and scratchy.

Susan nodded.

"I hear tell you're lookin' fer word from your man."

"I'm waiting for my husband, yes." Susan kept her voice cool.

"I might have somethin' to tell you 'bout him." He wiped a hand nervously across his mouth and his smile displayed yellow, uneven teeth.

"What is it?" He couldn't know Adam—or could he? Despite the shifty expression in his eyes, he spoke with confidence. "Well now, I reckon since you've been waitin' so long it might be worth a little somethin' to you." He eyed her slyly.

"I don't have any money." Susan began to move away.

He caught up with her and put a hand on her arm. Susan shook it off, and glared at him. "No need to get in a huff," the man protested. "Don't mean no harm—just thought, you bein' alone and all . . ."

Susan looked at him with distaste. "I'm not alone," she snapped. "My mother-in-law's waiting for me at the hotel."

He looked up the street. "Maybe *she'd* have a little somethin' to give me for news of her son."

Susan quickened her steps, risking a spill into the churned mud of the street, but the man easily kept pace with her. "It'll be worth your while to hear what I have to say," he persisted when she turned into the walkway leading to the hotel.

Susan hesitated. The man's greed was obvious. What sort of story could he tell that would convince Ellie to part with her money? Susan shrugged. Why not let Ellie decide?

"All right then. I'll get my mother-in-law. It's up to her whether she wants to pay you."

He followed her eagerly into the lobby and sank into a leather chair, his mud-covered boots scraping against the worn carpet, as Susan went upstairs to find Ellie.

Ellie greeted the news with excitement. "Word of Adam? Well, where is the man? What did you tell him?"

"He's downstairs. He wants to be paid for his information."

"Paid?" Ellie's eyebrows arched, then she sighed. "I suppose we'll have to pay him then." She went to the bureau drawer, extracted her leather pouch and slipped a few coins into her pocket.

"Well, don't just stand there, Susan. Aren't you anxious to hear what he has to say?"

The man was still slouched in the chair when they entered the lobby. Ellie regarded him with a look of distaste.

"Who are you?" she demanded. "How do I know you've even met my son?"

"Name's Dawson," he drawled, then spat a wad of tobacco toward the fireplace. "I knowed your son all right—met him in Californie—tall, good-lookin' fella, blond hair."

"What is it you know?"

Dawson stretched his denim-clad legs toward the fire. "Well, like I told the little lady here," he jerked a dirty thumb toward Susan, "seems like my news might be worth a little somethin' to you—seein's how you've been waitin' so long 'n all."

"How much?"

"Twenty dollars."

"I'll pay you ten and not a penny more." Ellie's voice was firm.

Dawson eyed her for a moment, then he shrugged. "All right, but I want it now, afore I say a word."

Ellie reached into her pocket and counted out the money.

"Now, tell me when and where you saw my son."

"Met him in Sacramento. Had a claim up round Spanish Flat, but he didn't seem to work it much though. He'd be gone a week or two, then come back with enough gold dust to buy a bottle—and a woman." Dawson glanced toward Susan and she thought he had mentioned the women deliberately for her benefit.

"Get on with your story," Ellie snapped.

"Well, ma'am, he hung around this here saloon, called the Gold Bar, it was. I got to know him pretty good. We shared a few bottles from time to time. He was downright gen'rous with his whiskey." Dawson licked his lips as though he could taste the drinks he had shared with Adam.

"Where is he now?" Ellie's voice was sharp with impatience.

"I'm gettin' to it, I'm gettin' to it." Dawson gazed into the fire. "Well, one day there's some men comes ridin' into town, see. Tough-lookin' varmints they were—black hair, looked like maybe they was Injun or somethin'."

Susan caught her breath. Could they have been Delia's brothers who had sworn to track Adam down? She glanced at Ellie and saw the muscles tighten around her mouth.

"These here fellas started askin' questions round

town, wanted to know if anyone knew an Adam Baker from back east. Said they was willin' to pay, too. Weren't long till they learnt 'bout Adam, and they settled in to wait for him.''

Susan had no doubt Dawson had been the one to claim the money for his knowledge, but she didn't speak.

"One night Baker comes ridin' into town and they're a sittin' there in the saloon when he walks in the door. Well, sir, you never seen the like of it. All of a sudden he turns the color of that there wall. Starts to leave quick, but one of these here fellas jumps up, throws back his chair and hollers out, 'Hey you—Baker.'

"Well, Adam he turns real slowlike and you can see his hand easin' for his gun. 'Keep your hand off that gun,' this fella shouts and Baker, he freezes. 'We got a score to settle with you,' the other one says and he gets up from his chair real easylike.

"Baker says, 'I ain't got no business with you,' and he starts for the bar.

"'Is that what you told our sister?' the first fella says.

"After that things happened so fast it's hard to tell what came first. Baker goes for his gun and these two fellas open fire on him. One of 'em took a shot in the shoulder, but they cut Baker down right afore my eyes, ma'am, and that's the gospel truth. Then they lit outta there like they was headin' for hell.''

"And my son?" Ellie's face was pale.

"Deader than a church on Saturday night, and that's a fact. I didn't stick round for the fun'ral or nothin', but he's dead and buried, ma'am, like I said.''

Susan wondered why Dawson had left town so soon. Perhaps there had been some who didn't approve of his way of earning money. Whatever the reason, his story had an undeniable ring of truth.

Waves of relief swept over her. She was a widow. Never again would she have to face Adam. The sound of Ellie's loud cries startled her from her musing.

"My son," Ellie sobbed. "My only son to be killed like that, for no reason. Whatever could have caused it?"

"Well, ma'am, seems to me—" Dawson began, but Ellie turned on him.

"I don't want to hear what you think," she cried. "Just get out of here! I hope I never have to see you again as long as I live."

Dawson hesitated a moment, then got to his feet. He smiled as he passed Susan. "Widder ladies are right scarce round here, 'specially good-lookin' ones like you. You won't have yourself no trouble atall, findin' another man."

Susan shuddered as the door closed behind him.

Chapter 33

In public Ellie wore her grief graciously. She dabbed at her eyes with dainty, lace-edged handkerchiefs and the black dress she ordered from the local seamstress was a masterpiece of femininity. Jesse Wilton hovered over her with solicitous offers, which she accepted as her right. The fluttering of her eyelashes grew more pronounced and she clung to Wilton's arm at every opportunity.

In the privacy of their room, however, Ellie was petulant.

"How could he?" she demanded. "To be shot down in a saloon like a common drifter. What will become of me?"

Ellie never mentioned Adam's killers, although Susan felt she must know their identities. Daily Ellie counted her carefully hoarded money and the lines around her mouth became more harsh. Once more Susan suggested that she look for work, and this time Ellie agreed.

"I suppose you must," she said. "Though whatever you'll be able to do is more than I know."

After a week of searching for work, Susan was tempted to agree. No one wanted to hire a young widow with no experience in even the barest rudiments of business. She approached all the small stores in town hoping to find work as a counter clerk, but with no success. The local seamstress had no need of an unskilled assistant. She had even sought work as a chambermaid at one of the boarding-houses.

It seemed the only thing left was to try for a job at a saloon. As Susan made her way back to the hotel after a day of endless rejections, her desperation grew. Raindrops fell from the bare branches of the trees, and dampness crept through the thin fabric of her cape. Tomorrow she would see Mike Chapman.

She had hesitated to ask him for work, even in the boardinghouse section of his establishment. She had no wish to take money from Ross Morgan, and although he was gone from Oregon City he still owned the Tamarack. She would be working for him. And what if Mike turned her down? He was her only hope—something she had kept at the back of her mind as a last resort. If that failed, what would she do?

She climbed the stairs to her room slowly, reluctant to face Ellie with news of her failure.

Susan opened the door to a scene of wild disorder. Clothing was tumbled across the bed and onto the floor. Two of her best dresses were thrown into a crumpled heap in a corner. In the middle of this chaos stood Ellie, her hands clenched at her sides, her eyes narrowed with malice.

As Susan closed the door, Ellie thrust her hand out accusingly. "Where did you get this?" she demanded. Her voice shook with rage.

Susan glanced at the money in Ellie's hand. She didn't need to see her open valise to know that Ellie had found her small hoard.

"You took it, didn't you?" Ellie accused. "You stole it from me, you ungrateful little . . ." Ellie sputtered to a stop as if unable to find a word that would properly describe her feelings.

Susan felt her face flame with embarrassment. "I didn't steal it. I earned it."

"Earned it!" Ellie screeched. "When did you ever earn anything?"

"I got us here, didn't I?"

"You! A fat lot you did! If it hadn't been for you, we could have gone back home where we belonged. But oh no, you knew best, didn't you? You forced me to traipse across half the country—and for what? To steal me blind the minute we arrive! Is that the gratitude I get for giving you a home, for taking care of you?"

Susan clenched her hands until her nails dug into her flesh. "You never gave me a home," she spat. "You don't know what a home is, and as for taking care of me, I did more for you than you've ever done for anyone in your entire life."

Ellie's mouth dropped open. Two bright splotches of color flared in her pale cheeks. "Get out!" she screamed. "Get out of my sight and don't ever come back—do you hear?"

Susan grabbed her clothing and pushed it haphazardly into her valise.

"I'll be glad to. There's nothing that would make me happier." Her meager possessions gathered, Susan turned on her heel. The door slammed behind her as she hurried down the stairs to the street. She had a fleeting glimpse of Jesse Wilton's startled face as she pushed past him on the walkway, and then she was hurrying down the street, away from Ellie and all she represented.

Susan's anger carried her for several blocks before she became aware of the damp fog that crept through her clothing. She pulled her cape closer and slowed her steps. She was free of Ellie, but what had it cost her? She was penniless, without friends or family, in a town that neither knew nor wanted her.

Her steps lagged as she turned toward the Tamarack. There were no alternatives left. She must ask Mike Chapman for help. He was the only person who could give her shelter and perhaps pay her a small pittance for what work she could do.

The winter daylight was beginning to fade and fingers of fog clutched at her hair. Tears welled in her eyes and spilled down her cheeks, but she didn't bother to wipe them away. There was no one to see. The streets were deserted. Lamplight shone from some of the windows and she glanced at them with yearning as she passed. How wonderful to be inside one of those warm houses, peaceful and content, looking out at the mist-draped afternoon. She had never realized before how much she had always taken for granted. Even on the trail there had been the shelter of the wagon. Now she had nothing.

When she saw the figure ahead, Susan stopped still in amazement. It couldn't be. Surely her mind had created this image to taunt her. She passed a hand over her eyes and looked again. The color of his hair was indistinct, but the shape of his body, the way he walked—it had to be Neal Laughlin.

Susan ran toward him, calling his name, but her

voice was muffled by the fog. She felt as if she were running through a dream, never getting closer to her goal.

"Neal," she sobbed again and at last he stopped and turned. She skidded along the muddy walkway toward him. His face was questioning in the dim light.

"Susan," he cried as she drew near, and his eyes lit with pleasure. She threw herself into his arms.

"Oh, Neal, Neal, thank God it's really you."

She clung to him, uncaring of what passersby might think. He was solid, warm—an answer to her prayers. She burrowed her face into the warmth of his coat as sobs ripped through her body.

"Susan, what's wrong? Tell me." She felt him smooth the hair back from her face. At last she raised her head. She tried to smile, but her lips trembled as she spoke.

"Oh, Neal, I have nowhere to go—no one . . ." Her voice broke and Neal pulled her into the warm circle of his arms once more.

"Hush, Susan. It's all right. Tell me what's happened. Where's your husband?"

"He's dead." She felt Neal stiffen, then he held her more tightly.

"How?"

"He was shot—gunned down in California."

"Where's Ellie?"

"She's at the hotel. She . . . she threw me out." Susan took a quivering breath. "I . . . I took some money—money that I got for the oxen. I know I shouldn't have done it—it was wrong. But I thought when Adam came . . ." She left the sentence unfinished. What would Neal think of her now that he

240

knew she had stolen from Ellie? Would he draw away—reject her? But he continued to pat her back as though soothing a baby.

"Poor Susan," he whispered. "Life's been pretty hard for you lately, hasn't it?"

"You have to understand, Neal," she pleaded as she drew away. "I—I didn't think of it as stealing. I believed I had earned it, by bringing the wagon through. Do you see?"

"Yes, my dear, I understand." His voice was gentle.

Susan breathed a sigh of relief. Wonderful, kind Neal. He always understood.

"And now you have nowhere to go?" he asked.

Susan shook her head. "I've been looking for work ever since we heard about Adam. But no one wants to hire me." Another sob shook her. Neal put his arm around her and they began to walk slowly down the street.

"It's all right, Susan. I'm here now."

She leaned against him. It was so wonderful to let someone else handle her problems. Neal would take care of everything. Suddenly her steps faltered.

"But Neal, why are you here? Why aren't you upriver?"

His face was shadowed with pain. "It's Mercy," he replied. "She took a turn for the worse shortly after we arrived. She's been getting steadily weaker, and then two days ago . . . She's unconscious most of the time. She doesn't know me or anyone. She just lies there, with her eyes shut, as if she were dead. I came to Oregon City to fetch the doctor, but he says there's nothing he can do. He won't even come back with me."

"Oh, Neal." She clutched his arm in sympathy. "Should you have left her?"

"There was nothing I could do. Mrs. Jameson—from the settlement—she's staying with her. But there's nothing anyone can do. I'm going to lose her, Susan. I know it."

"You mustn't think that. She's been sick before. Perhaps she'll get better."

"It's never been like this."

They had reached the Main Street House and Neal stopped.

"Let me rent a room for you," he offered. "In the morning I must start back. Will you—will you come with me?"

Susan gazed into his soft brown eyes. She had vowed to be independent, not to allow herself to fall into the trap of depending on a man. But Neal wouldn't desert her. He would take care of her forever, if she let him. Slowly she nodded.

"Yes, Neal, I'll go with you."

Chapter 34

Susan stood at the window of the Laughlin cabin and stared at the dark evergreens that bordered the clearing. They towered over the tiny structure as though threatening to reclaim the land the moment she turned her back. She knew there were other log cabins lining the path that zigzagged down the hill to the river, but they were hidden from view and did nothing to alleviate her sense of isolation. The only sounds were those of a log shifting on the fire and Mercy's labored breathing from the far corner of the room.

She had been shocked by Mercy's condition. Although the girl tossed and moaned, she hadn't been aware of their presence. Why had the doctor refused to come? Surely he could have done something to ease Mercy's suffering.

Neal had spent the night at the schoolhouse and she wondered if he had slept. She appreciated his concern for convention. As tired as she had been the night before when they arrived, she hadn't failed to notice the gleam of speculation in the eyes of the woman who had stayed with Mercy during Neal's absence. What were people saying? She tried to shrug the thoughts from her mind.

Wind whistled through chinks in the logs and Susan shivered. It seemed impossible that only two days before she had been in Oregon City.

She thought of the brief note she had left for Mike Chapman. She had told Neal she couldn't leave without telling Mike where she had gone. He had understood, but Susan knew it wasn't really Mike she had wanted to tell of her whereabouts—she hoped that when Ross Morgan returned Mike would tell him where she could be found. Would he return? If he knew she was free, would he care?

She envisioned Ross following her into the wilderness to claim her as his own. She would happily go with him anywhere. Where was he?

She clenched her fists in frustration. All she could do was wait and hope that he would return.

Mercy moaned and Susan crossed the room to her side. The girl's eyelids fluttered open and she stared at Susan in confusion. "What are you doing here?" she asked.

"I came back with Neal last night. Can I get you anything?"

Mercy weakly shook her head. "Where's Ellie?"

Susan adjusted the covers and averted her face from Mercy's searching eyes. "In Oregon City."

"What about your husband?"

"He's dead."

"Oh, Susan, how awful." She closed her eyes for a moment, then asked, "Why was Neal in Oregon City?"

"He went to get the doctor for you."

"He shouldn't have. There's nothing anyone can do. Neal must learn that." Mercy's face was wistful as she looked at Susan. "There are so many things I'll never be able to do," she whispered.

For the first time Susan saw tears in Mercy's eyes, Mercy who had always been so brave. She would have been a wonderful wife and mother. But she would never have the chance. Susan felt tears burn her own eyes.

"It was good of you to come, Susan. It'll make it easier—for Neal—when . . . when I die."

"Hush. That won't be for a long time. You'll get better."

Mercy's laugh was cut short by a coughing spasm. When the coughs subsided, Susan wiped Mercy's face with a damp cloth.

"You always were the optimist, weren't you?" Mercy whispered. "It's all right, Susan, I understand. But it won't be long. I think I'll be almost glad when it's over. I'm so tired. And it hurts now—all the time." She put her hand to her chest.

"Let me get you something to eat. There's soup in the kettle."

"All right. Maybe a little."

But Mercy turned her head away after only a few sips. Susan smoothed the covers and eased her back to a prone position.

"Sleep now," she said. "When Neal comes home you can talk."

"Is he at school?"

Susan nodded.

"That's good." Mercy's gaze was steady. "Will you take care of him, Susan?"

"He's fine."

Mercy shook her head against the pillow. "I mean

245

after it's over. He's never been alone. Please promise you'll take care of him."

Susan wanted to avoid the look in Mercy's eyes. How many promises had she made that she regretted? Once she had promised Mercy to tell no one of her worsening condition; perhaps if she had not agreed, Mercy would be strong and well now. Susan thought of the vow she had made to take care of Ellie; what humiliation that had caused her. She didn't want to make another promise she might not be able to keep.

"He'll be all right, Mercy. If he—if he needs anything, I'll do all I can."

Mercy's gaze was unwavering and Susan shifted uncomfortably.

"I know I have no right to ask you, Susan, but . . ." Her voice faltered.

How can I refuse, Susan thought. She asks for so little. "All right, Mercy." She clasped the girl's thin hand in her own. "I promise. I'll take care of Neal if I possibly can. But he's stronger than you think."

Mercy smiled. "Thank you. He thinks so much of you. I've seen him watch you when you didn't know it. I'd be happy if I knew you were here to see he's all right."

"If he wants me to, I'll stay."

Susan felt a mixture of relief and concern as she watched Mercy's face relax and her eyes close. She had granted Mercy's request, and it had comforted the girl. It was the only thing she could have done.

But what will it cost me, Susan wondered. Even Mercy had noticed Neal's feelings. What would she do if he decided to propose? Perhaps he won't, she told herself, if I can make him see that I only feel friendship for him.

She leaned back in her chair, her eyelids heavy. Her head nodded and at last she fell into an uneasy sleep filled with dreams of faceless people who pursued her down a hallway, all of them crying, "Come back, come back, Susan. You promised."

Chapter 35

Susan was startled to wakefulness by the clatter of logs thrown on the fire. The late afternoon sun had disappeared behind the trees, and for a moment she could barely see the outlines of the room. Then she saw Neal bent over the fire. He prodded the embers until the new logs caught in a sudden burst of flame.

"Oh, Neal, I'm sorry. I didn't hear you come in."

He turned from the fire, his face in shadow. "I didn't mean to startle you, but it was getting cold and I thought I'd better see to the fire."

She wondered how long he had been there. The thought of him watching her while she slept made her uncomfortable.

"Mercy was awake a little today."

Neal glanced toward the bed. "Did she recognize you?"

"Yes. She seemed better."

Why was she lying to him? They both knew Mercy wasn't really any better. He walked to the bed and looked down at his sister.

"Mercy."

The girl stirred and opened her eyes. Susan saw the look of love that passed between the two of them and turned away to busy herself with the fire. She heard Mercy's soft voice, but couldn't distinguish her words. She turned in time to see Neal bend and kiss his sister's cheek.

"Susan, why don't you get a breath of air? I'll fix supper," he said.

She moved gratefully to the door. Perhaps the night air would shake the lethargy from her mind and body. She stood in front of the cabin and looked around the peaceful clearing. The wind had died down and a few stars glimmered through the trees. It was difficult to believe that just down the hill the people of the settlement were going about their nightly chores.

"It's beautiful, isn't it?" Neal stood behind her. The light from the doorway cast a long shadow before him.

"Yes, it's lovely."

"No matter what happens, I'm glad I came," Neal said. "What about you? Do you wish you'd stayed back east?"

She thought for a moment. All that had happened in the last year had changed her drastically from the girl she had been when she met Adam. It was difficult to remember what she had thought and felt then. "No, I'm glad I came. There's something appealing about this country—something new and fresh. It isn't tired and used-up, like it is back east. There's hope here, hope for a new beginning."

"A new beginning." Neal echoed her words, and his hand touched the hair at the nape of her neck. "Yes, sometimes we all need to start again."

His nearness made her uneasy and she fought the urge to move away.

"Perhaps I shouldn't say anything, what with your

just learning of Adam's death and all . . ." He paused and she wanted to agree with him, but instead she waited for what she knew was coming. She might as well face it now.

"You must know how I feel about you," he continued. "And I've always suspected you didn't really love your husband. Is that presumptuous?"

Susan shook her head. "No, you're right. I married Adam for all the wrong reasons. I guess I got what I deserved."

"You were young. You couldn't be expected to know what marriage was all about. But I could give you more than he did. I love you, Susan. I want to spend the rest of my life making you happy, giving you things you've never had before. I think I can do that."

She started to speak, but he pressed his finger against her lips. "Don't say anything, not now. You came here because you had nowhere else to go. I don't want to take advantage. I just want you to think about it. Will you do that? Just think about it for a while?"

"Yes, I'll think about it, but—"

"That's all I ask. I'm not making any demands, please believe that."

He made it so easy for her. She was grateful for the warmth and understanding in his eyes. It would be so simple to tell him yes, she would marry him—but it wouldn't be fair.

The image of Ross Morgan's mocking face flashed before her. Why couldn't he have felt this way? Was she a fool to throw away the peace and contentment that marriage to Neal would give her? But she didn't have to decide now—Neal had said he didn't expect an answer yet. She could wait and think about it. Perhaps in time she would forget Ross. Yes, that would be best. She would try to forget she had ever met him, forget the way his touch had made her tremble, the way his lovemaking had sparked flames of desire within her. That was in the past now. It was time to consider the future.

Neal's hand gently cupped her chin and he gazed into her face.

"I only want to make you happy," he murmured, and he bent to kiss her.

She submitted to the feeling of his lips against hers. It was as though she stood at a great distance from herself and watched two strangers kiss. She allowed her lips to part and felt his arms pull her close, sensing the longing he controlled. Why can't I respond, she wondered, even as he lifted his head and glanced toward the cabin.

"Supper should be nearly ready." His voice was husky, and she knew he was shaken by their embrace although it had left her unmoved.

She followed him into the cabin and took refuge in the homely chores of setting the table and dishing up their food. Neal wouldn't press for an answer. He would be content to bide his time, to wait for her to come to a decision. And why shouldn't he be confident that she would finally agree to marry him? He didn't know about the dreams that tormented her and kept her from accepting his offer. He knew nothing of her love for Ross Morgan.

Chapter 36

Although she had expected it, Susan was shaken by Mercy's death two weeks later. She stood beside the freshly turned earth and tried to hold back her tears as clumps of damp dirt fell with sodden thuds on the wooden coffin.

The cold had crept down from the mountains, and Susan shivered.

Neal's face was grim, as it had been for the last four days. He had sent to Oregon City for a preacher to speak over Mercy's grave, refusing to bury her without a proper ceremony. During the time they had waited for the minister, she and Neal had shared the cabin in silence.

Neighbors made hushed visits to offer condolences. Their speculative gazes slid over Susan, and she longed to shout at them that there was nothing between herself and Neal. But she remained silent. It was not the time to cause a scene, and Neal hadn't noticed the glances.

He hadn't cried since the day of Mercy's death. Even now, as he watched the earth fall on her coffin, his face was immobile.

The neighbors began to drift away from the grave toward their homes. A few paused to speak, but

Neal only nodded. At last they were alone. Susan shifted uncomfortably. She yearned for the dry warmth of the cabin, but Neal looked so lonely. She couldn't leave him.

A shudder ran through his body, and finally he turned to her as if surprised to find her there.

"You should be back at the cabin, Susan." His voice was soft. "You're not dressed for the cold. You'll get chilled." He took her hand and together they walked away from the grave.

Silence hung over them as Susan busied herself preparing a meal neither of them wanted. She spoke hesitantly as she placed Neal's food before him. "Please eat something."

He glanced at the plate and obediently picked up a piece of corn bread. His eyes met Susan's and she wanted to cry out at the misery she saw in them.

"She's happy now, Neal. I know it's what everyone tells you, but she's not suffering anymore. You can be glad of that."

"Yes, you're right. I can't seem to believe she's really gone. I still see her as she was when she was little. She used to cling to my hand and gaze up at me. She wasn't sick then. We had happy times together. And she trusted me—oh, how she trusted me. I let her down." For a moment he stared at the bread he still held in his hand, then he put it back on the plate and pushed his chair away from the table.

"Mercy never thought you let her down," Susan protested. "That's all in your mind. She thought you could do no wrong—and she was right. There was nothing more you could have done."

His smile was weak, but he began to eat and Susan sighed.

"I think I'll go to Oregon City for a few days," Neal announced. "There are things I need to buy for the school, and it would probably do me good to get away for a few days. Would you mind being here alone?"

"No." She shook her head slowly. "But I think perhaps I should go with you. I can't stay here now. Before it was different, when I could help with Mercy, but now—"

"Don't leave." Neal's voice was alarmed. "What would you do in Oregon City? You couldn't find work before."

"Maybe I didn't try hard enough. Anyway, I can't stay here. People will begin to talk whether you spend the nights at the schoolhouse or not. And that's not fair to you."

"They can't talk if I'm away. At least stay until I come back. Stay with me until Christmas is over."

Christmas. She had forgotten all about the coming holiday. She remembered the Christmases of her childhood, carefree and happy. It would never be that way again—but how much worse it would be for Neal if he had to spend it alone in this isolated cabin with only memories of Mercy to keep him company.

"Please, Susan."

She remembered the promise she had made to Mercy. Although it was impossible to stay here indefinitely, she could at least postpone her departure until after the holidays.

She nodded, and was embarrassed by the relief she saw in his eyes.

"Thank you, Susan. I don't know if I could face the thought of coming back here to . . . to nothing."

The next day he left. Susan welcomed the solitude. She spent hours trying to think of what she would do when Neal returned. It was difficult to keep desperation from her thoughts. What would await her in Oregon City? She had told Neal she could find employment, but she was doubtful.

Ellie would have nothing to do with her; and Susan vowed in any case that she would never accept anything from her. In the back of her mind was the thought of Mike Chapman. She would have to go to him. She would learn to ignore the men who frequented the bar. She had faced real threats and dangers on the trail—surely she could handle a few rude remarks.

As the days passed and Neal did not return, her resolve strengthened. There were no other options. If she had to work in a saloon, then that's what she would do, at least until she earned enough money to leave Oregon City. After that—well, she would consider that when the time came.

Her decision made, Susan began to plan for Neal's return. She had promised to stay through Christmas and she wanted him to have as pleasant a homecoming as possible. She brought pine boughs in from the woods and used them to decorate the stone mantle of the fireplace. She chopped down a small fir tree, put it in one corner and decorated it with tiny bows fashioned from strips of material from an old dress. The pungent odor of pine permeated the cabin. Susan spent hours baking breads and pies.

The day of Neal's return she was warm and flushed from working over the fire, but the look in his eyes was worth all her efforts.

"Susan," he cried. "It's wonderful."

He hugged her spontaneously and she laughed as she pulled away.

"All that for a couple of tree boughs?" she teased.

"It's more than that—it's home. For the first time I feel like I've come home." His eyes were bright.

"How was Oregon City?" Susan turned back to the fire to pull out a loaf of bread.

"Busy. Seems like every time I go into town, they're building another store or office. Now they're talking about a new courthouse—and a girl's school. I can't believe it. Someday Oregon City will be the biggest city in the territory."

Susan pushed her hair back from her face. "Sit down and tell me about your trip."

Neal took an exaggerated whiff of the warm bread. "It'll cost you. Not a word until I have a slice of that bread."

Susan laughed. It was wonderful to see him in such good spirits. She had forgotten what it was like to exchange light conversation with a man. As she sliced the bread and put it on a plate, she surreptitiously observed his face. He seemed at peace. Perhaps the worst was over.

"Here's my side of the bargain," she smiled. "Now, tell me what you've been doing."

He took a bite of bread before speaking.

"I saw Ellie," he said at last, and the laughter faded from his eyes. "I thought she might want to know how you were." He shook his head.

"What did she say when you told her where I was?"

"She'd already heard you were here. Didn't say

how, but she said it hadn't surprised her much. She wasn't kind, Susan. Perhaps you'd rather not hear it."

"Nothing Ellie says can hurt me."

He studied her face for a moment before he continued. "She said it was just like you to find a man to take you in, even if it was without benefit of marriage." Neal paused. "I was angry with her at the time, but then I got to thinking. I've been unfair asking you to stay on. I wouldn't admit it before, but I can see now what people are going to think, even if there's no reason for it."

"I don't care about that," Susan replied, but her words lacked conviction. It wasn't so much for herself that she cared, but rather for what the gossip and speculation could do to Neal.

"Ellie's planning to get married—to that fellow who runs the boardinghouse where you were staying."

"Poor Jesse."

"He seems to be able to take care of himself."

"He'll have a time of it with Ellie." Susan shook her head. "Well, I wish her happy. She once told me that without a man there wasn't any reason for a woman to exist. She really believes that—and then to lose both her men so close together. I hope she'll be happy."

"It's kind of you to say that after how she talked about you. Why does she feel that way—surely not just because you kept a little of the money from the oxen."

Susan shrugged. "It's more than that. She doesn't think I was much of a wife to Adam—and I guess she's right."

"From what little you've told me, I don't think he deserved much of a wife."

"Maybe. But that's all over now. Did you see anyone else?"

"As a matter of fact, I did. Ran into Ross Morgan at the Main Street House."

For a moment the room seemed to spin. Ross was back. Her heartbeat raced as she waited for Neal's next words.

"He'd been down to California. Got back a couple weeks ago. He asked about you, said he'd heard that Mercy was sick and that you'd come down to take care of her."

Two weeks. He'd been back for two weeks and had known she was here, yet he hadn't come to look for her. There was a roaring in Susan's ears.

How foolish she had been to believe that her message to Mike would have sent Ross chasing after her like a lovesick schoolboy! He had never given her reason to think he cared.

"Susan, did you hear me?" Neal's voice broke through her thoughts.

"I'm sorry, Neal. What did you say?"

"I said Ross has taken over the Tamarack. Did you know he owned it?"

Susan nodded. Neal's eyes were intent as he studied her and she looked away. For weeks Ross Morgan had been uppermost in her thoughts. She had dreamed of his return, but nothing was to be as she had hoped.

She thought of how she had envisioned him coming to her and telling her how he had always loved her, what she would say in return. She had lived in a fantasy world while, for the last two weeks, he had known exactly where to find her and had not made the slightest effort to do so.

"I know it's none of my business, Susan, but sometimes I've wondered if perhaps there was something between you and Ross . . ." Neal's voice faltered. "I mean—"

"You're absolutely right," Susan snapped. "It isn't any of your business." She was instantly ashamed as she saw the hurt in his eyes. She reached for his hand.

"I'm sorry, Neal. Forgive me. I shouldn't have spoken like that."

"It's all right. I didn't mean to pry."

"You weren't." Susan drew a deep breath before she continued. "No, there's nothing between me and Ross Morgan. As a matter of fact, I think he's probably the most arrogant man I've ever known."

Susan fought back tears. She hated Ross. She wouldn't waste one more moment dreaming of him.

And to think she had believed he had left Oregon City because of her. How could she have believed Mike Chapman's words implying Ross had run from her because he didn't want to admit his love? She knew why she had believed—because she wanted to think that there would be some future for them. She had been so stupid.

A harsh laugh rose to her lips, but she bit it back before it could turn to a sob.

"I did some shopping in Oregon City." Neal spoke hesitantly as if afraid she would turn on him again.

"Oh?" Susan tried to muster interest in what he said. All she wanted to do was run from the room and hide from the thought of Ross's rejection, but she knew she must pretend that nothing had happened. If Neal were to guess the truth he would be sympathetic and tender, covering his own hurt. She couldn't face that—not now.

"I found three more readers to use at school. Some folks were selling out, heading south, and they had a lot of their things up for sale."

"That's nice."

"Susan, have you thought about what you're going to do?"

She remembered her resolution to ask Mike Chapman for a job. Now that was impossible. She would starve to death before she asked Ross Morgan for work! She shook her head.

"I've been too busy."

"Well, I thought about it."

He reached into the pocket of his coat and pulled out a small box. "I told you before how I feel about you, Susan. I know I promised not to make demands or push you into a decision. I'm not trying to do that now either, but . . ." He stopped and cleared his throat. "I'd like you to be my wife. I . . . I bought a ring—just in case you said yes."

He pushed the box across the table toward her. Susan stared at it, unable to move.

"I've said it all wrong," Neal muttered. "I want to tell you how I feel and all I do is make a mess of it." He sighed. "I love you, Susan. I know you don't feel the same about me, but in time I think you could learn to love me. I want to take care of you—to spend the rest of my life with you."

Susan's hand crept toward the box on the table. If she took it she would be committed to Neal. It was such a small gesture, yet such an important one. What he offered was something she had never had—the security of someone who cared about her, the comfort of making a home and sharing day-to-day pleasures. Would she ever have such a chance again? It was true that she didn't love him, but she cared about him. She wanted to comfort him when he was sad, rejoice in his triumphs. Perhaps that was really what love was all about; perhaps that was closer to love than the searing emotion she had felt for Ross Morgan.

Her hand touched the box and she looked at Neal. He remained silent. Only his eyes pleaded with her to accept what he offered.

Susan's fingers closed over the box. Slowly she picked it up and removed the lid. Inside, nestled against dark blue velvet, was a plain gold wedding band.

"It's beautiful, Neal," she whispered, but she couldn't meet his eyes.

Chapter 37

Marriage to Neal was totally different from what Susan had known with Adam. They were married immediately after Christmas, and the neighboring families were quick to offer their congratulations. Now that she was no longer a stranger they treated her with friendship, and she wondered why she had ever thought them distant and suspicious. Even Agnes Jameson, who had once seemed so disapproving, was quick to offer a jar of preserves or share a side of venison. Susan felt as if she belonged.

Neal was kind and understanding. He demanded nothing from her, but Susan constantly tried to please him. His lovemaking was tender and gentle, and there were nights when she clung to him with a desperate, unappeased hunger. She felt as though if she tried hard enough she could attain the one thing that was missing from her life. Neal never questioned her responses. Perhaps, in his mind, her desperation passed for desire.

The days took on a comforting pattern of sameness. Each morning she rose at dawn to fix breakfast before Neal left for the schoolhouse. No matter how inclement the winter weather, he always made the journey to the small whitewashed building. During heavy snows there were days when only one or two of his pupils arrived to struggle with their letters and numbers, but to Neal even that was worth it.

Most mornings Susan baked and cleaned. She often brought Neal his lunch, thankful for a reason to be out in the clear, invigorating air. In the afternoons she visited some of the neighbor women or did household chores. Neal had ordered material for her from Oregon City and Susan made two new dresses in modest styles. When she glanced in the mirror she was startled by her housewifely image. Where was the girl who had once dreamed of silk and velvet gowns? She shrugged off those memories. She would no longer allow herself regrets for unrealized fantasies.

The long winter months were depressing, and the coming of spring brought little improvement. Constant mist and drizzle blurred the horizon and drops of moisture hung from tree branches like miniature ornaments. The cabin was constantly permeated with the smell of damp clothing hung up to dry.

As the days lengthened, buttercups began to dot the clearing and on the fringes of the forest Susan found wood violets, trilliums and the crimson flame of wild currants. Meadowlarks and sparrows were joined by hummingbirds and warblers, a sure promise of summer.

At times the thought of Ross Morgan crept into Susan's mind. When she was alone and unoccupied she wondered what he was doing and if he ever thought of her. Sternly she told herself that that part of her life was over and that she no longer had any feelings for him, but she was grateful they didn't live where she would face the constant chance of meeting him on the street. Each time Neal went to Oregon City, she made excuses to stay home, although she knew he was puzzled by her actions.

Thoughts of Ross made her feel guilty and she tried to be especially kind to Neal on days when her mind had slipped to the past.

It was on such a day that she chanced to come across the ivory hairpin Adam had bought for her so long ago. It had lain forgotten in the bottom of a dresser drawer for months. She held it for a moment, feeling the carving where the two prongs met, remembering how she had admired it in the general store's display case before Adam bought it for her. It was the only thing he had ever given her that was truly hers. Even her wedding ring hadn't been bought to fit her finger.

She started to throw the pin away, then thought better of it. She would use it—why not? It was a pretty thing. She would put her hair up with it this afternoon, put on one of her more flattering dresses and surprise Neal. Perhaps that would make up for the fact that she had spent half the day dreaming of another man.

She spent several hours washing her hair, pressing a dress and primping before the mirror. The image that met her eyes was encouraging. Her figure had filled out since her marriage. The dress clung in the right places and its golden color brought out the topaz brilliance of her eyes. Her cheeks were flushed as she drew her hair to the top of her head and fastened it with the ivory hairpin. She could imagine the admiration in Neal's eyes.

I'll learn to be a good wife, she vowed. I won't

think about the past anymore. Neal deserves the best and that's what I'll give him.

Susan was standing at the open door of the cabin when Neal rounded the bend in the path. He raised a hand and waved. She felt a warm glow as he strode toward the cabin. He was so good to her.

It was several moments before Susan became aware that someone was hurrying up the path behind Neal. There was something vaguely familiar about the man, but from that distance she was unable to see him clearly. He overtook Neal and the two of them stopped, a motionless tableau silhouetted against the dark green of the trees. With an uneasy frown, she gazed at the stranger. The brim of his hat shaded his face, but his hands were clenched at his sides as if in anger.

With a quick movement he swept the hat from his head and motioned to the doorway where Susan stood. She gasped as the afternoon sun glinted against the silvery-blond hair.

It couldn't be. One hand went to her throat as she took an involuntary step forward. She had to be wrong. It couldn't be Adam. He was dead.

As she moved, Neal glanced toward her and shouted. She couldn't make out his words, but the man who couldn't be Adam and yet could be no one else turned to look at her. Now she saw his face and there was no doubt in her mind. Neal put a hand on Adam's arm as though to urge him away from the cabin. Adam flinched away from Neal's touch.

Even as Susan stumbled down the path toward the two men she saw the glint of sun against metal, saw the gun in Adam's hand and heard its echoing vibration as he fired. Stunned, she saw Neal crumple to the ground.

"No!" she screamed and hurled herself down the path.

She careened into Adam, who stood before her, his mouth curled into a sneer. "You needn't be in such a hurry to greet me," he jeered. "I'm not going anywhere."

"Let me by!"

She tried to twist away from the hand that grasped her arm.

"What? No welcome for your long-lost husband?"

"*That*'s my husband." Susan struggled toward Neal's still form.

"Not anymore he's not. Never was neither, unless they've changed the laws."

"Let me go!" She jerked her arm free and ran to where Neal lay.

"Neal, Neal," she sobbed, feeling desperately for a pulse, some sign that he still lived. She rolled him over on his back and gazed at his bloodstained shirt. She shook his shoulders, willing life back into the body that refused to respond to her urgings. He couldn't be dead.

"Neal!" she cried.

Adam yanked her to her feet. "He ain't gonna answer you."

"Don't touch me!"

Adam's eyes narrowed and his grip tightened on her arm. "I'll touch you all I want. You're my wife."

"No! You're dead. They said you were dead."

"I'll show you how dead I am." Adam laughed and shoved her toward the cabin. "It'll take more than a bullet from some half-breed's gun to finish me."

"But he saw you—he said . . ." Susan stumbled toward the cabin on the uneven ground. It was impossible. It had to be a nightmare. Soon she would wake to find Neal beside her.

"Ma told me what happened. Seems your informer didn't stick around long enough to make sure I was a goner. Guess there were some who thought I wouldn't make it—but they didn't know how much I had to live for, did they?" His eyes slid over her body and Susan saw the hard glint of desire in them.

"You'll hang for this," she cried. "You can't kill a man and get away with it!"

"I reckon I can since he stole my wife. What court is gonna blame me—'specially after he threatened me and all. I don't figure I'll have much to worry about."

"He never threatened you. Neal would never do a thing like that."

"And who do you think will believe that? Here I am, come home to claim my wife, only to find her married to another man. Why, there won't be a dry eye on the jury."

Susan glanced around. Surely someone would come to investigate the shot. But there was no one in sight.

"Don't bother looking for help," Adam snarled as he tightened his grip on her arm. "Gunshots are as common as jackrabbits round these parts. It's just you and me now."

They reached the door of the cabin and he pushed her inside. "Nice place you got here. Too bad we can't stay—but I reckon we don't have to rush right off."

"Get out! Get out of here and leave me alone."

"Oh no. I've thought about you a lot. I missed you—I surely did. I don't intend for you to get away from me again." He reached for the bodice of her dress and his fingers played with the fabric.

"Shame to spoil your pretty dress. Why don't you just take it off real nicelike, so I can see if you still look as good as I remember."

"No! I'll never have anything to do with you. How can you imagine I'd even share the ground you walk on?" Susan spat in his face and watched his eyes harden to anger.

"Ain't you learned yet how to treat a man?" he growled. His hand suddenly clutched the thin material of her dress and in one movement he ripped it to the waist. She cringed away from him.

"Ain't no sense fightin' me," he muttered. "Never helped before, did it?"

His mouth covered hers as his fingers clawed at her clothes. She pummeled him with her fists, but he twisted her arms behind her back and pushed her to the floor. She squirmed beneath him, numb with disgust and horror but driven by the need to get away. He thrust his tongue between her lips and she clamped her teeth down hard.

With a cry he drew back and Susan scrambled to her feet and stumbled toward the door. She had to get away. She knew she had no hope of outdistancing him if she fled down the path for help. Her only chance was to lose him in the forest. She clutched her skirt and raced across the clearing into the trees. She stumbled over roots and rocks, but somehow managed to keep going. She heard Adam plunging through the forest after her.

Deeper and deeper she pushed into the woods, her breath coming in ragged gasps, but still she heard him behind her. Suddenly her foot caught on a vine and she tumbled headlong to the ground. She fought to get up, but it was too late. He was upon her.

The weight of his body pinned her to the ground. He wrenched her hands behind her and held them in an unrelenting grip. She screamed, a piercing cry, and tears ran down her cheeks unheeded. He slapped her across the face and Susan tasted blood.

"Shut up," Adam snarled. "Another scream like that and you'll wish I'd shot you along with your friend."

His hands seemed to be everywhere, hurting and tearing at her. Her limbs trembled weakly. How much longer could she continue to fight him off? He grasped a lock of her hair, which had tumbled to her shoulders.

"Always did love your hair," he muttered as his fingers wound through the loosened strands. His grip tightened and Susan stifled a cry of pain. Something hit her shoulder and she turned her head to the side. It was the pin she had fastened in her hair such a short time ago in her plans to welcome Neal.

She stared at it for a moment, heedless of Adam's bruising fingers. Suddenly the hate she felt for him surged out of control. She would not allow him to defile her here on the forest floor. She had to get away no matter how.

His grip had loosened and she moved one hand warily toward the hairpin. If she could only reach it.

His mouth clamped down on hers and Susan forced herself not to struggle. He laughed as he felt her relax.

"Knew you wouldn't hold out for long," he muttered as his lips moved to her neck and down toward the torn bodice of her dress. Susan's fingers closed over the hard ivory of the hairpin and she held her breath. His head was a blond blur and she steadied her shaking fingers. She had only one chance. If she failed . . . but she refused to think of that.

She clenched her fingers around the hairpin, raised her arm above his head and with one sharp movement brought the points of the pin down with sure aim to imbed them in the side of his neck.

Adam screamed with pain and blood gushed from the wound. She struck him again and again. At last, shaken and weak, she pulled herself from under him. He lay still, his eyes glazed in a frozen look of surprise.

Hours later she staggered into Agnes Jameson's cabin, her bloodstained gown nearly torn from her body, and collapsed against the amazed woman's shoulder.

"I killed my husband," she sobbed over and over. "I killed him."

Chapter 38

The room they gave her in Oregon City didn't seem like a jail cell, but the door remained locked except when meals were delivered. Susan slept, ate and relived the events that had led to her confinement.

She remembered leading someone to the place in the woods where Adam lay. Apart from that, the time since the afternoon of Neal's death was a blur of faces and voices.

The sheriff who escorted her to Oregon City had been polite, but Susan knew that in his mind she was guilty of a crime no gentlewoman would commit.

It would have been better to let Adam rape me, she thought as she paced the small room. It had been futile to defend herself, because in the eyes of society she was still Adam's wife and therefore his possession to do with as he pleased. By resisting his demands she had breached an unwritten code, for which she could never be forgiven.

She had lost track of how many days she had spent in the tiny room. She knew the number of steps between the door and the window; she had memorized the grim view of the cliff that bordered the back of the boardinghouse. She had become accustomed to the sounds outside her door as the house's regular occupants went about their daily tasks. She supposed she should be grateful that the Oregon City jail had burned down and not yet been replaced —how much worse it would be to spend each day in a barred cell.

Her only contacts with the outside world were the sheriff and a thin, pasty-faced girl who delivered her food.

She was startled by a sound at the door and turned from the window. The sheriff stood in the doorway. A shadowy figure peered over his shoulder.

"I've brought you a visitor," the sheriff announced gruffly. "This is Thomas Milberg. He'll be preparing your defense." He moved aside and Susan saw a slender young man with receding hair. His clothes were meticulously arranged, but he twisted his hands and plucked at a button on his vest.

"I can't afford a lawyer," Susan protested.

"Thomas here has volunteered his services," the sheriff replied. "He'll see you have a fair trial, all right and proper."

Susan looked at Milberg and her heart plummeted. Surely she could more ably defend herself.

"Why would you do that?" she asked.

Milberg's gaze slid away from hers. "Everyone should have a right to counsel," he replied stiffly.

"Very well." What did she have to lose? "Won't you sit down?" She motioned to the only chair in the room, but Milberg continued to stand, shifting from one foot to the other.

"I'll leave the two of you alone." The sheriff backed from the room. "Be back in an hour. Will that be enough time?"

"Yes, fine." Milberg watched the door swing shut and Susan heard the scrape of the key in the lock.

"Please, sit down," Susan repeated. "Shall I call you Tom or Mr. Milberg—or what?"

"Thomas."

"Well, Thomas, where do we start?"

He moved to the chair and seated himself on its edge. His fingers pleated the sharp crease in his trousers. "Just tell me what happened—how it started." He kept his head lowered.

She began with the day she had met Dawson in the streets of Oregon City and his story of Adam's death, and proceeded quickly to the events that had left two men dead and herself in custody for murder.

"What was your relationship with your husband—Mr. Baker, that is—before you were told he was dead?"

"I can't see how that has anything to do with this."

"You'll be asked in court. It's best to be prepared."

"But he attacked me—he'd just killed my . . . killed Neal. Surely that's self-defense."

Milberg shook his head. "He was your husband."

"But I thought he was dead."

"That doesn't change the law." The muscles contracted along his smooth-shaven chin. Susan felt a wave of despair. If she couldn't get her own lawyer to understand her predicament, how could she ever convince a jury?

"Now then, what were your feelings toward Mr. Baker?"

"I hated him."

Susan's words fell into the stillness of the room

and Thomas's head jerked up as though yanked by an invisible string.

"You hated him?" he repeated as though he could not believe what he had just heard.

"Yes. Had he met us here in Oregon City I planned to ask for a divorce. I had no intention of living with him ever again."

"I'd advise you to keep that to yourself. A jury isn't likely to feel sympathy for you if you tell them you hated the man you've been accused of murdering." He pursed his lips thoughtfully and looked past Susan. "Do you have friends here?" he asked. "People who would vouch for your character?"

Susan thought of the few people she knew in Oregon City. Ellie would never speak up for her— and it was her son Susan would be tried for murdering. There was Ross—but what would he say in a court of law? He had thought little enough of her the last time she had spoken with him, at The Dalles. No, that would never do.

"There was the wagon master, Mr. Taggerty, and his wife, from the wagon train we came out on. If you could find them . . ."

Milberg nodded. "Anyone else?"

Susan shook her head. Her only friends were dead and buried. There was no one.

"I suggest you plead guilty—throw yourself on the mercy of the court. It's the only way."

"No! I won't do that." Susan was stung from her lethargy. "I didn't do anything wrong. I was defending myself from a man I had reason to fear."

"Did he actually threaten your life?"

"No . . ."

"Then for what reason did you fear him?"

"He was going to take me by force. He had no right."

"He was your husband."

"He was never a husband. He lied when he married me. He sent me to Oregon when I was expecting a baby—a baby who died because of him. He was cruel and inhuman."

Milberg shrugged. "I can only give you advice. If you won't listen . . ." He rose from the chair.

"Does that mean you won't defend me?"

"No. I'll do the best I can, but to be perfectly honest, I don't think you stand a chance if you persist with your present attitude. The men of the jury will never agree that you didn't owe your first loyalty to your husband once you learned he was alive."

"I had a husband. Neal was my husband."

Milberg shook his head. "We're talking about the law—not emotions, but what's written in the law books. By those laws you'll be judged, and by those laws you were never married to Neal Laughlin. You were, in fact, committing adultery, although I believe the jury could be persuaded to overlook that in view of the circumstances."

Susan despised his dry voice and pompous manner. He was convinced of her guilt. She wanted to shout at him to leave, but she realized how futile the gesture would be since he couldn't leave until the sheriff let him out.

"I want you to think about what I've said," he continued. "I'll be back to see you in a day or so. Your trial is set for a week from Monday. Try to see that I'm giving you the best legal advice. Your only chance is to plead guilty."

Susan shook her head vehemently and began to answer, but the sound of the key interrupted her.

"I'll be going now." Milberg turned with obvious relief to the door. "Remember what I said." He left quickly.

Susan stared at the closed door. "That stupid man! Stupid, stupid man!"

She grabbed the pitcher from the washstand and hurled it at the door. It shattered with a loud explosion and shards of pottery fell to the floor in a puddle of water.

Susan turned away. Let someone come and clean it up. She didn't care. She didn't care about anything. They were going to convict her of murder—she had seen it in Milberg's eyes. Her death warrant had already been signed and sealed. The trial would be only a formality.

She threw herself across the bed and beat at the pillows in frustration.

"Why? Why? How did I ever let this happen to me?"

Her anger spent, she stared at her clenched fists. Somehow she must find a way to convince them, to make them realize that she had been within her rights to defend herself from Adam.

I won't let them beat me, she vowed. Somehow I'll make them understand.

Chapter 39

The first day of the trial was warm and sultry. Dark clouds scudded across the horizon as Susan walked between Milberg and the sheriff to the office building that served as a temporary courthouse. She held her head high, but she was uncomfortably conscious of the stares and comments of people they passed.

"She don't look like a sinner, Ma," one small boy cried from the yard of a house they passed.

"Hush, Jamie." His mother pulled him into the house and closed the door, but Susan saw the curtains move.

"Have you changed your mind?" Milberg whispered in her ear as they neared the door of the courtroom. She shook her head and heard him sigh. For a week he had tried to persuade her to change her plea to guilty. He truly believed it was her only hope, but she refused to give in.

The courtroom was packed with observers. Everyone turned to stare as she walked up the narrow aisle between hard-backed chairs to the front of the room. The smell of unwashed bodies combined with the heat of the day nauseated Susan. Why didn't they all just go home? What business was it of theirs?

She collapsed into the chair Milberg held for her, but had to rise a moment later as the judge entered the room.

"Court is now in session. We will begin proceedings of Oregon Territory versus Susan Baker. You may be seated."

The formalities over, Susan glanced at the jury. For two days Milberg had questioned prospective jurors, reporting the results to her. He hadn't been happy with some of the choices, but had done his best. The twelve men who faced her appeared ordinary. For the most part they were working men, many of whom had come west by wagon train only a short time before. As decreed by law, all owned property, all had an interest in the future of the territory. She knew that eight of them were married. Milberg had hoped to find more single men, believing they might be more sympathetic to her case, but the prosecution had done its job well.

Edward Stanton, the prosecutor, was gray-haired and had a slight paunch and carried himself with dignity. Compared to Stanton, Thomas seemed younger than ever. How could he hope to gain the favor of the jury against an opponent whose bearing radiated authority? She sighed and listened to the opening remarks. They did nothing to alleviate her sense of hopelessness.

The eloquent phrases that rippled from Stanton's tongue seemed to impress the members of the jury. She saw two of them exchange glances and nod when he stated that the people of Oregon City could not allow a murderess to go free in society.

Milberg's opening statements were fair and reasoned, but nothing to match the rhetoric of his opponent.

The morning was spent taking statements from the witnesses who had discovered the body. Agnes Jameson related how Susan had stumbled into her cabin, her dress torn and covered with blood, declaring that she had killed her husband. The sheriff described the scene as it had been told to him, and several men from the settlement told of finding Neal's body and of Susan leading them to Adam.

The ivory hairpin was introduced as evidence. From where she sat Susan could see the rustlike marks that stained its long prongs.

There were whispers from the assemblage behind her as they craned forward at each new revelation. She could almost feel their breath on the back of her neck, but she didn't turn around.

There was a two-hour recess at noon. It was a relief to step outside and breathe fresh air.

"Things will get tougher this afternoon," Milberg warned her as they walked toward the boarding-house. "Your mother-in-law has been called as a witness."

"Ellie?"

Milberg nodded.

"But what could she have to say?"

"I warned you this would happen. They'll bring out as much of your past as they can. Are you sure there isn't anything else I should know before we go back?"

Susan shook her head. She remembered the venom in Ellie's voice the last time she had seen her. How could anyone predict what Ellie might say? She couldn't bring herself to tell Milberg about some of the things Ellie might consider pertinent. After all, they didn't really have any bearing on the case.

Afternoon brought no relief from the muggy oppressiveness of the courtroom. Perspiration trickled down Susan's back and between her breasts under her dress. She had taken Milberg's advice and worn the most modest, high-necked garment she owned.

The prosecuting attorney rose from his seat as soon as the crowd quieted.

"I'd like to call as a witness Eleanor Wilton."

For a moment the unfamiliar name startled Susan. Who was he talking about? Then she saw Ellie mincing between the rows of chairs. She wore a walking dress of black serge and a small hat with a veil that covered the top half of her face. A gold brooch at her throat was her only ornament.

She didn't glance at Susan as she was sworn in and took her seat near the judge. She clutched a white, lace-edged handkerchief in one hand, as though anticipating the ordeal ahead. Stanton approached her with gentle dignity.

"Mrs. Wilton, would you please tell the jury your relationship to the accused."

"She's my daughter-in-law—or she was," Ellie drawled.

"How long did you know her before she married your son?"

"Never laid eyes on her till the night he brought her home as his wife. I made her welcome though, I surely did. Gave her a home and never questioned her none about her background. Figured Adam knew what he wanted. Never reckoned on her killing my own flesh and blood—my only child. If I'da known, I'da thrown her out the minute I set eyes on her."

"Objection, Your Honor." Milberg's voice was dry and raspy.

"Objection sustained. Mrs. Wilton, please confine your statements to the facts."

Ellie shot the judge a guarded look from beneath her veil, then settled back in her chair. "Yes, Your Honor," she replied meekly.

"Now then," the prosecutor continued. "Would you tell the jury how you happened to come to Oregon City?"

"Well, sir, Adam—my son—he decided our future lay out west. He decided to go to California ahead of us and we all planned to meet here in Oregon City, me and Susan and my husband, George—my first husband, that is. Adam planned to make us a fortune in the gold fields and he was going to meet us here in the fall."

"And did he meet you?"

"No. She brought home some drifter one night who told us a story about Adam bein' shot in California. Now I know better, I reckon she just paid him to tell that story so's she'd be free to run off and marry someone else."

"Objection." Milberg was on his feet before Ellie had finished speaking.

"Objection sustained. Please, Mrs. Wilton."

Ellie nodded, but her eyes were spiteful as they met Susan's.

"By 'she,' do you mean the accused?" Stanton asked.

"Yes."

"What happened after you were told your son had been killed?"

"Well, I was in a fine pickle, I'll tell you that. Didn't know how to make ends meet and that's a fact. If it hadn't been for Mr. Wilton, why, I don't rightly know what I'd have done, bein' all alone like that. My husband was killed on the trail, you see, and so it was just Susan and me. She said she'd find a job, but she was gone all day and there never was a sign of work. Seemed peculiar to me, if you know what I mean. Well, one night I got real desperate and I was huntin' through some old things, hopin' I might come across some money I'd forgot about, when I happened to find some money all right— money she stole from me, hidden away in her suitcase."

"Objection, Your Honor. The witness has no reason to accuse the defendant of stealing from her."

"Mrs. Wilton?"

"Oh, I knew it all right, Your Honor. She admitted it to me right off. Said she figured she earned it by bringin' the wagon out and all."

Milberg turned to Susan, his eyebrows raised in question. She nodded slightly and his shoulders sagged.

"Very well. Proceed."

"And when you discovered this money and confronted your daughter-in-law with it, what did she do?"

"Why she just lit out of there—just grabbed her clothes and ran. I figured then she had someone else she was plannin' to run to, and no more than a week later I learned she'd gone to live with Neal Laughlin."

Susan waited for Milberg to object, but he merely drew circles on a piece of paper.

"And did you see her again?"

"No, sir. And thankful I am for that."

"When your son arrived, what did you tell him?"

"Why, I told him his wife had run off with some other fella. Told him not to waste his time goin' after her, said she wasn't worth it. But he wouldn't listen to me. He said what was his was his and he wasn't gonna let no other man take it." Ellie paused and dabbed at dry eyes with her handkerchief.

"How many nights since then I've laid awake a-wondering what I could have said to keep him from goin' after her. But it's too late now." Ellie sniffed loudly, and there were murmurs from the crowded courtroom.

Stanton paused for a moment to allow his witness to regain her composure. "Can you continue, Mrs. Wilton?"

"Oh, yes."

"Can you tell me about the relationship between your son and the defendant? Did they have a happy marriage? Did they seem to love each other?"

"Adam worshiped the ground she walked on. But nothin' he ever did was good enough for her. She was always criticizin' him about something, seemed like. Then when he decided to come out west, she didn't want to come at all. Wanted to stay there in Illinois."

Susan clenched her hands in her lap. How damaging Ellie made everything sound! She didn't mention that Susan had been pregnant, that Adam had left home in part because of Delia's brothers. And to say that Adam had worshiped the ground she walked on . . . !

"On the way west, did the defendant look forward to being reunited with your son?"

"Not by a long sight. I'll tell you this, she was so busy chasin' after every man on that train, it's a wonder we ever made it to Oregon at all. If it weren't the scout, Ross Morgan, it was Neal Laughlin. She was always makin' eyes at some man—and not stoppin' there either, I'll tell you."

"Objection."

The judge leaned from his seat to question Stanton. "I presume your line of questioning has a purpose, Counselor?"

"Yes, Your Honor. I plan to show a direct bearing on the character of the defendant."

"Very well. Proceed."

"Do you mean," Stanton continued, "the defendant was romantically involved with other men?"

"She surely was, and there's witnesses to prove it."

"And these men were . . ."

"The scout, Ross Morgan, for one. Can't say for sure about the others, though I wouldn't doubt it."

"And this affected her feelings about meeting her husband?"

"What would you expect?"

There were chuckles from some of the men in the courtroom and Ellie ducked her head and said, "Don't mean no disrespect, but why would she be anxious to go back to bein' married when she had the freedom to run after whoever took her fancy?"

"Did you confront her with this?"

"I did."

"And what did she say?"

"Said she had no intention of ever living with Adam again, that she'd stay with me till he met us and after that she'd be on her own. I told her no matter what she intended, she was still married to my son and I wouldn't tolerate that kind of behavior."

The prosecutor paused for a moment, glanced at the jury, then back to Ellie. "I think that will be all, Mrs. Wilton. Thank you."

"Your witness, Mr. Milberg."

Ellie dabbed at her eyes once more as Thomas approached the stand.

"Just a few questions, Mrs. Wilton, if you don't mind."

Ellie nodded.

"You say your daughter-in-law didn't want to come west. Wasn't there a good reason for that?"

"Depends on what you call a good reason."

"Wasn't she expecting a baby?"

"Yes."

"And wasn't that why she didn't want to make the trip?"

"That's what she said." Ellie's lip curled scornfully.

"Did she not, in fact, lose the baby after leaving Independence?"

Ellie nodded. "Didn't have to happen, though. Lots a women have babies on wagon trains. Ask them. If she'da been more careful—but like as not she didn't want the baby in the first place, woulda tied her down too much."

"Your Honor." Milberg looked beseechingly at the judge.

"Mrs. Wilton, please confine your statements to fact and avoid conjecture."

"You say your daughter-in-law had relations with other men on the train," Milberg resumed. "Did you actually see this?"

Ellie hesitated for a moment, and Susan wondered if she would dare to perjure herself.

"No, I didn't," she admitted at last. "But I know someone who did, and she told me."

"But you yourself have no way of knowing whether or not such was the case?" Ellie shook her head with obvious reluctance.

"Would you answer the question, please?"

"I never seen it." Ellie glared at Milberg. "But that don't mean it weren't so."

"How long after you left Independence did your husband die, Mrs. Wilton?"

"Why, I don't know exactly. A few weeks, I reckon. Before we got to Fort Laramie."

"And from that time on Susan was solely in charge of getting the wagon to Oregon City. Is that correct?"

"Well, I helped as much as I could."

"But it was Susan who drove the oxen, who was responsible for getting from one night's campground to the next and pitching camp?"

"Yes."

"And you don't think she was entitled to some sort of payment for that service?"

"I paid for the trip. She wouldn'ta made it if I hadn't had the money to pay for the crossings. No, she wasn't entitled to a thing. After all, I gave her a roof over her head and food to eat—that was payment enough."

"Is it true that your son was followed from Illinois to California by two brothers who held your son responsible for their sister's death—death in childbirth?"

"I'm sure I couldn't say. I was never in California."

"But could that have happened?"

"I suppose most anything *could* have happened."

"Was there a reason for two such men to take an action like that? To hate your son enough to kill him? In fact, is that not why your son married when he did—to escape a forced marriage to a half-breed girl whose child he had fathered?"

"Objection, Your Honor. It's not the deceased who's on trial here."

"Mr. Milberg, I'll have to ask you to withdraw your question."

Thomas sighed. "Very well, Your Honor. I have no further questions at this time."

"In that case, I suggest that court be adjourned for today. We will resume at eight o'clock tomorrow morning."

As Susan was led through the crowd, she felt their hostility. Her entire life had been spread before them by Ellie—a slanted, biased version of it, but how were they to know that?

As she stumbled into the bright sunlight she was startled and shaken to meet the gaze of Ross Morgan. She clutched Milberg's arm and hurried him down the street, but she was conscious of Ross's eyes on her. What was he thinking? Had he been there in the courtroom today, listening to the accusations Ellie had made with such satisfaction?

Susan shuddered. She wished he had never returned to Oregon City. It would have been far easier to face what was to come if Ross Morgan were miles away.

Chapter 40

"Was it true what she said?"

Thomas had been questioning her ever since their return to her room.

"You have to tell me the whole story, Susan, if I'm to defend you. I can't continue to have surprises thrown in my face. Were there any other men?"

His voice beat against her senses until Susan wanted to scream. His expression held a hint of distaste at the entire affair, and she knew he wished he wasn't connected with her sordid trial.

"There was one." Her voice was a whisper.

"Who? This Ross Morgan? Where is he now?"

"I don't know." Susan lowered her eyes to hide her lie. "I had to do it."

"What do you mean, you 'had to'? Did he force you?"

Susan shook her head. "No, not exactly. But I . . . I thought it was the only way I could get him to agree to let us stay with the train. After George was killed, he wanted to send us back to Independence."

"He? Morgan, you mean?"

Susan nodded.

"Wasn't that what you wanted anyway?"

"Not then. I'd lost the baby. My father had died—though I didn't know it until we reached Laramie. But there was nothing to go back to. So I did what I felt I had to do."

"And that was all?"

Susan nodded. What was the point of telling him that there had been other times—times when she had ached to feel Ross's body next to hers? He wouldn't understand. Let him excuse her actions in his own mind with the consolation that she had done it merely to survive.

Milberg thoughtfully twirled the button on his vest. "We may be able to get away with that. If you'll tell the jury what you told me."

"Tell the jury?" Susan cringed at the thought of facing those twelve men with the story of how she had deliberately seduced Ross Morgan to gain her own ends. She could imagine the speculation that would glint in their eyes. She shook her head vehemently. She couldn't do it.

"You'll have to. When the prosecution is done calling witnesses, you'll have to testify. I haven't been able to find the Taggertys, and from what you tell me they wouldn't be much help in any case. All they can say is that you saved their daughter from a snake. That isn't going to change your character in the eyes of the jury, at least not to any appreciable degree. You'll have to tell your story in your own words. Unless you want to change your plea—and it may be too late for that now."

"No. I won't do that, no matter what."

"Then I suggest you prepare yourself to face the

jury and pray to God that this Morgan doesn't show up to shoot your story full of holes."

After he had left, Susan paced the room. She tried to think of what she would say when she was called to the stand, but her mind was blank. Although Thomas had suggested she should pray that Morgan didn't turn up to ruin her story, she had a totally different reason for not wanting him there. How could she say there had been no feelings involved if he was watching her from that sea of hostile faces? She would be lost if that happened. She prayed he would stay away.

A knock on the door announced the sheriff's arrival. Susan was surprised to see him. Her evening meal had come several hours earlier.

"There's someone downstairs wants to see you. I said I'd ask, but I can only let you have five minutes."

"Who is it?"

"Wouldn't give me his name. Says he's a friend of yours. Tall, dark hair, sorta cold gray eyes."

Ross. It had to be Ross. Susan's pulse quickened and hope flared. He had come to see her at last. Then she remembered the ordeal she had yet to face. She forced herself to turn away.

"I'm sorry, I don't know anyone like that and I'm not in the mood to visit with strangers. Tell him I can't see him."

The sheriff shrugged. "Whatever you say."

The door closed softly behind him and Susan heard the scratch of the key in the lock. She had to strain to keep from calling the man back. How she longed to hide in Ross's arms, to let him shelter her from the hostile world, if only for a moment. Tears burned her eyes as she turned her back on the door. She couldn't face Ross knowing what she would have to say tomorrow.

The storm that had threatened the day before broke during the night and stopped around daybreak. There were puddles in the street and Susan lifted her skirts to avoid the mud, but the air smelled fresh and clean, newly washed by the rain. She lifted her face to the sunlight. How wonderful it felt. How long would she be allowed to enjoy these sensations she had always taken for granted? She refused to speculate on the outcome of the trial.

It seemed impossible that more people could crowd into the small room than had been there yesterday, but she was aware of new faces turned to watch her. She kept her eyes straight ahead. She didn't want to know if Ross was there somewhere in the crowd.

The day's first witness came as a surprise to Susan, although when she reflected on it, she knew it shouldn't have.

Mrs. Jordan, her face set in stern lines, took the stand with the air of doing her duty, however unpleasant. She answered the opening questions in a brisk, clear voice, the voice of one who feels totally righteous.

"You were on the wagon train that brought Susan Baker to Oregon?" Stanton's voice had the same steady assurance as the day before.

"I was."

"And you knew the defendant?"

292

"I knew who she was."

"There was an occasion, I believe, when you saw the accused in a . . . shall we say, a compromising situation?"

"I did."

"Could you describe for the jury, in your own words, what took place?"

"It was at the Green."

Susan's heart lurched at the name. Ellie had told her that Mrs. Jordan had seen her, but not the occasion. Of all times, this was the most incriminating.

"The Green River, that is," Mrs. Jordan explained, glancing at the jury. "We'd crossed a great stretch of desert and everyone was hot and dusty. I left the train to get a breath of air, thought I'd wash out some of my clothes away from the others. I'd been there maybe two or three minutes when I heard someone come runnin' through the woods toward me. I was afraid it might be an Injun, so I got down behind a bush."

"But it wasn't an Indian?"

"No, it was her." Mrs. Jordan pointed an accusing finger at Susan. "Barely dressed she was, carrying her underthings in her arms and her hair all undone and streamin' down her back. Well, I didn't know what to think, so I just stayed where I was and before she got to me she stopped and started fastening her dress. Then along comes Ross Morgan—the scout for our train. He didn't have a stitch on, but he was laughin' and carryin' on."

"What did the defendant do?"

"Well, I didn't watch all of it, you know. I was downright embarrassed—somethin' awful, seein' Mr. Morgan like that and all, but the next time I looked, there they were, lyin' on the ground with their arms around each other and she wasn't tryin' to get away, let me tell you."

"What did you do then?"

Mrs. Jordan pursed her lips together in a thin line. "I did what any God-fearin' body woulda done. I hightailed it back to the wagons." She paused a moment.

"I thought about it a long time, but finally I decided it was my bounden duty to tell Mrs. Baker— Mrs. Wilton now—to let her know what her daughter-in-law had been up to. She did somethin' to put a stop to it, but I don't know what she said or done—and I don't want to know neither. I believe in tending to my own business. But I know what's right and proper, and there weren't nothin' right about what that woman there was up to." Again she pointed an accusing finger.

Milberg leaned toward Susan, an expression of horror on his face. "Who is that woman?"

"She was on the wagon train."

"I know that. But what did you have to do with her?"

"It's a long story."

Milberg rose to his feet. "Your Honor, with the Court's permission, I'd like a short recess to confer with my client."

"Very well. Court is adjourned for half an hour."

Susan followed Thomas from the courtroom, her

eyes fastened on his back. The moment they were alone he began to question her.

"Could that woman have seen what she claims?"

"Yes."

"I thought you told me there was only one time—before you reached Laramie?"

Susan lowered her eyes and studied the hem of her skirt.

"You'll have to say he forced you—that he chased you and you couldn't get away." Milberg gazed at her with troubled eyes. "Susan, I can't defend you if you won't cooperate. Why is this Jordan woman so set against you?"

Quickly Susan told him the story of how the Jordan wagon had been lost. "She blamed me for it. It was to have been our turn to be last in line, but they weren't ready when we started. She knew the rules of the trail, but she blamed me anyway."

Thomas nodded. "Well, that's something at least. I hope there won't be any more surprises. This afternoon you take the stand."

Susan forced a smile to her lips.

"Thank you, Thomas. You've done the best you could under the circumstances. I . . . I had no idea I'd be on trial for more than Adam's death. But it seems like I'm on trial now for everything I've ever done."

"It'll be over soon."

She thought she saw a softening in his eyes, but she wasn't sure.

Milberg's cross-examination of Mrs. Jordan was brief. He brought out her resentment toward Susan for the accident on the trail with the skill of a much more seasoned attorney, and Susan examined the faces of the jury as they listened. Perhaps the obvious vindictiveness of the woman would lessen the impact of her testimony. But Susan couldn't help but wonder whether the jury had already made up their minds.

Chapter 41

"I'd like to call Susan Baker to the stand."

The buzzing of flies was the only sound Susan heard. Her palms were sweaty as she placed one hand on the Bible and swore to tell the truth, the whole truth and nothing but the truth. Then she sat carefully in the chair recently vacated by Mrs. Jordan. She fastened her eyes on Milberg and refused to glance at the jury or the crowd of spectators who leaned forward in their chairs.

"State your name, please."

"Susan Baker . . . Laughlin." She added the last word defiantly and Thomas frowned before he continued.

"You were the wife of the deceased?"

"I was."

"Would you tell the court how you met Adam Baker?"

Thomas led her through the series of events that had led to her departure from Independence.

"After your father-in-law was killed on the trail, what happened?"

"I was told that we could no longer remain with the train—that we would have to turn back when we reached Fort Laramie."

"Who told you that? Who was in charge of deciding these matters?"

"The scout."

"His name?"

"Ross Morgan."

Susan raised her head. She had to look. Her eyes swept the crowded courtroom twice before she saw him. He stood in a corner near the door, his back stiff, his hands in his pockets. His gaze met hers, but it held no recognition. It was as if they had never met.

"You were alone, with a sick woman on your hands, and nowhere to turn. Is that correct?"

Milberg's voice made her wrench her gaze from Ross. "That's correct."

"How did you feel?"

"Objection, Your Honor." Stanton was on his feet. "The defendant's feelings have little to do with this case."

"Objection overruled. Proceed."

"I was desperate. I had to get us to Oregon somehow."

"And so you did the only thing you could think of—you went to Ross Morgan and bartered your body for a chance to stay with the train."

The words were harsh. Susan wanted to cry out that it hadn't been like that, that it hadn't been cold and calculated. Or had it? Of course, at the beginning it had been just that. She looked toward the corner where Ross stood, his expression unchanged.

"Susan," Thomas prodded gently.

"Yes." Her voice was a whisper. "That's what I did."

"Did you feel at that time that you had any other choice?"

"No."

A wave of comments ran through the courtroom and was quickly subdued as Thomas resumed his questioning.

"After you married Neal Laughlin, were you happy? Did you love him?"

Susan glanced at Thomas in surprise. What difference did it make whether or not she loved Neal?

"I felt comfortable with him." She knew it wasn't the answer he had looked for, but he continued.

"When Adam Baker arrived at your home, what was your reaction?"

"Shock. I couldn't believe it—I thought he was dead. I saw him catch up to Neal on the path. They stopped to talk."

"Did you hear their conversation?"

"No, I was too far away. But I . . . I saw Adam pull out his gun and kill Neal." Susan lowered her head, fighting to control her quavering voice. Quite sharply she could see the clearing once again, smell the damp pine needles, hear the sharp crack of Adam's gun.

"Then what happened?"

"Adam attacked me. He . . . he tore at my dress and pushed me down on the floor. He was going to . . . to . . ."

"All right. I think we understand. But you got away?"

"Yes. I ran into the woods. I thought I could lose him, but I tripped and he caught me."

"Did he threaten you?"

"I screamed. He hit me and said if I did that again I'd wish he had shot me when he shot Neal."

"So you had reason to fear for your life?"

"Yes. I was terrified."

"What happened then?"

"I . . . I had a hairpin. It fell out of my hair in the struggle. I grabbed it and . . . and stabbed him with it. I . . . killed him."

There was a hush in the courtroom as Thomas returned to his seat. Susan raised her eyes and looked at Ross, but his face was shadowed. She couldn't tell what his reaction was to her words. It doesn't matter, she thought, I should worry about what the jury thinks instead of Ross.

Stanton rose to begin the cross-examination and she tried to still the trembling of her hands. She would not allow him to frighten her.

"Would you describe for us your feelings for your husband, Mrs. Baker?" he began.

"My feelings?"

"Yes. Did you look forward to meeting him in Oregon City?"

"No. He had beaten and abused me. I didn't look forward to seeing him again."

"Yet you came to Oregon with that intention?"

"At first."

"When did that change?"

"On the trail."

"Would that have been before or after you met Ross Morgan?"

"I don't remember. After, I suppose. I met him before we left Independence."

"Was it before or after you began your . . . association with this same Mr. Morgan?"

"I don't know."

"But your intentions did change?"

"Yes. I could no longer accept the way Adam treated me. I wanted a chance to live my own life—not be dependent on him or on anyone else."

"And yet you didn't hesitate to be dependent on other men, did you?"

"I don't know what you mean."

"I mean you were dependent on Mr. Morgan to see that you were allowed to remain with the train. When your mother-in-law justifiably rejected you, you became dependent on Mr. Laughlin for support."

"Yes, but I—"

"Tell me, Mrs. Baker," he broke swiftly across her rebuttal. "Were there other times when you were with Ross Morgan? The incident you related was before you reached Fort Laramie, and yet Mrs. Jordan says she saw you with him at the Green, long after you had left Laramie. Was it necessary to reconfirm his agreement to let you continue to Oregon?"

This was the question Milberg had warned her of. She had known it was coming; yet she could not readily give her rehearsed answer. How could she deny what she had felt for Ross, what she still felt in spite of his indifference? She glanced toward the back of the room. Ross's face held no emotion, but she sensed his alertness as he awaited her reply.

"You haven't answered my question, Mrs. Baker. Were there other times you spent with Ross Morgan?"

"Yes."

Susan's eyes blazed into those of the prosecuting attorney, defying him to continue.

"And for what reason, may I ask?"

Susan met Ross's steel-gray eyes above the crowd. She would not lie to save herself. She would face the consequences, but she would let Ross Morgan know once and for all how she felt.

"Because I loved him."

Her voice was clear in the stillness. For a moment there was no sound. Then a murmur swept the room, rising in volume until the judge was forced to use his gavel to regain order.

"That will be all." Stanton turned from the witness stand. "I have no further questions, Your Honor."

Chapter 42

"Why, Susan?" Thomas's voice was tight with anxiety and anger. "I told you what to say. Why didn't you do it?"

"I couldn't lie."

Susan sat in the room that had been her prison for so many weeks.

"All that's left is the summation." Milberg spoke more to himself than to her. "After tomorrow morning it will be up to the jury. What am I going to say?"

"Whatever you decide, Thomas, I'll never blame you. I had to do what I felt was right. I couldn't sit there and tell them everything I did was because of circumstances. I'm responsible for my actions, and it's time I started to act like it."

"It may well be one of the last things you ever do." His voice was despondent, and for the first time Susan felt sorry for him. She wondered how many cases he had tried before this one. Hers had certainly not been easy.

"I'm sorry, Thomas."

He nodded. "Get a good night's sleep. Tomorrow will be difficult for both of us."

She saw him to the door, where he rapped for the sheriff to let him out.

"I'll see you in the morning, Susan."

She wondered if he would go home and ponder how best to present her actions to the jury. She wondered what the members of the jury were thinking tonight. But most of all, she thought about Ross.

He had disappeared from the courtroom shortly after she left the witness stand. Had he been moved by her declaration? Did he have any idea what it had cost her to admit her love for him before all those people? Perhaps it made no difference to him; that was probably the case. Had he come out of idle curiosity, like so many of the others who crowded into the room each day to see the show and hear the accusations that flew around her? She dared not hope he had come because he cared. But she was glad she had said what she did. At least now Ross could never doubt she had loved him.

Surprisingly, she slept well and awoke refreshed. This was the day her fate would be decided. In a few hours it would be over.

The prosecuting attorney looked particularly confident. His somber black suit was relieved only by the gold of his heavy watch chain, which he fingered idly as he waited for the jury to take their seats. His initial summation was brief and to the point. His tone clearly implied there should be no room for doubt in the minds of the jury.

He watched with a slight smile as Thomas began to speak, and Susan was filled with doubt. What could Thomas say that had not already been said? How could he convince these men to let her go free?

She listened as he described the hardships of the trail and praised her strength and her loyalty to Ellie.

"Gentlemen of the jury," Milberg continued, "you are not here today just to judge one woman. You are here to judge the rights of a fellow citizen.

"Granted, by her own testimony, she admits to mistakes in judgment. There were times when we might be tempted to condemn her actions. But who among us is so pure they can say with certainty that they would not have done the same faced with similar circumstances? We are not here to decide her fate based on past mistakes, but only based upon the actions that led to the death of Adam Baker.

"What you are here to decide, gentlemen, is whether or not a marriage license gives a man the right to abuse and degrade a woman to any extent, to use her as he might an animal. Even an animal would receive better treatment from a man such as Adam Baker, because to him it would have a degree of value.

"After physically and mentally abusing this young girl who sits before you today, he forced her to begin a two-thousand-mile journey through dangerous wilderness while she carried his child, a child she subsequently lost. Is that the mark of a man who cares about his wife—the woman he has sworn to love, honor and care for?

"And when he returned to find her married to another man, what were his reactions? Did he go to her and try to discuss the matter? No, instead he violated an innocent man's home, shot him in cold blood and began a brutal assault on the woman he believed to be nothing more than a personal belonging. Is it any wonder that she feared for her life?

"Is it not apparent from what you have heard in this room that Adam Baker was little more than a beast? Truly, he got what he deserved, and had his enemies been more successful, he would have received his just reward at the hands of the men who followed him hundreds of miles from Illinois to avenge their sister's death. But instead, his fate rested in the hands of the woman he married to escape his responsibilities.

"If you find the defendant guilty of murder, then no woman is safe in Oregon Territory. You will be giving every man a license to take out his failures and frustrations on the woman to whom he is married simply because he has a piece of paper that says she belongs to him. I ask you today, do not judge Susan Baker as a wife. Judge her as a woman —as a person who has proven her strength in the face of adversity—as another human being with rights the same as yours, the right to live in this great land as a free individual, without fear of degradation or dishonor because of her sex."

As Thomas returned to his seat, Susan reached out to touch his hand. It was damp with perspiration and he mopped his forehead with a handkerchief. She had never thought that he understood her, but he had put her own feelings into words so well that she marveled at his perception.

"Thank you," she whispered before she turned to listen to the prosecuting attorney.

Stanton recapped the events of the trial, pointing out that not only had Susan killed her lawful husband, but she had had no love for him from the very first, that her morals were questionable at best. He

306

ended with a final plea that she should not be allowed to go free and unpunished.

With shuffling feet and averted eyes, the jury left the room and court was recessed.

Susan scanned the crowd as they left the court-room, but there was no sign of Ross Morgan. What had she expected? She had refused to see him when she had the opportunity. She couldn't expect him to be here now.

The meal brought to her at noon was tasteless and she was too keyed up to eat. The hours dragged by. She wondered why it was taking so long—surely the jury should have reached a verdict by now.

When the call finally came to return to the court-room it was almost dark. The streets were empty as she walked the familiar route.

"Are you all right?" Thomas murmured anxiously as they neared the building.

Susan smiled reassuringly. "I'm fine. It'll be over in a few minutes."

"Yes." His worried frown left little doubt in her mind that he expected the worst.

The jury filed slowly into the room. Susan tried to read some expression in their faces, but it was impossible to tell what they had decided. Soon she would no longer have to speculate.

"Has the jury reached a verdict?" The judge looked solemn and forbidding in his judicial robes.

"We have, Your Honor."

Hurry up, Susan thought. Hurry and get it over.

"Will the defendant rise."

Susan stood and faced the jury. She clenched her hands at her sides. No matter what was said she would maintain her composure. She would meet their decision with dignity.

"Would you please read the verdict."

Susan watched a tall, sunburned man rise from his chair at the end of one row. He cleared his throat and shuffled his feet.

"The jury," he began at last. "The jury finds the defendant, Susan Baker, not guilty of murder as charged."

The courtroom was completely still for a moment, and then Thomas was hugging her jubilantly, whirling her off her feet. She couldn't believe it. She was laughing and crying at the same time and she clung to Thomas, afraid she would faint.

"We did it! We did it!" he crowed, and hugged her again. Susan couldn't believe this was the same carefully dignified man who had first come to her room.

"Am I free now?"

"As free as you like." His smile threatened to reach from ear to ear.

"I can't believe it."

"It's wonderful, Susan. I didn't think we had a chance. I'm so happy for you."

The spectators crowded from the courtroom. The show was over. Now they could return to their everyday world where nothing more astonishing happened than the birth of a calf or the harvesting of the crops. A few nodded as they passed. One woman reached out to take Susan's hand and said, "Congratulations, my dear. You deserve the best."

Susan was amazed. Only minutes before these same people had avidly awaited a verdict of guilty, and now they actually seemed pleased she had been freed. She would never understand.

Through the crowd she glimpsed Ross Morgan. He took a step toward her, but suddenly a hand clutched Susan's sleeve and she turned to meet Ellie's spiteful eyes. Her mouth twisted in anger as she glared at Susan.

"So you got away with it," she hissed. "Should have known—with men to judge you. Always did have a way with men, didn't you?"

Susan recoiled a step and felt Milberg's steadying hand on her arm.

"The jury made their decision." His voice was calm.

Ellie gave him a look of hatred. "That don't change the facts," she spat, and turned on Susan again. "You're a murderess and someday you'll get what's coming to you. You mark my words."

With relief Susan saw Jesse Wilton approach. He took Ellie's arm and she looked up, her hatred and spite masked as she leaned against him.

"Come, my dear," Jesse drawled. "This has been an ordeal for you." He led Ellie from the courtroom.

Susan turned back to where Ross had stood, but he had vanished. She tried to hide her disappointment as Thomas led her outside. He walked her back to her room, but the sheriff no longer accompanied them. When she closed the door behind her it would not be to the sound of the key clicking in the lock.

"What will you do now?" Thomas asked as they stood in the hallway outside her door.

"I don't know. I hadn't planned for this really. I

hoped—but I never dared to dream beyond a verdict of not guilty."

"Do you have any money?"

"A little—at least, the sheriff has it. Neal had some money. I guess it would go to me now."

"Enough to get away from Oregon City?"

"Yes."

Away. She hadn't thought of leaving, but perhaps Thomas was right. What was left for her here?

"That might be best, at least for a while," Thomas continued. "Why don't you think about going to San Francisco? I hear it's quite a town. It'll help you forget. And if you do decide to come back—well, people won't have everything still fresh in their minds."

Susan nodded. "Thank you, Thomas. Thank you for everything. You've been so good through all of this."

"Don't thank me, Susan. They found you not guilty because of what you are and what you stand for. I just helped them see things more clearly. Good-bye, and good luck."

She let herself into the room and closed the door. It felt strange after all these weeks to know she could go anywhere she wished. But for the moment she was content to sit and watch the moonlight reflecting off the window. She didn't even want to light a lamp.

Tomorrow she would make plans to leave. Thomas had been right—she could start over somewhere else where there were no painful reminders of Neal or Ross. She would make a new life for herself and perhaps, someday, she would even love again. A tear formed at the corner of her eye, but she wiped it away impatiently. This was no time to feel sorry for herself. She had her whole life ahead. She would take charge of it this time, she would make things happen the way she wanted them to. No longer would circumstance force her to make decisions she regretted.

The knock on the door was so soft she barely heard it. With a sigh, she rose and made her way through the darkened room to open it. Ross stood silhouetted against the light of the hallway.

"Susan?"

It was the first time she could ever recall hearing uncertainty in his voice.

"May I come in?"

She opened the door wordlessly and watched him cross the threshold. His nearness made her feel weak. She took a step back and braced herself against the wall, waiting to hear what he had come to say.

"Were you asleep?"

"No. I just didn't feel like lighting a lamp. I can do it now." She made a move to do so, but he stopped her.

"No, don't. It's better like this."

The silence between them grew uncomfortable.

"I'm leaving tomorrow." Susan spoke at last.

"Oh?"

"Yes. I thought it best." Why was she telling him? Did she expect him to beg her to stay?

"You're probably right."

Susan smiled wryly in the darkness. There went another daydream. Someday she would learn that things did not happen according to her preconceived ideas, that other people seldom fit into the script she wrote in her mind.

"I'm leaving myself," Ross added.

"Why?"

"There's nothing here for me."

"But the Tamarack. I thought you wanted your own business."

"That seems like a long time ago. There isn't any satisfaction. Mike will be happy to run it. Maybe someday I'll decide I'm ready to settle down. I can always come back."

"Why did you come back at all?"

"Because of you."

Susan caught her breath.

"Because of me?"

"God knows I tried to stay away. I thought it was for the best. But when I came back it was to see you. Then I learned you were with the Laughlins, and I realized I'd been wrong to return. You belonged with them. I thought you'd be happy, contented—I had no way of knowing what would happen, all this . . ." He made a sweeping gesture with his arm.

Susan didn't know what to say. He seemed so distant, a dark blur against the lighter background of the wall. He shifted uneasily.

"Once, a long time ago . . ." He paused, then went on. "You said you'd go with me—anywhere. Do you remember?"

"Yes, I remember. You're right—that was a long time ago."

"Did you mean it then?"

"Yes."

"I didn't believe you."

"You had reason to doubt me."

"Perhaps. Or maybe I was just afraid to trust anyone. I wouldn't let down my guard."

Susan remained silent. What he said was true. She too had been guilty of holding back her feelings, afraid of his rejection.

"You're not making this easy, Susan."

She started at his words. Was there really a hope he was trying to say what she wanted to hear?

"I can't make it easy for you—you have to do it for yourself." How could she say that? She wanted to run to him, throw herself into his arms, tell him she would go with him anywhere. He had only to ask. Instead she waited cautiously in the darkness for the words she knew he must say if they were ever to have a future together.

"I'm not afraid anymore, Susan." His voice was soft, a caress. "I believed what you said in the courtroom yesterday. I didn't want to believe it, but I did. And I knew then that no matter what had happened, for whatever reason, that I . . ."

He stopped, and Susan willed him to continue. Don't stop now, she cried silently.

"Damn it, Susan, I'm trying to say I love you." He nearly shouted the words, and Susan choked on a laugh that was almost a sob.

On feet that were sure and certain she crossed the room to stand before him. This strange, silent man who had held her at a distance for so long had finally moved to break the barriers between them. She knew that the next move was up to her.

Slowly she wrapped her arms around his neck and lifted her face for his kiss. As his arms enfolded her, Susan knew this was where she belonged.